WEB of
the CITY

by Harlan Ellison®

IN ASSOCIATION WITH

A HARD CASE CRIME BOOK

First Hard Case Crime edition: April 2013

Titan Books
A division of Titan Publishing Group Ltd
144 Southwark Street
London SE1 0UP

in collaboration with Winterfall LLC

Web of the City, copyright © 1958, 1975 by Harlan Ellison.
Copyright © 1983 by The Kilimanjaro Corporation.
Renewed © 1986 by The Kilimanjaro Corporation.
"No Way Out" (under the title "Gutter Gang"), copyright © 1957 by Harlan Ellison.
Renewed © 1985 by The Kilimanjaro Corporation.
"No Game for Children," copyright © 1959 by Harlan Ellison.
Renewed © 1987 by The Kilimanjaro Corporation.
"Stand Still and Die!" copyright © 1956 by Harlan Ellison.
Renewed © 1984 by The Kilimanjaro Corporation.
This edition of *Web of the City*, © 2013 by The Kilimanjaro Corporation.
All rights reserved.
www.harlanellison.com

Cover painting copyright © 2013 by Glen Orbik

No part of this book may be reproduced or transmitted in any form or by any
means electronic or mechanical—including photocopy, recording, Internet posting,
electronic bulletin board—or any other information storage and retrieval system,
without permission in writing from the Author or the Author's agent, except by a
reviewer who may quote brief passages in a critical article or review to be printed
in a magazine or newspaper, or electronically transmitted on radio, television
or in a recognized on-line journal. For information address Author's agent:
Richard Curtis Associates, Inc., 171 East 74th Street, New York, New York 10021 USA.

*All persons, places and organizations in this book—except those
clearly in the public domain—are fictitious, and any resemblance
that may seem to exist to actual persons, places or organizations living,
dead or defunct is purely coincidental. These are works of fiction.*

Print edition ISBN 978-1-78116-420-4
E-book ISBN 978-1-78116-421-1

Design direction by Max Phillips
www.maxphillips.net
Typeset by Swordsmith Productions

Harlan Ellison and Edgeworks Abbey
are registered trademarks of The Kilimanjaro Corporation.

The name "Hard Case Crime" and the Hard Case Crime logo are trademarks of
Winterfall LLC. Hard Case Crime books are selected and edited by Charles Ardai.

Printed in the United States of America

Visit us on the web at www.HardCaseCrime.com

The original edition of
this, my first book, bore the
following dedication:

*"Whoso neglects learning in his youth,
loses the past and is dead for the future."*
                                    — *Euripedes*

To my teachers:
        Charby,
        Mother,
        AJ

But time passes, debts are
canceled, and sometimes the
student surpasses the teacher.

In which case one curses the
lesson and blesses the knowledge.

And so, years later,
I need only rededicate this
fledgling effort to

MY MOTHER,

with love and deep respect.

WEB OF THE CITY

INTRODUCTION: UNNECESSARY WORDS

There's really no point to writing an introduction to a novel. A book of short stories, sure, okay. A collection of essays, definitely. A scholarly tome, naturally. But what the hell should one have to say about an entertainment, a fiction, a novel? Nothing. It should speak for itself.

And I intend to let it.

Even so, I'd like to make one brief statement about the book. Bear with me; I won't be long.

There's a story told about Hemingway—I don't know if it's true or not, but if it isn't, it ought to be. The story goes that he was either on his way to France or on his way back from France, one or the other, I don't recall the specifics of the anecdote that well. He was on shipboard, and he had with him his first novel. Not *The Sun Also Rises*; the one he wrote *before* that "first novel" that made him a literary catchword almost overnight.

Yes, the story goes, Hemingway had written a book *before The Sun Also Rises*, and there he was aboard ship, steaming either here or there; and he was at the rail, leaning over, thinking, and then he took the boxed manuscript of the book…and threw it into the ocean.

Apparently on the theory that no one should *ever* read a writer's first novel.

Which would mean—were all writers to subscribe to that theory—we'd never have had *One Hundred Dollar Misunderstanding* or *The Catcher in the Rye* or *From Here to Eternity* or

The Seven Who Fled or *The Painted Bird* or *Gone With the Wind* or...

Well, you get the idea.

I don't know whether to argue with the theory or not, but I suppose I'm lobbying against it by permitting (nay, *encouraging*) this reprint of my first novel, *Web of the City*. It was my first book, written under mostly awful personal circumstances, and I'm rather fond of it. I've re-read it this last week, just to find out *how* amateurish and inept it is, and I find it still holds the interest. I even gave it to a couple of nasty types who profess to being my friends when they aren't sticking it in my back, and even *they* say it's worth preserving.

So the book is alive once more.

The time about which it speaks is gone—the early fifties; and the place it talks about has changed somewhat—Brooklyn, the slums. But it has a kind of innocent verve about it that commends it to your attention. I hope, of course, that you'll agree with me.

In case you might wonder, I began writing it around the tail end of 1956 and the first three months of 1957. I was drafted in March of 1957 and wrote the bulk of the book while undergoing the horrors of Ranger basic training at Fort Benning, Georgia. After a full day, from damned near dawn till well after dusk, marching, drilling, crawling on my belly across infiltration courses, jumping off static-line towers, learning to carve people up with bayonets and break their bodies with judo and other unpleasant martial arts, our company would be fed and then hustled into a barracks, where the crazed killers who were my fellow troopers would clean their weapons, spit-shine their boots, and then collapse across their bunks to sleep the sleep of the tormented. I, on the other hand, would take a wooden plank, my Olympia typewriter, and my box of manuscript and blank paper, and would go into the head (that's the toilet to you civilized folks), place the board across my lap as I sat on one of the potties, and I would write this book.

After the first couple of fist fights, they stopped complaining about the noise and let me alone. But Sgt. Jacobowski called me, in his dragon's voice, "The Author." The way he pronounced it, it always came out sounding like The *Aw*-ter.

The editor who bought the book originally, who took the first chance on me as a novelist, was a wonderful guy named Walter Fultz. He was the editor at Lion Books, a minor paperback house that gave a lot of newcomers a break. Walter is dead now, tragically, before his time, but I think he would have liked to've seen how long-lived this book has become, and how the kid he gave a break has come along.

Lion Books went out of business before they could release *Web of the City*, and the backlog of titles was sold here and there. Pyramid Books then bought the manuscript.

It was almost a year later, in 1958, while I was serving out my sentence as the most-often-demoted PFC in the history of the United States Army, at Fort Knox, Kentucky, when this book finally hit print. I was writing for the Fort Knox newspaper, and getting boxes of review paperbacks for a column I was doing, when the August shipment of Pyramid titles came in. I opened the box, flipped through the various products therein, and almost had a coronary when I held in my hands, for the first time in my life, a book with my name on the cover.

Except, the book was titled *Rumble*.

Nonetheless, it was an experience that comes only once in a writer's life, the first book, and I was the tallest walkin' Private in the Army that week.

Maybe I should have taken sides with old Ernie, dumping this book in the Pacific as he dumped that first novel in the Atlantic;

but I cannot forget the hot August afternoon in Kentucky during which I realized my life's dream and became, for the first time, an *author*.

And even if *Web of the City* isn't *War and Peace*, you just can't kill something you've loved as much as I love this book.

So read on and, with a little compassion on your part, you'll be kind to the memory of the punk kid who wrote it.

HARLAN ELLISON

ONE:
THURSDAY NIGHT

- *rusty santoro*
- *the cougars*

The city lay cool and dim beneath a vaulting sky of high-scudding gray clouds. A gray shroud that covered the corpses of buildings, stiff in brick-and-steel rigor mortis, pale in their eternity of sooty death.

The heat of the afternoon had slowly passed away, the trembling waves of warmth disappearing like wraiths to be replaced by mugginess and unrest; the sweat had gone back into the pores, the cats back into the alleys, the wineheads back into the bars, the amateurs back to their pads.

It was evening, and evening was free time, and free time was the time to go! Rusty was abroad in the night.

His name was Rusty, but it wasn't really Rusty, and he had cut the umbilicus that bound him to the gang. A half hour before he had faced the gang and snarled, "I told ya a couple months ago I was through, that I was split with the Cougars, an' ya been buggin' me ever since to come back. Now you better know what I'm sayin'—'specially you, Candle—that I'm done.

"That's my answer. Now I'm splittin' and I don't want no trouble."

That had been the speech, and those had been the emotions, and that was what had started it, what had set the spider to weaving. The spider was a city, gray and observant and jealous once in a while, though deep inside it didn't really care at all.

But the black widow cannot stop weaving, and the city cannot stop weaving. Alike in temperament, they feast on their spawn.

It was good to get away from them. Rusty felt the sweat that had come to live on his spine trickle down like a small bug. He had made his peace with them, and he was free of the gang. That was it. He had it knocked now. He'd built a big sin, but it was a broken bit now. The gang was there, and he was here.

He was no longer Prez of the Cougars, and the road was starting to open up. He'd be able to walk past the fuzz on the corner, and not have the bluecoat stare at him like he was hot or something. He was out and gliding.

The streets were silent. How strange for this early in the evening. As though the being that was the neighborhood—and it was a thing with life and sentience—knew something was about to happen. The silence made the sweat return. It was too quiet. Like it was down, man. A down down bit. What was up?

He came around the corner, and they were waiting.

"Nobody bugs out on the Cougars," was all one of them said. It was so dark, the streetlight broken, that he could not see the kid's face, but it was light enough to see the reflection of moonlight on the tire chain in the kid's hand. Then they jumped him.

He took a step to run. A fist crashed into the side of his head. He felt the brains within him scramble and jumble, and then he went down. The tire chain took him in the small of the back with a crack that numbed both his legs, sent lancets of liquid fire up to his neck.

He tried to cover, to dummy, folding in like a foetus with head and gut and groin protected, but there were hundreds of them, and they used their feet.

Metal-toed barracks boots, reinforced motorcycle boots, sod-brogans; they stomped him again and again. His ribs were numbed in a second, his back was a plain of welts and blood.

One of them got through his protectively covering arms and caught him on the right cheekbone.

"Holy Jesus, Mary, god save me…" he murmured softly through bloody lips and they continued working on him.

It only went on forever.

Then the sound of a cop's whistle broke the silence that had been host to only the sounds of stomping and his grunts of pain. The whistle came from far away beyond the veil of foggy pain that swirled in on him, and one last resounding kick took him in the crotch. He screamed like an animal. Then he heard them running away. The whistling grew louder.

"G-got to, to make it…" he bubbled, trying to rise. He fell back and lay there panting. The pain was so big, man, so big. He crawled to the gutter and slipped over, trying to raise himself on the fire hydrant. He got to his feet and saw that the world had been sawed in half across the skull-top. "Ma—Make it away…" was his plea to the night.

He stumbled away, into the alley, and down its stinking length to a hideaway behind the rubbish bins and cardboard boxes. He fell into a sitting position, his eyes closed, and waited.

The cop hit the scene on the street, and looked around. Deadly all-pervading silence. Gone. They were gone, and he had missed again. Damned juvies!

The cop checked out. Rusty Santoro lay there, eyes closed, and hurt.

Then he opened his eyes, for someone was watching him.

In one of the bricked-up doorways in the alley, slumped down with a ketchup bottle full of Sweet Lucy, lay his father. Eyes red and puffed, his face a mask of interest and stupor intermingled, Mr. Santoro stared brightly at his son. Rusty could tell, the old man had seen it all and had not moved to help.

Rusty lay there with the pain like a torch in him, barely drawing breath, seeing his father for the first time that week. He lay there gasping and wetting his ripped, bloody lips with a dry tongue-tip.

"They beat'a hell outta ya, didn't they?" Mr. Santoro cackled.

Rusty shut his eyes and let the darkness that marched in behind the irises take him. He swirled down and down, with pain his partner, and knew this was a typical night. It was the same.

Always the same.

You can't get free. Once stained, always stained. The seeds of dirt are sown deeply. And are harvested forever.

Darkness outside, while his father laughed and fell asleep also.

TWO:
FRIDAY MORNING

- *rusty santoro*
- *candle*
- *pancoast*

There was no doubt about it: they were getting ready to stomp him again. They were going to wait for him in an alley and slice his gut out. That was the way the Cougars did it to a member who left the club. That was the way of it, and no escaping.

Rusty Santoro knew they were going to get him, if it took forever. They had asked, "You comin' back?" and he had stalled, trying to find a way out. But now there was no way out. They had jumped him the night before, and the pain was still big in him. Rusty choked as the chisel bit into the leg of wood, sprayed sawdust across his face and T-shirt. He puffed air between his thin lips, continued working, and continued to ignore the boy who stood behind him.

The boy who had come to kill him, surely. Candle; their Prez, their assassin.

The wood shop had quieted down. No one else moved, and their tools were silent.

He had wakened in the alley this morning, and hurried right to school. He couldn't cut out, or the boom would lower on him… after all, he was in Pancoast's custody, and any infraction of the rules would stone him good. He ignored Candle, behind him.

The alley had been cold, and his back had been stiff and he had ached terribly, but as the hours had passed, the pain had simmered down to merely a constant throbbing. Three teeth were broken, but they were in the back, and when he had washed his face, only a group of blue and ugly welts were left on his face. Broken flesh and shattered capillaries studded his right cheekbone, but it would pass. His lips were raw.

His back was in worse shape. But he knew he would live. He had to—because the Cougars wanted him dead.

The school shop was empty of voices. Only the constant machine hum of lathes that had been ignored, left running, filled the shop with sound. Yet somehow the room was silent.

The boy behind Rusty took a short half-step closer, shoved his shoulder hard. Rusty was thrown off-balance, and the chisel bit too deep into the chair leg between the lathe points. The design was ruined. The chisel snapped away, and Rusty spun, anger flaming his face. He stared hard at the other boy, changed his grip on the wood chisel. Now he held it underhand—knife-style.

The other boy didn't move.

"What's a'matter, spick? Y'don't wanna talk to your old buddy Candle no more?" His thick, square face drew up in a wild grimace.

Rusty Santoro's face tightened. His thin line of mouth jerked with the effort to keep words from spewing out. He had known the Cougars would try to get to him today, but he hadn't figured on it during school hours.

Over him, somehow—tense as he was, knowing a stand was here and he couldn't run without being chick-chick—Rusty felt the brick-and-steel bulk of Pulaski High School.

You just can't run away from them, he thought.

The boy, Candle, had come into the basement wood shop a minute before. He had told the shop teacher, Mr. Pancoast, that he was wanted in the Principal's office. Mr. Pancoast had left the shop untended—oh, Kammy Josephs was monitor, but hell, that didn't cut any ice with *anyone*—and Candle had moved in fast. First the little nudge. Then the shove that could not be ignored. The dirty names. Now they were face-to-face, Rusty with the sharp wood chisel, and Candle with a blade. Someplace. Somewhere. It wasn't in sight, but Candle had a switch on him. That boy wouldn't leave home without being heeled.

Rusty looked across into Candle's eyes. His own gray ones were level and wide. "You call me spick, craphead?"

Candle's square jaw moved idly, as though he were chewing gum, when he was not chewing gum. "Ain't that what you are, man? Ain't you a Puerto? You look like a spick…"

Rusty didn't wait for the sentence to linger in the air. He lunged quickly, slashing upward with the chisel. The weapon zipped close to Candle, and the boy sucked in his belly, leaped backward. Then the switchblade was in his square, short-fingered hand.

The blade was there, and it filled the room for Rusty. It was all live and lightning, everything that was, and the end to everything else. Rusty Santoro watched—as though what was about to happen was moving through heavy syrup, slow, terribly slow —and saw Candle's hairy arm come up, the knife clutched tightly between white fingers. He heard the *snick!* of the opening blade, even as the other's thumb pressed the button.

Then there was a green plastic shank, and a strip of light that was honed steel.

The shop was washed by bands of lazy sunlight, slanting through the barred window; and in those bands of light, with sawdust motes rising and turning slowly, slowly, Rusty saw the blade of the switch gleam. Saw it turn in Candle's hand, saw the way his flesh cleaved to it with more than need; this was part of Candle. Part of his thought and part of his life. His hand had been formed to end in a knife. Anything else would have been wrong, all wrong.

"Don't you ever call me that again, man. Just don't you call me no spick again!"

Candle dropped his shoulders slightly. He automatically assumed the stance of the street-fighter. No spick bastard was going to buck him. There was more to this than just a wood chisel. Nobody, but nobody, leaves the gang.

"Well, ain't you gettin' big these days. One minute you're too good for the Cougars, and the next you're particular who calls ya what." His green eyes narrowed, and the knife moved in aimless, circling little movements, as though it were a snake, all too anxious to strike.

"I don't dig you, spick man…"

And he came in fast.

The knife came out and up and around in one movement that was all lightning and swiftness. Rusty slipped sidewise, lost his footing, and went down, his shoulder striking hard against the base of the lathe. He saw Candle strut back and get ready to pounce. Then there was all that knife in his vision, and he knew he was going to get it at last. Not later, not sometime never, but here, gutted and cut, right here on the floor, and there was nothing he could do about it. He saw Moms and Dolores.

Candle rose high, and his arm drew back, and then his arm was dragged back of his head by someone else. Rusty looked up and everything was out of focus, and his shoulder hurt, but a man with dull red hair had Candle around the throat, had the knife-hand bent back double. Candle screamed high and loud, over the whine of the machines, and the man twisted the arm an inch more.

The blade clattered to the floor.

The man kicked it out of sight under a drill press, into sawdust debris. Then the man had Candle by the front of his dirty T-shirt, was leaning in close, and saying, "You get the hell out of here, or I turn you over to the Principal and tell him you lied to get me out of my shop while you attacked a pupil with a switch. With your record around here, Shaster, you couldn't stand it. Now beat it!" He shoved Candle Shaster away from him, sent him spinning into the door.

Candle threw it open, spat on the floor, and was gone in a moment.

Rusty still found himself unable to focus in properly, but Mr. Pancoast was lifting him to his feet, and yelling to the other boys, "Okay, let's get back to work."

The rising clatter of shop work filled his universe, and then he was out in the basement hall, in the cool depths of the school. "Sit down," Pancoast directed him, pushing him gently toward the stairs.

Rusty sat down heavily. Now he not only felt the incessant throbbing of his shoulder, but for the first time felt the full force of the pain where, he now realized, he had struck his head. It throbbed mercilessly.

Pancoast slid down next to the boy. He was a short man, with hair just a few shades darker than orange. His face was tired, but there was something alive in his eyes that gave the lie to his features. He had been dealing with high-school boys so long, he had difficulty with adults, so geared were his thoughts to the adolescent mind.

He pursed his lips, then asked, "What was that all about, Rusty? I thought after that last scrape you were going to stay away from the Cougars, from Candle and his bunch."

Rusty tapped gently at the bruise that ached on his head. He swung his body back and forth, as though he were caught in some tremor that would not release him. His entire body shook. The aftereffects were setting in—they always did, just this way. It made him wonder if he was a coward. He shook and quivered and wished he'd never heard of the Cougars.

"I told 'em I was quitting. Last night. They don't like that. They tell me nobody leaves the gang. I said *I* did."

Pancoast rubbed the short stubble on his small chin. He stared levelly at Rusty. "That all, Rusty?"

"Isn't that enough?"

Pancoast replied, "Look, Rusty. When they caught you, along with those other Cougars, trying to break into that liquor store, I went out for you. Remember?" He waited for an answer. Finally, Rusty nodded.

The teacher went on. "I had them release you into my custody, Rusty, and you've been good as your word ever since. At first I thought you were like all the rest of them—hard, no real guts, just a little killer inside—but you've shown me you're a man. You've got real woodworking talent, Rusty. You could be a sculptor, or a designer, even an architect, if you wanted to be."

Rusty was impatient. Being praised like this, in the crowd he ran, usually meant a slap was coming. "So?"

"So, we're both going to have to go over there, Rusty, and let them know for sure, for finally, that you're out of the gang, that you don't want any part of it…"

Rusty was shaking his head. "It ain't that easy. You don't understand, Mr. Pancoast. It ain't like being a member of Kiwanis or the P.T.A. It ain't like nothin' else in the world. When you're in, you're in. And the only thing that gets you out is if you land in the can, or you get a shank in your gut. That's what I tried to tell ya when ya made me quit."

He stared at the teacher with mute appeal. He was boxed-in, and he knew it. There was going to have to be a face-up soon, and he wasn't sure he was man enough.

Carl Pancoast leaned closer to the boy, put an arm on his knee, tried to speak to him so the words went deeper than the ears. So they went right down to the core.

"Look, Rusty. Let me tell you something. You can go on doing what the Cougars do, all your life, and wind up the way Tony Green did. You remember Tony, you remember what happened to him?"

Pancoast could see the memory in Rusty's eyes. He could see the vision of Tony Green, who had been top trackman at Pulaski, laid out on a slab, with a D.O.A. tag around his big toe. A zip gun .22 slug in his head. Dead in a rumble.

"Remember why he got killed, Rusty?"

Pancoast was pushing thoughts tightly, forcing them to the fore, making Rusty analyze his past. It wasn't a pleasant past.

Drenched in violence. Product of filth and slum and bigotry. Mothered by fear. Fathered by the terror of non-conformism and the fate that waited for those who did not conform. Rusty remembered. His stomach tightened, and his seventeen-year-old brain spun, but he remembered.

Tony Green, tall and slim, and dead. Out there on a slab because someone had danced with his steady girl at a club drag. Nothing more important. Just that.

"I'm through, Mr. Pancoast. You don't have to worry about that. I'm through, but man, it's gonna be rough all the way."

Carl Pancoast clapped the boy on the back. It would be tough all right, tough as banana skins, but that was the way it had to be. Because Rusty had to live out there in that stinking city. He had to live and learn and sweat beside those kids.

"What are you going to do?"

Rusty bit his lip, shrugged. "Don't know, man. But I got to do something. They ain't gonna give me much longer. Maybe I'll go over there tonight, club night. Maybe I'll go over again and have a talk with some of the kids."

Pancoast's forehead assumed V-lines of worry. "Want me to go along? Most of the Cougars know me."

Rusty sloughed away his offer.

"No go. They know you, but you're still out of it, man. Way out. You're boss-type, and they don't dig that even a little. I come walking in with you, and I'm dead from the start.

"No, I can handle it."

He stood up unsteadily, clung to the bannister for a minute. It rocked under his weight.

"Lousy school," he mumbled, slamming the banister, "gonna fall apart under ya."

He walked back into the shop, and a minute later Pancoast heard the chisel on the ruined chair leg. Violently. Could Rusty come all the way back? Could he purge the kill stuff from his blood?

It was going to be rough. Real rough.

He went back to his class, worried as hell.

After school, Rusty avoided Carl Pancoast. The teacher had done too much for him, and whatever was coming, was going to have to come to him alone. Rusty slouched against the sooty brick wall of Pulaski High and drew deeply on a cigarette. The kids avoided him. The stench of trouble was all about him.

Finally, Louise came out of the building, books clutched tightly to her chest. She saw Rusty, and stopped. Rusty knew what was running around scared inside her head: should she go to join her steady, walk home with him, stop to have a Coke with him—or should she walk past and get the hell away from what might be coming?

It was a big choice. One way she would lose Rusty—he was like that, just like that—and the other she might lose her pretty face.

Rusty knew what was happening within her, and he abruptly felt so alone, so terribly desperately alone, he had to remove the burden of decision from her, had to hold onto one person in this thing…if only for a short while. He pushed away from the wall. He walked over to her.

"Wanna stop for a Coke, Weezee?"

Louise Chaplin, more "Weezee" than Louise, was a highly attractive girl, whose natural beauty was marred by imperfect application of makeup. Her eyes were a clear blue, her skin smooth, her hair a rich chestnut brown, drawn back into a full, rippling ponytail. Her young body was already making attractive bulges and curves within her sweater and skirt. She was aware of her growing body, and so the sweater was a size and a half too small.

Now her eyes darkened, and she blinked rapidly, pausing a moment before answering; an agonizing moment for Rusty. She finally answered, "Sure. Guess so. What's new?"

It was like that all the way down the street.

Chit-chat. She was scared. Really, terribly scared, and though Weezee wasn't a member of the Cougars' girls' auxiliary—the Cougie Cats—she was still in Cougar turf, and if a war started, she would be one of the first to get it. Right after Rusty.

The streets were crowded. Late Friday afternoon, with fat Polish women going from butcher to butcher, trying to get the best cuts of meat for the weekend; little kids playing hopscotch and stick-ball on sidewalks, against walls; radios blasting from every direction with the Giants or the Dodgers beating the pants off someone. Normal day, with a sun, with gutters dirtied by candy wrappers and dogs that had been curbed, with the sound of the subway underfoot, with everything normal. Including the stink of death that hung not unknown above everything else.

It was funny how the territory—the turf—knew when something was burning. Even the old women in their anti-macassared single rooms, waiting for their government checks, knew the gangs were about to rise. The shopkeepers knew it, and they feared for their windows. The cops knew it and they began to straighten in harness. The cabbies knew it, and they shifted territory, hurrying back uptown to catch the safe Madison Avenue crowd.

Everyone knew it, yet a word was never spoken, an action never completed. It hung rank in the air, dampening everyone's mood of weekend joviality. Rusty walked through it, dragging his feet as if he were underwater.

Weezee walked along beside him, clutching her books to her firm young breasts, too tightly, till her fingers whitened out on the notebook. The scare was so high in her, it came out of her pores, and Rusty wished he had not approached her. They were steadies, but their feeling went no deeper than movies, casual loving, kicks and mutual respect. Was it enough to die for? No sense dragging her into this.

But at the same time, he was perversely glad she was there; he was determined to make her sweat, if *he* had to sweat. They turned in at Tom-Tom's Ice Cream Parlor. Rusty gave the place a quick look-over before entering, and then pushed open one of the wooden doors with the glass almost covered by soft drink advertisements. They walked past the counter, past the magazine racks, to the booths in the back.

Weezee slipped into one far back, and even as Rusty watched, drew in on herself, slid closer to the wall, made herself ready for what *had* to come.

Rusty sat down across from her, two-fingered a cigarette from the crush-box in his jacket pocket. He offered it to the girl, but she shook her head slowly. Her eyes were very blue and very frightened. He lit the cigarette with a kitchen match and settled back, one foot up on the bench, watching her steadily.

Finally Tom-Tom came back to get their order.

He was a stubby man, built like a beachball, with rolls of baby fat under his chin, where a neck should have been but was not, with faint lines where his wrists joined his hands…like the lines on a baby's wrists. He had been in the neighborhood a long time, and his hair was white, but his appearance was always the same. So was his service. Bad.

Rusty looked across at Weezee. "Coke?" She nodded. "Make it a pair," he said to Tom-Tom.

The beachball rolled away, shaking its head. These damned kids sat here for three hours over one lousy Coke, and if he tried to bounce them he'd get a staved-in candy counter for his trouble. Damned neighborhood. One of these days, he was going to move, open a high-class little shop in the Village somewhere.

Rusty sat silently watching his girl. Weezee bit her red, red lips, and her hands moved nervously. Finally, she asked, "Why are you quitting the Cougars?"

Rusty made a vague movement with his hand, uneasy that she had broken the law. She had let her feelings be known, had asked him a straight question he could not goof out of answering. "Dunno. Just tired, I guess."

Her face grew rigid. "It's that goddamned teacher, that Pancoast, ain't it?" she asked.

Rusty leaned forward an inch, said tightly, "Just forget about him. He's okay. He saved my tail from the can a month ago, that's all I know."

"But it is him, isn't it?"

"For Christ's sake, can't you knock it off? I just quit because I wanted to, and that's it, period."

She shook her head in bewilderment. "But you was Prez of the Cougars for three years. They ain't gonna like you leeching out that way."

"That's their row to hoe."

She tried desperately to pierce the shield he had erected

before his thoughts. What he was doing was suicide and she felt a desperate need to communicate with him, to get him to see what he was doing to himself—and to her. For as Rusty's drag, she was as marked as he.

"Are you chick-chick?"

Rusty slammed forward against the table. His hand came down flat with a smash, and his eyes burned fiercely. "Look, don't you never call me that, unnerstand. I'm no more chickie than anybody else." His face smoothed out slowly, the anger ebbed away even more slowly.

Finally, he added, "Weezee, I been runnin' the streets with the Cougars for three years. I got in lots of trouble with 'em. Look at me. I'm seventeen, an' I got a record. Nice thing to know? Like hell it is! I been usin' my fists since I could talk, and I'm just up to here with it, and that's on the square. I just wanted out, is all."

The girl shook her head. The brown hair swirled in its ponytail, and she began twirling it nervously. "They're gonna make it rough on you, Rusty."

He nodded silently.

Tom-Tom brought the Cokes, collected the two dimes Rusty laid out, and went back to his fountain.

Five minutes later, they arrived. The silent word had passed down the neighborhood.

Not the entire gang; just ten of them, with Candle in the front. Many of Rusty's old buddies were there—Fish, Clipper, Johnny Slice, even the kid they called the Beast—and they all had the same look in their eyes. All but the Beast. He was half-animal, only half-human, and what he had behind his eyes, no one knew. But all the rest, they saw Rusty as an enemy now. Two months before he had been their leader, but now the lines had changed, and Rusty was on the outside.

Why did I come here with Weezee? Why didn't I go straight

home? His thoughts spun and whirled and ate at him. They answered themselves immediately. There were several reasons. He had to prove he wasn't chicken, both to himself and to everyone else. That was part of it, deep inside. There were worse things than being dead, and being chicken was one of them. Then too, he knew the running and hiding was no good. Start running, do it once, and it would never stop. And the days in fear would all be the worse.

That was why he was here, and that was why he would have to face up to them.

Candle made the first move.

He stepped forward, and before either of them could say anything, he had slid into the booth beside Weezee. The boy's face was hard, and the square, flat, almost-Mongoloid look of it was frightening. Rusty made a tentative move forward, to get Candle away from his girl, but three Cougars stepped in quickly, and pinned his arms.

One of them brought a fist close to Rusty's left ear, and the boy heard a click. He caught the blade's gleam from the corner of his eye.

"Waddaya want?" Rusty snarled, straining against their hands.

Candle leaned across, folding his arms, and his face broke in a smile that was straight from hell. "I didn't get called onna carpet by Pancoast. He kept his mouth shut."

"Why don't you?" Rusty replied sharply.

Candle's hand came up off the table quickly, and landed full across Rusty's jaw. The boy's head jerked, the night-before's pain started anew, but he stared straight at the other. His eyes were hard, even though a five-pronged mark of red lived on his cheek.

"Listen, teacher's pet. That bit this mornin' was just a start. Last night was a sample. We had us a talk in the Cougars, after I was elected Prez, after you ran out on us like a…"

Rusty cut in abruptly. "What's it all about, Big Mouth? What's your beef? You weren't nothin' in the gang till I left, now you think you're god or somethin'…"

This time it was a double-fisted crack, once! twice!, and blood erupted from Rusty's mouth. His lip puffed, and his teeth felt slippery wet.

"I'll hand all that back to you real soon, Big Deal." But Rusty was held tightly.

"Nobody checks out on the gang, y'unnerstand?" He nodded to one of the boys holding Rusty's left hand, and the boy drew back. Candle's fist came out like a striking snake, and the fingers opened, and they grasped Rusty's hand tightly. Rusty flexed his hand, trying to break the grip, but Candle was there for keeps, and the knife was still at his ear. He let the other boy squeeze…and squeeze…and squeeze…and…

Rusty suddenly lunged sidewise, cracking his shoulder into the boy with the knife. The force of his movement drew Candle partially from the booth, and he released his grip.

Then Rusty moved swiftly, and his hand, flat and fingers tight together, slashed out, caught the boy with the knife across the Adam's apple. The boy gagged and dropped the blade. In an instant it was in Rusty's hand, and he was around the booth, had the tip of the switchblade just behind Candle's ear.

"Now," he panted, trying to hold the knife steady, having difficulty with nervous jerks of his hand, "you're all gonna listen to me.

"I left the Cougars 'cause I'm through. That's all, and it doesn't gotta make sense to any of you. I'm out, and I want out to stay, and the first guy that tries to give me trouble, I'll cut him, so help me god!"

The other Cougars moved forward, as if to step in, but Candle's face had whitened out, and his jaw worked loosely. "No, for Christ's sake, stay away from him!"

Rusty went on, "Listen, how long you figure I gotta run with this crowd? How long you figure I gotta keep gettin' myself in bad with the school, with my old lady, with the cops? You guys wanna do it, that's your deal, but leave me alone. I don't talk to nobody about what goes on in the Cougars, and I don't bother you. Just don't you bother me."

Fish—tall, and slim, with long eyelashes that made him think he was a ladies' man—spoke up. "You been fed too much of that good jazz by that Pancoast cat, Rusty. You believe that stuff, man?"

Rusty edged the knife closer, the tip indenting the soft skin behind Candle's ear, as the seated Prez tried to move. "He dealt me right all along. He says I got a chance to become an industrial designer if I work hard at it. I like the idea. That's the reason, and that's it.

"Now whaddaya say? Lemme alone, and I let your big deal Prez alone."

At that instant, it all summed up for Rusty. That was it; that was why he was different from these others. He wanted a future. He wanted to be something. Not to wind up in a gutter with his belly split, not to spend the rest of his life in the army, not to end up as a useless bum on the street—because that was where *most* of these guys were going to close out their stories.

He wanted a life that had some purpose. And even as he felt the vitality of the thoughts course through him, he saw the Cougars were ready to accept it. He had been with them for three years. They had all rumbled together, all gotten records together, all screwed around and had fun together. But now, somehow, he was older than them.

And he wanted free.

Fish spoke for all of them. Softly, and with the first sincerity Rusty had ever heard from the boy. "I guess it sits okay with us, Rusty. Whatever you say goes. I'm off you." He turned to the others, and his face was abruptly back in its former mold. He was the child of the gutters; hard and looking for opposition.

"That go for the rest of you?"

Each of them nodded. Some of them smiled. The Beast waggled his head like some lowing animal, and there was only one dissenter, as Rusty broke the knife, tossed it to its owner.

Candle was out of the booth, and his own weapon was out. He walked forward, and backed Rusty into the wall with it. His face was flushed, and what Rusty had known was in the boy— the sadism, the urge to fight, the animal hunger that was there and could never really be covered by a black leather jacket or chino slacks—was there on top, boiling up like a pool of lava, waiting to engulf both of them.

"*I* don't buy it, man. I think as long as you're around, the Cougars won't wanna take orders from their new Prez. So there's gotta be a final on this. I challenge."

Rusty felt a sliver of cold as sharp as the sliver of steel held by Candle slither down into his gut. He had to stand with Candle. It was the only way. As long as you lived in a neighborhood where the fist was the law, there could be no doubt. Either you were chickie or you weren't. If an unanswered challenge hung around his neck like an albatross, his days on the street were numbered.

Slowly, hesitantly, he nodded agreement. Knowing he was slipping back. Knowing all the work Pancoast had done might be wasted. Knowing that the future might wind up in the gutter with him.

"When?" he asked.

"Tomorrow. In the morning, we'll send someone after ya. At the dumps. Come heeled, man, 'cause I'm gonna split you to your groin."

He broke his knife, shoved it into his sleeve, and walked

away, angrily shoving aside the Cougars. He was gone, then, and the ice-cream shop was silent for a moment.

Then Fish shrugged, said lamely, "Gee, I'm, well, hell, Rusty …there ain't…"

Rusty cut him off, running a hand through his own hair. "I know, man. Don't bother. Ain't nothin' you can do. I gotta stand with Candle. Gonna be rough bananas, though."

Why was his past always calling? Always making grabs on him? The blood was flowing so thick, so red, and it smothered him. He felt as though he was drowning.

Wouldn't he ever be free?

THREE:
FRIDAY NIGHT,
SATURDAY MORNING

- *rusty santoro*
- *the family*
- *the scum*

The apartment was cool and dark as Rusty threw his books on the sofa. The persistent ticking of the beat-up cuckoo clock kept the feeling of everything together, like a glue of sound. He sometimes felt if it weren't for that damned clock always going, the household would fall apart. He didn't know why he felt that way, but he had the queer feeling the clock was the magnet in the joint.

He heard a clattering sound from the kitchen and knew his mother was in there, moaning and working. Preparing chow for Dolores and himself—and for Pops, if he came home tonight. Which was pretty slim chancey.

"Russell?"

His mother's voice came echoing out of the kitchen. He nodded his head tiredly and knew she would call again. He got some sort of strange pleasure from making her call twice. "Russell, that you?"

"Yeah, Ma. Me."

"Where you been? School let out two hours ago. You been runnin' the streets again with them kids?" Her voice was like an ancient steam radiator puff-puffing, never stopping, till late in the night when it went cold with sleep.

"I stayed after school, worked in the shop," he lied.

"You tellin' me the truth?" She knew when he was cutting the corners of truth. He didn't know why he always did it, because telling her the truth would have been just as easy, but some perverse inclination always substituted another alibi.

"Yes, yes, yes, fer Chrissakes, I'm tellin' the truth!"

She came out of the kitchen, wiping her red hands on a dish towel. "Don't use the Lord's name in vain in this house!"

Oh no, Rusty thought tiredly. She's on the Savior kick today. *She must of stumbled across Pop's Bible*. This'll be a good night, I can tell. "Yes, ma'am," he said aloud.

"Now," she was relentless, "where was you? You didn't come home last night."

"I told ya, Ma! I was around last night, just out, like, and I stayed after school today, inna wood shop. Don't ya believe me?"

Her face drew tight about the eyes. "You lyin' to me again? What about last night?"

He knew there was no point in continuing. He changed the subject. "Dolo get home yet?"

As though it were understood that he had lied, but that the discussion was closed, Rusty's mother shook her head slowly, drawing a deep fatigue-breath. "No, she's just like you. Got all your habits in her. You hadda go and get her into that gang. Now she's never home, like a good girl, always runnin' with them other girls, an' swearin'."

She knew it cut Rusty. He had gotten Dolores into the Cougars' girls' auxiliary at his sister's constant insistence, and he had regretted it immediately. It wasn't good for a fifteen-year-old girl to run with them. They were worse than the boys sometimes. It worried Rusty how she was always with them, never at home helping Ma. But then, neither was he...

"How'd your lip get split, Russell?"

She was back on that kick again. "My name ain't Russell. Everybody else calls me Rusty, why can't you? You all the time gotta be different?"

His mother stepped forward, raised the dish towel as though to strike him, and in defense he put a hand before his face. "Don't you raise your voice to your own mother. Oh god! What have I done to deserve this? A rotten son, a wayward daughter and a husband…"

Rusty cut in. "Dolo's okay! You don't say nothin' against her, Ma. She's okay, she just—just wants a little fun, that's all."

His mother shook her head sadly, slumped into one of the cheap, overstuffed armchairs in the room. "Oh, yes, yes, yes, just fun. That's all you kids want is fun. Fun, fun, and nothin' else ever. Is this what I brought you up to be? A street hoodlum?"

"Oh, Ma, for Chrissakes!"

"I thought I told you not to —"

"Okay, okay. Sorry, sorry. I'm sorry I said it, just a slip of the tongue; you know."

She stared down at her red hands. "I know. I know."

Rusty suddenly felt an overwhelming wave of compassion for this woman. Was it his mother or just some stranger who had a strong claim on him for some unknown reason? He wasn't certain. He didn't know. But there was a tearing in him, and he said, "Anything I can help you with?"

Her face looked up at him, and he was surprised to note that he could never recall having seen that face before. But it was his Ma, he knew that.

"Do for me? What's there to do…when I've done it all, already. No, nothing to do."

He turned, and saw her face was marked by the zig-zag path of a tear down one cheek. The tearing came again and an actual physical pain deep in his stomach. He wanted so much to go to her and kneel down and put his head in her lap, and cry with her. But that was outside the code. That was being weak and he would never do it, though it would mean so much to both of them, he knew.

"Why don'cha call me Rusty, Ma?"

"Because your name is Russell!"

"But the kids all call me…"

"I don't care! I don't care what the kids call you. Have you no heart, no feeling for your own mother, for what she wants? Is it always the kids?"

What could he say. Rusty was his name, more than Russell could ever be. "Oh, forget it, Ma. Just forget it."

He turned and walked away.

She sat very still till he was down the hall, and she heard the slamming of the bedroom door. Then she twisted the towel so tightly about her hands, the skin wrinkled, and reddened terribly.

The sound of the record player from the bedroom struck her with force.

Then, and only then, did the tears come full.

Dolores did not show for dinner, and Rusty ate with his mother, a screen of silence between them broken occasionally by "Please pass the butter," or "Good bean soup tonight."

After dinner Rusty helped his mother do the dishes, she washing and he drying. He stacked them carefully, noticing each crack and chip on the old chinaware. If his father wasn't so stiff on Sneaky Pete all the time there might be more dough in the house. But that was just idle wishing. He couldn't figure why Ma stayed with a lush like his old man. It was a high dream to think of Pops being a steady nine-to-fiver. He was a mean man, that one. Rusty's mind shied away from thoughts of the old man. That was bad stuff, and he wished his old man was down under sometimes. He knew it was bad, thinking that way, fourth commandment and like that, but there was no heat you could generate about a rotten apple like his old man.

"What're ya gonna do tonight?" his mother was asking.

Rusty took a practiced swipe at the dish in his hand, and shrugged his shoulders.

"Well, what are ya gonna do?"

"How should I know? Maybe take in a movie. Maybe go down and sit around Tom-Tom's joint. I dunno, I'll see."

She pursed her thin gray lips, stared at him hard, wishing feverishly she could get through.

"Why'nt ya stay home tonight. Maybe somethin' good's on TV."

He thought of the set. The coin slot for quarters and the guy who came and emptied the receptacle once a week. Crummy, like everything else they'd ever bought. On time. A quarter in the slot and a million years to pay off. All the yuks ya want for one thin two-bit piece. Shit!

Rusty shook his head. "I don't feature that stuff, Ma. You know that. All that crap with Gleason or some other guy that ain't funny. I'd rather go out, check in some air."

She said incongruously, "Can't you talk natural? You all the time gotta use those crazy words?"

He was honestly confused. "Whaddaya mean?"

"Oh, you talkin' like them kids in the street all the time. You never talk natural, or cultured, like the people on television."

It was too much. Just too goddamned much! He threw the dish towel onto the scrubbed wooden table, and stormed to the door. "Goddamnit! I talk natural as everybody else! Can'cha stop beatin' on my ears for once? Just for once?"

He stumped through the apartment, dragged a half-empty package of cigarettes off the top of the television set, then slammed a fist against the blank-faced machine. He shrugged into his leather jacket halfway through the door, yelled, "Damn it!" as loud as he could, and slammed the door. The sound of his feet descending the stairs was a sharp tattoo in the dim halls.

Rusty's mother listened carefully, tensed with her stomach tight to the sink, and the wham of the slamming door downstairs brought her head around with a snap. He was gone, like a thousand other nights, he was gone.

She never knew if he would return.

The street was noisy as usual. The cabs tooled along with gnashing gears. The steady squares were out on the doorstoops with their fat wives, their cans of beer, their stupid expressions. Man, he couldn't stand them. All the time just roosting on their butts, never getting a cool time, just gathering dust in the world.

He beat for Tom-Tom's.

It wasn't still there. The Cougars were in, full force. He took a fast look through the glass doors to spot Candle, before he entered. But Candle was not there.

He shoved in, and the gang stopped their noise for a moment, awkwardly, before the rumpus started in again. Three couples were doing the fish, close together on the aisle between the booths. The juke was going loud—one of the boys must have turned it up, over Tom-Tom's fat objections—and Rusty identified a rhythm and blues number he was fond of. There were at least twenty kids in the malt shop. Lockup and his broad, Margie. Tiger, Greek, Shamey and that broad with a million miles on her, Caroline. He saw the Beast slouched way back in a booth, beating time with his massive hairy hands, his drooling face swinging back and forth.

Rusty edged down the counter, and came over as Fish beckoned to him from a booth.

"How goes it, man?" Fish asked.

Rusty slid in beside him, spread his hands to indicate so-so. "Where's the apple?" Rusty asked, meaning Candle.

"Out. Went off in Joy's heap with her. He'll be out for the rest of the evening. She just came off the rag and Candle ain't gonna waste no time."

Rusty nodded understanding.

"You seen my drag?"

Fish shook his head. Weezee had not been around all night. "I think she's scared out, man."

Rusty agreed. "She's okay. I don't blame her."

Fish shrugged. He couldn't care less.

The number ended, and the couples slunk off the floor, the girls clinging to their partners. Rusty felt alone, as usual. It was strange how these kids who had been his best friends, almost his whole universe, a few months before, were now nothing to him.

Fish was speaking, jerking Rusty back to where he was. "What you gonna do about tomorrow, man?"

"Whattaya mean?"

Fish arched his eyebrows. Rusty was playing it maybe too cool. "What about the stand with Candle?"

"Whattaya think? I'm gonna be there."

"He'll eat ya up, man. That's a rough apple, that Candle. You see him in that rumble with the Cherokees, couple months ago?"

Rusty shook his head. "What?"

Fish tensed his puffy fish-like lips. "Uhuh! He got one of them studs down on the ground and stomped the boy's head in with his one foot, man. Made me puke to see it. Took away that Cherokee's eye on the left, I think."

Rusty dragged out a cigarette, lit it by snapping his thumb against the head of a kitchen match. It flamed abruptly, casting a bloody shadow over his face. "He don't fear me none, Fish. I don't wanna fight to begin with, but I don't back off for no man, specially not that punky."

Fish shrugged. It wasn't his problem, but Rusty had been a good friend, and Candle was now Prez of the Cougars. It was smartest to stay out of it.

Caroline showed then.

She came around the edge of the booth and her huge, pointed breasts aimed over his head. She was a worked-out trick, with bags under her eyes, and there wasn't a stud in the club who hadn't sampled her offerings.

"Wanna dance, Rusty?" she said. Her voice was a nasal bang, and it grated on him. He thought of Weezee and her smooth, clean face, and the sight of this girl ate on him.

"No."

The juke started up then. A mover named "Blueberry Hill," Fats Domino singing, and she began hip-switching, moving her plushy, soft body in a suggestive rhythm. "Aw, come on, Rust. Let's go. Dance with me."

"I said no! Like move out, or I'll chop you out. Go!"

She said something nasty under her breath and slid away from him. In a minute she had another boy in her grip, and they stepped out smartly to the song. She pressed her fleshy breasts against the boy at every close-in, and he didn't pull away.

Rusty was sick to his belly. All this, every night, night in and night out. It was all a waste. It was a loser from the top.

He started to leave.

Fish stopped him with a hand on his arm. "Where you off to?"

"Nowhere, just out."

"You wanna get a little up tonight? I hear Boy-O got a little good-cut on him. Sound interesting?"

Rusty didn't particularly want to get high on pot or Horse

tonight, but if he went home, all he'd get would be the beat-
ears treatment from Ma and that goddamned TV. He slid back
into the booth, plopped down heavily.

"Talk to the man. See if it's top stuff or just crap. All I got on
me tonight's round money, man, so if he wants the moon for it,
no go." He drew forth a handful of coins, jiggled them mean-
ingfully. Among the coins was a souvenir Spanish silver dollar
his mother had given him. He put it inside his wallet as Fish
watched.

"I'll talk to him," and Fish stood up.

Rusty watched him walk toward Boy-O. They were so different, those two. Fish was slim, dressed sharp, had a quick wit
and an innate fighting man's senses. He was murder with a
gloveful of quarters—he had seen Fish bring down a mark with
one swing of the glove many times—and yet he had long, slim
fingers, excellent for picking locks on candy stores, or working
in clay. They had been in the same fine arts class at Pulaski last
semester, and Rusty had been amazed at how talented Fish
was, working with clay.

Boy-O was something else.

He dressed like a wharf-rat, with a stink on him that came
from alleys and taking his fun under bushes in Prospect Park.
His face was a puffy thing, all slides and fattiness, without a real
expression ever pausing on it for very long. His eyes were
junkie eyes, and he shook like a tree in a storm when he couldn't
knock off a stick or two for a few days. He had a record longer
than Seventh Avenue, in and out of Lexington Narcotics Farm
for the treatment. He was more yo-yo than human being. His
arms were cheeseclothed with needle holes. But he was the
pusher in this turf, and if you wanted a fast sky-trip, Boy-O was
the one to see.

In a while, Fish came back. He held a thin brown tube in his
fist, and dropped it into Rusty's lap. "Mex. But not bad."

Rusty picked up the dark cigarette, smelled the weed. "Pyeew…how much?"

Fish held up one finger.

"A buck? For this?" Fish shrugged, that was the way of it. A buck or no sock.

Rusty nodded okay, tossed a buck's worth of change on the table. Fish slid it off into his hand, then to his pocket.

"I figured you'd buy in. I paid him already. I got mine. Where you wanna hit for?"

Rusty felt rotten, felt nasty, felt rebellious. "Anything wrong with right here?"

Fish looked uneasy. "A fuzz walks in here, man, we've but *had* it."

"Cops don't bother me tonight. I stay here."

Fish still looked restless, unhappy about borrowing trouble. "You still under the hand of that Pancoast cat?"

Rusty replied, "Yeah. Cops put me under him for a year."

Fish tapped the table with authority. "Then what d'you wanna pull more trouble for? The fuzz are hard enough as it rides now. We better hit for the clubhouse and puff in the basement."

Rusty was adamant. "Here." To accentuate his words, he flicked a match alight, and put it to the end of the Mexican marijuana. He slumped back in the booth, putting his feet up on the seat, sinking into the cool leather of his jacket.

Fish shrugged, lit up also.

Around them the Cougars danced and chattered, while Tom-Tom cursed silently, and wished for sanctuary in the Village.

It took a longer while than usual for the stuff to hit. Rusty never liked the taste of the stuff, but the sock was more than enough to make up for the ratty taste. Pretty soon the world got fuzzy on the edges, and spanged out long, like what was at the end of your hand was way out on the top of the moon. Distances became distorted, and the shop spun a little bit, then settled right side up.

His vision grew even stranger, and way the hell off in never-never land Fish was puffing, too. Fish's kisser was like the faces in the funny mirrors at Coney, and Rusty knew he was edging away from all his worries.

Worries? Man, they were nowhere. This was gonna be a real dream night. Top, top, top!

He wanted to dance, because the music of the juke was roaring in his head like the front end of the Super Chief. He slid out of the booth—man, it took a whole *year* to get up, and he swayed unsteadily. Between his lips he could feel something puffing, like it was that dynamite stick, and it was goosing him more and stronger every second.

In front of him he saw Lockup—a buddy, that goddamn Lockup; he loved him like a brother—and Caroline rubbing up and down each other, rocking to the music from The Clovers in the juke. It was a solid cutting and he wanted that Caroline bitch more than anything.

"Hey man!" he called to Lockup, and his voice echoed down and down and down a long corridor, over and over. "Hey. Man. Let. Me. At. That." He held out his hands, and even through the smoke that enveloped the universe, he saw comprehension on Lockup's face. He was on a stick and Lockup saw it.

"No, man. I'm workin' here right now. Come later."

An uncontrollable hatred filled Rusty instantly for this wise bastard punk Lockup. He had always hated Lockup. To show how much he hated him, he swung Caroline's soft, gooey body out of the other's grip, and shoved Lockup hard in the chest.

Lockup was a dwarfy punk and he went back into another couple. He came back up as fast with something in his hand that Rusty thought might be a knife. But what the hell was that, a knife cut no ice, not now, not on sock! He went at Lockup hard and caught him in the cheek with a straight right. Rusty's arm came out forever, longer than a telephone wire, and way off down the end of the line it hit Lockup. He brought up his knee then and Lockup doubled with his hands clutching his groin.

He swung round, hard, and a bolo punch erupted from the north end of nowhere, missed Lockup entirely. He tried again and missed again. He was sore, man, really sore, about that punk making him miss such easy swats. Lockup was stumbling around with his hands down around his middle, and finally Rusty took back and whammed one home. Lockup sprawled backwards again, and three Cougars caught him. They helped the boy into a booth, and Rusty heard phantom voices from somewhere say, "Let him alone. He's on pot. He didn't mean it. Let him be."

Then he swung on Caroline, and the scared pasty expression on her face made her all the sexier to him. He wanted to do more than dance with her. He wanted to…

Dance. That was safest. Just dance, right now.

So he gathered her to himself, and felt the two soft areas of her press into his shirt, and it was warm.

It was a long, long dance, but he wasn't tired.

Then they went out together, and he took her in an alley behind Tom-Tom's joint.

When he woke up the next morning, he went into the bathroom and puked out his guts.

What a helluva night.

A fight and pot, and then that worked-out bitch Caroline. There had to be a better way to live. Couldn't he ever get free of all that slop? Couldn't he shake them off him like flies from carrion flesh?

He didn't have the answer.

✸

The bedroom was a mess. Clothes were thrown all over the floor, on the chair, on the desk, under the bed. He hadn't even bothered to shuck out of his underwear. He felt sticky and muggy. Through the window he got a clean, clear view of the airshaft, and the smell of Mrs. Hukaya's rice and meat, stinking on the stove. He wrinkled his nose and turned to the mirror over the dresser.

His lip, where Candle had cut it, was puffy and queer-looking. It reminded him of what he had to do today.

He tried to put it from his mind, but all during the shower, and getting dressed, and combing back his long, brown hair, he knew he would have to open the bottom drawer of the dresser.

Finally, before he went in to eat, he kneeled down and put his hands to the cool metal pulls of the bottom drawer. He hesitated for a minute, wishing there was some way he could stop himself from doing what he was going to do next. But he knew he was sucked in again.

His life was a sick thing, all caught up with brass knucks and swiped candy and fights in the gutters.

As he crouched there, without his even knowing it, he was reliving all the times he had stood with a knife or a broken bottle or a zip in his hand, and faced another boy. At times like that, just as this time, he felt like speaking some other language than English. Was it his native Spanish, a tongue he had never really spoken—never really appreciated—a third-generation Puerto Rican seemed so irretrievably lost to that slim heritage, or was it some other language? Some more guttural, more distant, more deeply buried language? Perhaps it was the growl and scream of the beast. Did the jungle call to him at those times? After all, wasn't that what he was reduced to, when he fought?

With nothing left to him but the fang and the claw?

He pulled the drawer open slowly, and stared at it.

He hadn't used the machine-steel, razor-honed, six-inch blade in over three months. Closed, the knife was dangerous-looking, but when he pressed that button on its side, out sprang six deadly inches of gutting metal. It had reach, that knife. It was sharp enough to slice through three layers of clothing and bite deep into flesh.

It was a kill, that knife.

He had laid it away when Carl Pancoast had gotten him free from the fuzz. He had promised he would never use it again, that he would stop running with the pack, that he would start to build a future, instead of building a sin.

He chuckled in his mind. His ma had been right. He did talk too gutter-way. "Building a sin." Getting ready to commit an immoral act. That was the way he talked. Flip, hard, cryptic, so no one would really know what went on inside his head.

He took the knife out and slid the drawer shut with his knee. He stood up, holding the plastic length of it closed in his hand. It felt wrong there, not like it had felt so often in the past.

Then, it had been right. But now he felt more at home with a compass and T-square. Was he actually outgrowing this thing, through the help of the teacher, or was it all an illusion?

He still knew what he had to do.

He bent over and stuck the knife into the top of his desert boot. The gang all wore these shoes, with high, soft tops, in case they had to pack a blade. But he knew Candle carried his knife in his sleeve. So when Candle rose high to let the knife slide out, Rusty would scoop low, and come up with the knife open—gutting.

A full-body swing, straight up from the groin. Slicing heavy and cutting from crotch to navel in one movement...

He stopped himself with a mental wrenching.

Wrong, wrong, wrong! All wrong. He had to stop this. He

couldn't let himself get involved again. It was more than just disappointing Pancoast. It was more than keeping Weezee out of trouble. He suddenly realized he owed a debt to himself. If he threw himself away, he was a waste to everything. He could not get it any clearer in his mind—he knew it was all wrong to be nothing, to get nowhere—but he sensed deeply that he must try to get this stand canceled. He would even back down. Let Candle think he was a punk. It didn't matter, just as long as he didn't have to fight, didn't have to kill.

For he knew in his heart that if he fought today, only one boy would come out of the rumble alive. He was determined to be that one, *if* they fought—but he wasn't going to fight.

He had to see Candle. Had to stop the argument now, cold, dead, final. Now!

But the knife felt reassuring in his shoe-top.

Dolores was at the table when he came in. Ma was in front of the stove, stirring a battered pot full of cocoa. "Where were ya so late?" Rusty asked his sister.

She was a pert, slim girl, with shiny black hair pulled into a ponytail like her friends. Her eyes were very wide and very black and her lashes quite long. Yet there was an insolence about her, an invisible smirk that seemed about to show itself on her full lips.

Her body was held proudly, and she rose an inch at his question. "You didn't show till three o'clock. Whaddaya coppin' low at me for?"

Rusty felt anger rising in him. Since his father had taken to sleeping out—god only knew where he was vomiting and crashing tonight—he felt more and more responsible for the girl. He had gotten her in with the Cougie Cats, and he had to watch out for her. These were bad streets.

"I ast ya something. Where were ya?"

Her face grew more defiant, and she spat, "I was out with the kids."

"What kids? Where?"

"Oh, fer Chrissakes, gawdamighty! Can't a person lead a private life without a bunch of snoopin'—"

Rusty's voice cut through, then was itself cut off as the tired woman at the stove smothered them both with, "Eat. It's mornin'. Let's not have it today. Just eat. As long as you're both home, it don't matter. Eat." Her voice was colored with weariness. She hadn't slept much, Rusty knew, waiting for him to come home. Yet she had not helped him undress.

How far apart they had grown. Again, he felt the tearing in his belly. He remembered the Spanish coin.

"It does matter," he started again, covering his own feelings. "I don't want ya runnin' with that gang no more, Dolo! They're bad medicine…"

Dolores leaped to her feet, and the chair went over with a snapping bang. "You should talk! You should talk to me. I'm so humiliated 'cause of you. I can't live it down. They all call me the chickie's sister. How'd you like it? I can't get away from it. You got me so humiliated!" Her voice had risen to a shriek. "I hate you! You're just a coward, is all! I hope Candle creams you today!"

So the word had spread in the neighborhood already.

Rusty heard the spoon his mother had been using drop to the floor with a thunk! and he turned to see her staring at him.

Her voice came out shaded with fright. "What—what's she mean? You fightin' today? Answer me, you gonna fight again?" Her hands were wrapped tightly in her apron and her face was the color of the sky outside—pale-sick white.

Rusty started to deny it, but Dolores yelled a vicious word, and then she was gone, flouncing out of the kitchen. A moment later he heard the front door slam and her progress bang-banging down the stairs.

What could he say to his mother?

"Answer me," she whispered.

"Nothing, Ma. Just nothing. Don't worry. I ain't gonna fight." Then he, too, was free of her. He left the dingy apartment.

But he knew he would fight. It was being called chicken. That bit deep. He had lived in the streets too long to let something like that slide away. If Candle would not see reason—the stand would come off just as planned.

He tried not to think about it.

Because the air stank with death.

FOUR:
SATURDAY AFTERNOON

- *rusty santoro*
- *candle*

The day went like a souped-up heap. The kids stayed away from Rusty like he was down with the blue botts. He tried to find things to do, but the scene was cold and dead.

Rusty saw Candle only once, and that was in the cafeteria. The hard-faced Prez of the Cougars was sitting at a table with Joy, feeling her up, and laughing loudly with his side-boys. They ate together. Rusty cut wide around them, for a while, and got a tray for himself. The food was the usual steam-table garbage and he only took a peanut butter and jelly sandwich, a piece of apple pie and a pint of milk. He wasn't hungry, not at all.

Finally, when he had polished off the food, he got up, leaving the tray, and turned around.

Everyone was watching him. He realized suddenly that they had been watching him all through lunch. But he had been thinking as he ate and had not noticed. Now they stared at him, and from the middle of the room he heard the derisive voice of a punk.

"Here chick-chick-chick-chick-chick! Cluck, cluck, cluck, cluck, cluck, cluck...chick-chick-chick..." It went on and on, leaving the first boy, swinging to another, then pretty soon the entire room was carrying it, like a banner. The sound was a wave that washed against the shores of Rusty's mind. It was the worst. It was a chop low like no other he'd ever heard.

He had been top man of the Cougars for so long, to have this kind of indignity pushed on him, was something frightful. He clenched his fists, and stood where he was. Customers got up quickly, most of them abandoning their trays of uneaten food, and left.

Rusty knew he had to talk to Candle now. Now was the time, because if he spent the day with that chick-chick festering in his brain, he'd fight sure as hell!

Somebody yelled, "Oooooh, *Russsell*! Oh, Russell, baby, do your hen imitation fer us! Go, man, go, Russell!"

He hated that name. It was the first time they'd called him that since it had been abbreviated to Rusty.

The boy stepped slowly away from the table, and walked over to Candle's place. The Cougars' Prez had been talking to his broad, not even looking at Rusty while the call had been going up. Now, as Rusty approached, he paid even more attention to Joy, but the three side-boys stood up slowly, their hands going into the tight pockets of their jeans. There were shanks in there, waiting to cut if Rusty made a snipe move.

Rusty stopped. "Candle."

The boy with the almost-Mongoloid features did not look up. He had his hand clutched to the girl's knee, and he seemed totally oblivious to what was happening behind him. But Joy's blue eyes were up and frightened. She stared straight at Rusty and the wild excitement in her face made him sick; they all wanted kicks. They didn't care who got nailed, so long as sparks flew and they could bathe in them. Then Candle turned carefully around. He looked up.

"Well, read this," he said arrogantly, more to his side-boys than Rusty. "Check who just dropped in for a chat. Welcome, spick."

Rusty felt the blood surging in him and he wanted to drive a fist straight into the bastard's mouth. But that was what Candle wanted. That would be the clincher. They'd slice him up like fresh bacon, right there, and everyone would dummy up. No one wanted the Cougars pissed off at them.

"Candle. I wanna talk to you," Rusty said softly.

The other grinned hugely, and he swung one foot up onto the chair, just touching the edge of Rusty's pants, putting a bit of dirt there.

"What you got to say to me you can say out at the dumps, spick."

"Look, don't make it rougher than now," Rusty cautioned him. "I wanna knock this off. I don't feature the idea of a stand. I got enough trouble with the cops already. No sense my getting picked up and tossed in the farm."

Candle reared back and laughed. Loud. His voice cut off all the chickie-chickie around the room, and everyone waited to find out what would happen. They knew Rusty was no chicken, they knew he had been rough as Prez of the Cougars and did not understand what had changed him. But they also knew Candle was a rough stud, and it would be top kicks to see these two go at each other.

"You don't wanna stand, man? You don't wanna come out and show all these kids you ain't yellow?" His grin grew wider as he grabbed a cardboard pint carton of milk, ripped open across the top. "That sits fine with me, but I still got a beef with you.

"So," he said, lifting the carton, "if you wanna bow out, that's ace with me, and I'll settle my beef like *this*!" He threw the milk at Rusty.

They laughed. The crowd burst into sound and Rusty stood there with the milk running down over his face, soaking quickly through his shirt and running through to his pants.

Before he could restrain himself he had lunged and had his hands around Candle's throat. The Prez of the Cougars gave a violent gasp and brought his own hands up in an inward swinging movement, breaking Rusty's grip. Then he choked out, "Grab—grab him!" and the side-boys had Rusty's arms pinned.

Candle swung out of the chair and stood up. His face was a violent blued mask of hate. "Now you read this, man. I'm not gonna work you over like I should now. Mostly 'cause I want to have more time at you, without nobody holding you back, yellow-belly. So you be out at the dump and we'll settle this down once and for all."

Then he shoved Rusty in the stomach, not hard enough to knock him out, but hard enough to suck the energy from him. Then they walked away quickly, several of them sweeping full trays off the tables. Garbage lay everywhere in their path.

Rusty stood there for a few minutes, listening to the cackles and catcalls ringing around him.

He could not move.

There was no way free. He would fight and he would win. He would carve that sluggy sonofabitch from gut to kisser and leave him for the dump rats to chew on.

It was gonna be tough as banana peels.

Pancoast got to him just before four o'clock. He caught him on the street.

"Rusty, I heard what happened yesterday. You going out there?"

Rusty shifted from foot to foot. What could he say? He knew Pancoast was pulling for him, and he knew if he went out there and fought he was throwing it all away. He couldn't yank loose now if he wanted to and yet he knew it was the worst thing he could do.

"I—I *gotta*, Mr. Pancoast. I got inta this and if I don't finish it once and for all, they won't never let me alone. One way or the other, I got to put a tail to this thing."

Pancoast shook his head, grabbed the boy by the biceps. "Listen to me, Rusty. Listen to me now. You've been doing real well. You've been growing with every day. You go out there and come down to their level and you'll be right back where you started two months ago when I fished you out of jail. Do you understand?"

"I understand," Rusty said, not looking at him, "but it's gotta be this way. Final."

Pancoast dropped his grip. His voice got steely hard. "I'll call the police, Rusty. I'll come out there with them and stop it."

"You come out there or you call the fuzz and I'll cut you off even, myself."

Pancoast had been around the kids long enough. He knew that "cutting off even" was tantamount to a threat of revenge. He said nothing, but his eyes were filled with hurt. His hands moved aimlessly at his sides. Then he turned and walked away.

Rusty was alone.

So damned, finally, horribly, all alone.

He walked down the street. After a while, he knew two Cougars followed him. He moved down the street and when Fish pulled alongside in his heap Rusty was not surprised.

"Hey, man. They give me the word to bring you out. You know, like they told me." He was always alibiing, Rusty thought ruefully.

"Yeah. Yeah, I know. Just a job like."

"So, like get in, huh, man?"

Rusty got into the car and Fish waited while Tiger and the Greek got in the back seat. No one said a word. The car pulled away from the curb, swung out into traffic heading uptown toward the dumps.

Rusty was scared and his mouth was dry.

But at least the knife in his shoe felt reassuring.

But not much.

*

As they passed the burning piles of garbage and refuse, the sky darkened appreciably. It was still early, not quite four-thirty yet, but the day seemed blacker than any Rusty could remember.

Fish tooled the beat-up Plymouth along the bumpy road, avoiding chuck holes and pits in the packed dirt. "One of these days, damn it, I'm gonna crack a parts shop and get me enough cams and crap to juice up this buggy."

Rusty didn't answer. He had more important things to worry about.

If he chickened here, he would not only have to ward off the antagonism of the neighborhood for the rest of his days; that was minor compared to what else would happen. Dolo would have to live him down, and that could mean any number of things in the streets. She might have to get more deeply involved with the Cougie Cats and their illegal activities. And then his ma. She would be bugged in the street. His old man…

That crumbum wouldn't have to worry, but if he was here maybe he could have done something, maybe he could have helped. Rusty set those bitter thoughts aside. Pa Santoro was a wine-gut and there wasn't no help coming from that angle.

The heap pulled around a bend and Rusty saw a dozen or so cars all drawn into a circle, their noses pointed into the center. The place was crawling with kids and a great cheer went up as they saw him through the window.

Rusty's belly constricted. He didn't want to fight Candle. He didn't want to fight anybody. He wanted to go home and lie down and put on some records and lie very, very still. His belly ached.

Fish took off at top speed around the ring of cars, spraying dirt in a wide wedge as he rounded the circle on two wheels. It was all Rusty needed to finish the nerve-job on him. He leaned against the right side of the car and puked so hard he thought the tendons in his neck would split. Fish was spinning the wheel as Rusty came up with it, and his eyes bugged. "Hey! Man! What the hell ya doin'?"

He slammed his foot onto the brake pedal and the Plymouth ground to a skittering halt, the tires biting deep into the dirt of the dump grounds and spinning wildly.

The car stalled and Fish was out, around the other side, and opening the door in an instant. He grabbed Rusty by the jacket collar and hauled him bodily from the car.

The kids were running over from the circle, violence light on their faces. What was happening there? This was a real kick!

Fish pulled Rusty down and he fell to his knees in the dirt, Fish still clinging to his jacket. He began dry-vomiting, hacking in choking spasms.

Finally, he slapped Fish's hand away and laid his palms flat on the ground, tried to push himself up. It took three cock-eyed pushes till he was standing unsteadily. Everything was fuzzy around the edges and he could only vaguely hear —

"Man, what a punk *he* turned into!"

"Chicken all the way. No guts!"

"Candle's gonna slice him up good, you see!"

Every face was one face; every body was a gigantic many-legged body. He was swaying and he felt a hand shoved into his back and, "Stand up, fer Chrissakes!"

His throat chugged and he thought for an instant he was going to bring up what little of his lunch was left lying uneasily in his stomach. But it passed as he gulped deeply and he began to get a clear picture of what was around him.

He saw all the faces. Poop and Boy-O, Margie, Connie, Cherry, Fish beside him looking angry and worried at the same time, Shamey, the Beast, Greek, Candle, with his eyes bright and daring, and—he stopped thinking for a moment when he saw her.

Weezee. She was here, too. Who had brought her?

He started forward in her direction, but Candle moved in and stopped him. "She came with me. I brought her. Any complaints?"

Before he could answer, Weezee started to say something. "I couldn't help it, Rusty, he saw me—"

"Shaddup!" Candle snapped over his shoulder. He turned back to Rusty. "You got any beefs, you can settle 'em the knife way."

The sickness and the fear had passed abruptly. Rusty was quite cold and detached now. If it was a stand Candle wanted, all the rest of these sluggy bastards wanted, then that was what they'd get. Right now.

"Who's got the hankie?" he yelled.

Magically, a handkerchief fluttered down onto the ground between the two boys. Neither touched it. Candle's arm moved idly in his sleeve and the switchblade dropped into his hand. Even as he pressed the stud and the bright blade flicked up, Rusty was bending sharply and he came erect with his own weapon in his fist, already open.

They faced each other across the white handkerchief, and then Candle watched stonily as Rusty bent down and picked it up. From the crowd cries of, "Get him! Sling him!" and once in a while, "Go, go, go, Chickie-man!" rang out.

Rusty shook out the hankie and put one corner in his mouth, wadding it slightly behind his clenched teeth. He extended the opposite corner to Candle delicately and when Candle took it, his eyes were sharp on Rusty's own.

Caution: when you knife-fight…don't bother watching the knife as much as the other guy's eyes. *They* tell when he's gonna strike.

Candle knew it and took the hankie in his mouth with care. He maneuvered his tongue and teeth a bit till the cloth was settled properly. They were separated across a two foot re-straining line of taut cloth, their backs arched, their bodies curved to put them as far away at swinging level as possible. The arm-swinging range was just two feet—with the other man's knife in the way. The first man who dropped the hankie lost and was at the mercy of the other.

Poop was going to be the starter and Rusty motioned him with an offhand gesture to hold up for a second. Rusty saw the heavy black leather jacket Candle wore and realized his own jacket was thinner, more easily ripped. The dangerous area—the lower arms—was mostly unprotected. He held his knife tightly and reached back, took his own handkerchief from his hip pocket and wrapped it tightly about his free hand. That helped a little.

Poop stared at them anxiously. He lit a cigarette and puffed it violently as Rusty banded himself with the hankie. Then the boy threw down the cigarette, stamped it into the dirt of the dumps, and said, "Ya ready to go now?"

Rusty felt a wry laugh bubble up from his belly. Poop was getting anxious. Maybe they wouldn't kill each other; then he wouldn't get his kicks.

Both boys nodded.

Poop raised both hands above his head, as a drag-race starter would. Then he brought them slashingly down, screaming, "*Go! Go! Go! Go!*"

Candle jerked back heavily and the hankie started to slip from Rusty's teeth. The cloth gave an ominous tearing sound and Rusty swung the knife in flat arcs, moving forward and teeth-winding the hankie so he had more of it firmly tight in his grip. He stopped as he saw Candle's knife-arm edging closer. Then they were equal, with the hankie tight, and their knives ready to draw blood.

They circled, stepping, stepping, stepping carefully, measuring each movement. Footwork had to be close, because the slightest fouling of feet, and down a man could go. And that meant not only down. It meant out.

The ground was worn into a rough circle as they went tail-around-head past each other. The gang fanned out and watched, making certain an idle sweep of the blades could not touch them. The two boys bent forward from the shoulders, putting their bellies as far back as possible, for that was the direction in which trouble lay.

Feet widely spread, they stopped every few seconds, swinging, making certain they did not throw themselves off-balance.

Grunts and explosions of sweat marked their circular passage and soon Rusty felt his arms getting weak. He stooped slightly and it was a soft sight to Candle that the effect of the retching, the movement, the swinging, the tension, had taken hold. He moved in for the kill. But he was premature. Rusty caught the other's arm as it came up, caught it on his other wrist, the hankie wound tightly, and Rusty let a squeal of pain loose as the blow ricocheted off. Candle's hand had struck his wrist with impact and the shake threw Rusty off-balance. Candle was on him, then, with the knife coming back for a full overhead swing, and Rusty tossed himself sidewise. Candle went past, and the hankie snapped tight, dragging Candle almost off his feet.

Rusty moved back away, dragging Candle with him, and in a second, before the advantage could be gained, they were circling each other, both steady, both wary. The air was filled with the flash and flick of steel as each tried to slip one past. Rusty countered and parried each thrust from the deadly Candle and the stout boy did the same.

Rusty's hair loosened from its rigid wave and flopped over his eyes. He could not waste a hand to swipe it away however. He could not blow it up with his lips, so he tossed his head quickly, right at the height of a full-arm swing.

It fell back and he resigned himself to the handicap. Candle's hair was sandy, crew-cut, and gave him no trouble. But what he had considered an advantage—the heavy black leather jacket—was not. The jacket bunched against the inside of his elbows, made swinging difficult and cut short Candle's reach at times.

Candle kicked out with a faking movement and Rusty leaped back, jerking his neck at the end of the hankie. The stout boy had been steadied for that. Then Candle was in close and the knife was around back of Rusty somewhere, his own arm pinned at his side. He fought in close to Candle, and they shoved at one another with their shoulders, edging one another a few inches, then back again.

Finally, Rusty shoved off and got his feet steadied for the swing he knew was coming. But it came from an entirely new direction. Candle's knife hand stayed in sight, and his free hand caught Rusty in the kidneys.

Rusty's face went pasty and he staggered back. Candle hit him again, this time with the handle of the knife, wrapped in his fist, in the side of the head, and Rusty started to fall. He grabbed out, and Candle came across with the knife once more. Rusty felt the razor-keen blade slice flesh between thumb and forefinger. He wanted to scream, but could not without dropping the hankie, so he wadded it more behind his teeth, and sank to his knees. Blood poured across his hand.

Candle stepped back for the death-swing and it came up like a jet from around the stout boy's knees. Rusty jerked sidewise, throwing out one leg. Candle went down in a heap and the hankie popped from his mouth with a snap.

Rusty was on his feet in an instant and Candle lay there staring up at him, the hankie hanging ludicrously from Rusty's thin lips.

The gang went insane. "Kill him! Jab him! Knife! Knife! Knife!" they screamed, and one hand shot out of the crowd to snatch away Candle's blade from where it lay in the dirt. Another hand caught Rusty's arm and shoved him forward. He stumbled and stopped.

"Get him, he was gonna put you down!"

Rusty stared down at Candle, lying on his elbows, at his feet. There was a queer mixture of fear and surliness on the boy's heavy features. He had lost, but he was going to be angry about dying. It made no sense, but that was the way he looked. Rusty stood silently as the storm of directions grew behind him.

As he stood there, Candle's cool, green eyes met his own and he saw right to the center of the boy. He saw all the garbage that Candle had substituted for guts, for integrity, for honesty; and Rusty was frightened again. Not so much frightened at how close, but scared because this was the way *he* had been, before Pancoast had showed him there were other ways than the ways of the gutter.

He knew he had slipped back and knew the gang would now expect him to resume his position at the head of the Cougars. He didn't want that! He wasn't going back to all that. Inside him, two warring natures fought for the mind of Rusty Santoro.

The hand holding the knife moved itself, of its own volition, and the blade reversed itself—overhand, so that one downward stroke would slash the throat of the terrified Candle. The stout boy sat looking up at Rusty, knowing his life hung by a thread, hung on that thread of decency—that he called cowardice—he knew was in the boy.

Rusty moved an inch forward and the gang went crazy.

"Kill him! Kill him! Knife 'im!"

Rusty tried to stop his feet, tried to say to himself, this is no good, but the days of the gang were back with him, smothering him like a blanket and he knew the only way he would be safe from an enemy was to kill the enemy. His arm came back and the blade poised there in nothingness for an instant, then started the downward arc that would slice deeply. The hand moved, and then it stopped.

All the hatred passed away. Everything was clear again. Clear and smooth.

"Clear and smooth," Rusty said, to no one at all.

No one understood.

But they understood what he did next.

He put the blade under his boot and with all his strength bent upward. The blade did not give and he pulled up his foot, brought it down with a crack on the blade. The knife snapped in two, at the base of the steel, and Rusty let it lay there.

"I'm through," he said.

No one argued with him.

This time no one demanded a stand, for he had proved his strength in the only way they could understand. Now that he had proved it, he was free. Free of them forever and the days would not be filled with wandering and hating.

"Anybody going back to town?" he asked.

There was a tacit agreement that the affair was concluded, an agreement that no one would help Candle to his feet. They walked away, back to their cars and Fish gave the finger-circle to Rusty, to show him the outcome had been right by him.

"I got room in mine," Fish said, and nodded his head in the direction of the battered Plymouth.

"Ain't you afraid I'll whocko on your floor again?"

Fish laughed, then, and they walked to the car together. Only then, when she called from behind, did Rusty remember Weezee.

"Rusty?"

He turned and looked at her and there was nothing really wrong. She was what she was and for the time being she was all the woman he needed; weak and watery and scared and only doing her best by living the rules as they'd been put to her; building a sin once in a bit, and trying to make it from day to day—that was the best anyone could do, till a passage opened up.

He walked back and stood before her, not saying anything. He still had his pride. He still had to let her make the first move.

"I'm—I'm glad ya won, Rusty…"

He let the slow smile build off the corner of his mouth and he fumbled with his jacket to show it had been nothing really. Then he said, "Wanna go back to Tom-Tom's with us and have a soda?"

She nodded brightly, the past wiped away like clouds from the sky and he decided to let it settle that way.

What was the use of carrying the hurt? It didn't matter. There were worse hurts than this little one. He took her with him in the way the rules decreed. Not by the hand, gently, as he wanted to for that would have left her confused—but with the hand at the back of her neck. Commanding, leading, directing, roughly, the way a mean stud did it to his broad.

She came up close to him as they walked back and her body said she was his girl again, to whatever extent he wanted her.

Strangely, though, Rusty felt no heat for her, felt no desire to be the big man. She was his girl and he would treat her as he was expected to treat her, but the distantness of their relationship was too profound, too unexplainable, for him to try to love her.

They were together and that was enough for the time being. Alone was bad enough. Together was at least not alone.

In the car, with the others behind them, churning up the dirt of the dumps, with the dual exhausts deep-throating a challenge at the land and the city, they tooled around in a winner's circle, and sped around the grounds once, like a parading matador with the downed bull still bleeding in the center of the arena.

Candle lay where he had fallen.

The days were finished for him, too. Now he was a mean stud, but he wasn't the big man. He was just another cat without a tail. He knew his place now and if he tried to overstep it, they would toss this affair at him. That was the code. Silent and eternal, that was it on skates.

The cars tooled around, honked their horns at one another, missed colliding because, hell, that was the way to do it, and ripped back toward town on the shore drive.

It seemed like a good day, a free day, the last day of it all.

Rusty settled back with the hankie around his bleeding hand and let the peace of release flood through his body. He was out of the woods at last.

Free at last. Free of the past and free to move ahead.

He was dead wrong.

FIVE:
SATURDAY NIGHT

- *rusty santoro*
- *dolores*
- *the war*

News spread down through the neighborhood like a swollen river rushing to the sea. By the time he got home, after the many congratulations in the streets—as though he had actually accomplished something—Dolores was waiting, pride and affection shining in her face. She rushed to him as he entered and kissed him warmly on the mouth.

"I heard," she said.

He grunted a noncommittal answer and shoved past.

Dolo turned uncomprehending eyes on his back, and said, "What's a' matter? You got the botts or somethin'?"

Rusty flopped into the chair beside the TV, and threw a leg over the arm. "I don't like you runnin' with the Cougie Cats."

"What's that got to do with anything?"

"I just don't like it is all."

She bristled and flipped her ponytail insultingly. "That doesn't much matter to me. I got my life, you got yours. You wanna stand with Candle like that, you do it. I wanna split with the kids, that's my biz, none of yours."

Rusty slung the leg to the floor and leaned forward, hands clasped between his knees. He stared intently at the pretty girl with the brown hair. He loved her more than anyone he had ever known. Since she was old enough to talk he had been her self-appointed guardian. Her addition to the family had not been a loss of affection from his mother and father, for there had been little enough of that to begin with. Instead, she had been a light toward which he could direct his own affection. And she had needed it, received it with gratitude. But as she had grown older, with the poison of the neighborhood in which they lived flowing through her young veins, she had changed—grown apart from Rusty. He needed her as he knew she needed him. His relationship with Weezee could never have been complete, or deep, for they took each other lightly, as playthings; but his love for his sister was a completely realized thing. Now he was deprived of the one outlet for his warmth, and having introduced her to the Cats, he felt more than just responsible for her. He felt as though he had given her cancer.

Today had taught him something. The break had to be a violent and final one. No one gradually grew away from the streets. To gradually grow away meant you became a different kind of street bum—one of the fat slugs who sat on the front stoops with cans of beer and listened to the cha-cha music beating out of the windows. That was no good, either. It was a dead end. And he wanted something better for Dolores than a quick lay in a back alley or a police record.

"You got to stay away from them kids, sis."

"They're my friends!"

"Friends, hell! You got to drop 'em."

Her face flamed. *"Mienta!"*

Rusty snapped at the swear-word, leaped from the chair and cracked her solidly in the face. Dolores stumbled back, her eyes went wide with disbelief. It was the first time her brother had ever hit her.

She had hardly known what she was calling him, had regretted it the moment it had left her lips, but he had not given her the opportunity to take it back, to apologize.

Now the barrier was erected. Solid as the Great Wall of China, older than life itself and insurmountable. She backed away, turned and ran into her room. He heard the skeleton key turn in the lock and he slumped back dejectedly, hating himself for his temper.

This was indicative of what the gang had done to him; he could no longer reason. Violence was the only answer he knew; violence was the only approach. He had to learn to curb his temper, to stamp out that blood-hunt in his veins.

He let his head flop back against the cushions and tried to stop thinking.

Perhaps dinner would kill the animosity, the fury, the hatred boiling in the house. But he knew it wouldn't.

Dinner was a silent affair, all tinkle of glasses and clatter of silverware. They ate in silence and Moms looked from one to the other with a knowing hesitance. Should she ask what was the matter? No, stay out of it.

"Where you goin' tonight?" the gray-haired woman asked her daughter.

Dolores did not answer. Her eyes lifted sidewise from the plate to stare at her brother for an instant, then they returned to the plate.

"I ast ya where you was goin' tonight."

Dolores looked up again and a flash of defiance coursed across her dark eyes. Her long lashes lowered and she addressed the inch of table just beyond the plate. "To a dance."

Rusty butted in, "Where at?"

"What're you, the F.B.I.?"

"No, just askin'."

"The clubhouse."

"The Cougars' rooms? Down in the bowling alley?"

She nodded. "You know any place else they hold their dances?" Her fork skewered a piece of meat, shucked it off.

Rusty looked across at his mother and she sensed his concern. Her own words were carefully chosen, carefully selected in softness. "You goin' with anybody we know, Dolores?"

The girl flipped her hair again, insolently, defiantly, "Just by myself is all. Just alone, with some of the kids."

Rusty said, "You know there's been trouble with the Cherokees. I heard over at Tom-Tom's they might crash the drag tonight." Rumors had been flooding the neighborhood, not only about Rusty's stand with Candle—which somehow had been kept from Moms—but of a proposed war that seemed about to break. Rusty was worried. The Cherokees had been bested in a battle three weeks before and the winds had it they were still nursing their wounds.

"You never can tell," Moms said, picking at her food nervously. "You better go to a movie tonight, or something."

She waited for what she knew must come.

"I'm goin' ta the dance. Alone."

Rusty inched forward, till his hard belly pushed the edge of the table. "You know what happened to Margie?"

Dolo decided to play it cool. "Margie who?"

Rusty stared at her with exasperation. "Come off it. Lockup's stupid broad. You know she had it right on the school grounds and put it in a paper sack an' left it leaning against a tree."

Margie's stillbirth had been the talk of the school for months. Her miscarriage had been a big thing in the Cougars' social whirl. Rusty feared a like situation with his sister. The main job of the Cougie Cats was to keep the Cougars' studs happy. Rusty wanted nothing like that to happen to Dolores.

"You want somethin' like that to hit you?"

Dolores shoved back from the table, anxious to bluff high

and snappy, not yet ready to storm away. She dropped her fork
with a clatter and her mouth twisted venomously.

"You got a dirty mouth," she snarled.

"I'm just tellin' the truth. An' Paulie Ricco's sister got a busted
spine in that Prospect Park thing a few weeks back. You wanna
spend the rest of your life in bed like that? You keep runnin'
with them girls, that's what's gonna happen."

"Don't you chop low on my friends."

"Friends, crap! They don't know from friends!"

Moms had been sitting there, her faded gray eyes open wide
at these tales of horror from just beyond her walls. She had
sensed the crowd with which Dolores ran was a wild one, but she
had never suspected that they were—were like *this*. Her heart
stopped beating, she was sure, and she was sure her daughter
heard the silence. This was her baby, her Dolores, just baptized
and just having her first party and just wearing her first high
heels and now suddenly grown, and playing with a deadly sort
of fire.

She had to stop her.

"Dolores, I forbid you to go there tonight. You gonna stay
home and dry dishes with me, then we'll go take in a show, huh?"

The girl sensed the time for total retaliation had come. She
leaned over, as if to clamp down on everything her mother had
said, and she came back with, "Can't you ever leave me alone?
Can't you let me have a little fun once in a while? I'm not hurtin'
you. I don't care if I never see my old man or if you got no time
for nothin', always here in the kitchen, and *you*," she turned on
Rusty, "*you* got big crazy ideas, the big brother thing all the
time, and just cause you was yellow, you think I have to be.
Well, it ain't gonna be that way. Leave me alone, both of you
crapheads!"

The word hit Rusty with all the force of a steam drill. He saw
the effect it had on Moms and for the second time, hardly

knowing what he was doing, his hand came out and cracked hard against Dolores' cheek.

She fell back against the chair and her face told everything there was to tell. It told the past was rotten and the future was a disappointment and the present was the rock that lay in the pit of her stomach. She slid back the chair and ran from the room, yelling, "I'm never comin' back here again! Never! *Never!*"

Then the sound of the vase on the shelf near the door smashing to the floor and the sound of the slamming door, then that going-away-forever sound of Dolores hitting for the street.

The word "never" hung like fog in the kitchen. Rusty avoided his mother's eyes until he heard her crying.

By then it was too late. They were all lost to one another down a dark lonely road that led nowhere. She cried too easily, damn her. Cried too easily, showed she was human, fallible, too easily. There's only one way to escape the hurt; that way is the safe way. Just keep it locked in, down inside you somewhere, where they can't get to you. No mother, no father, no sister, no one, because when they know they got you suckered, they know they can hurt you. And ain't no one who doesn't like to play god once in a while. No one who doesn't like to hurt when they know they can be god and so they try it every once in a while. So play it cool, play it steady, keep it back where they can't see it. Let the others—the mothers, the fathers, the friends—let them make the move, then you can play god! That's the way.

Rusty wadded up the paper napkin lying unused beside his plate and tossed it into the waste basket. He played with his food for a few moments, trying not to let the sound of Moms sobbing get to him. Finally, he could take it no longer and he slid away from the table, went to his room. It was going to be like that, all day, he was sure.

He turned on the record player absently, letting a stack of 45s start turning on the center post. Without knowing it, he pushed the reject button, allowing the first disc to slip down. Music had become very important to Rusty. When he had no one else around, when solitude was forced on him, he could use the music to stave off loneliness, fear. The words were pointless, the tunes vapid, but he desperately needed the sounds. Nothing more, just the sounds.

Come on over baby, Whole lot of shakin' going on— Come on over, baby, Whole lotta shakin' goin' on—

The music reminded him where Dolo had gone.

He sat down heavily on the edge of the bed letting his arms hang between his legs drawing tightly at the shoulder joints. It wasn't good to let Dolores run loose like that, particularly not tonight. Besides the rumors of Cherokee action, there was always Candle—who might still harbor enough of a grudge to want to take it out on Rusty's sister—and Boy-O with his always handy supply of sticks. There were the girl-hungry Cougars, and the lousy influence of the Cougie Cats, many of whom had police records.

Dolores was clean so far and Rusty intended to keep her that way.

As he sat there he glanced toward the bureau and saw the picture one of the kids had taken of him and Dolo at Coney, last summer. She stood shorter than he, slim and happy in the sun with the crowded beach behind her and the cloudless sky above. And he started undressing, so he could put on some better clothes and follow Dolores to the dance.

He was going to make certain nothing happened to his sister. She had too much to live for, to let any gang of juvies louse her up.

He dressed hurriedly.

*

Whoever had intimidated Greaseball Bolley into letting the Cougars turn his back rooms into a club, had done a fine job. For the fat man was terrified of the hard-eyed kids who walked through his bowling alley, into the rear. He studied each one carefully, getting to know them by sight and name, against the day they decided to wreck the joint and put him down. He was more than fat; he was gigantic in that seldom-seen fantastic way that brings to mind thick dough puddings and overstuffed Morris chairs. One of the men who bowled regularly in League, Wednesday nights, who was also an avid reader of science fiction, compared Greaseball to a spaceman who had been infected with a spore that had bloated him into moon-proportions. It was a striking analogy, for Bolley's body was not only hasty-pudding squishy, and waggled flappingly as he stumped forward, but the skin was an unhealthy yellow, pimpled and puckered and strewn with moles, pustules, explosions of flesh, that made him look like some weird diseased fruit, overripe and rotting within.

He was well-liked by everyone in the neighborhood.

But someone in the Cougars, years before Rusty had become the Prez, had decided the gang needed a clubhouse, and had decided with equal ease that the back rooms of the Paradise Bowling Alley were the site. So Greaseball Bolley had become unhappy host to the Cougars and their girls' auxiliary. The place resounded to the stomping feet and high-flung wails of rock'n'roll, and the occasional moan of an apple who had been put down for a while.

Greaseball Bolley was unhappy about the situation, but he maintained a philosophical neutrality, for his size cut away any ideas the gang might have had about causing him trouble. He watched them and they watched him and they hung suspended in a state of alert tolerance. Enough that Bolley allowed them to use the place, as they allowed him to stay in business. It was not at all the same sort of arrangement the gang had with Tom-Tom, who was merely terrorized. This was a grudging acceptance of strength, and a decision to permanently put off hostilities, for the good of the majority.

Greaseball was glad the spanging of pins cut off most of the Cougars' noise.

But tonight, they were doing it up sky-blue. More than usual had tramped past the showcase with its FOR SALE sign, model pins, balls, carrying cases, shoes and other paraphernalia inside. They had all given him the eye of recognition, the two-fingered greeting and gone quietly back to the club rooms.

Greaseball never went back there. They had their own locks on the doors and they kept their house. He knew about the several bedrooms, about the girls and boys who stayed overnight, about the slashings and the narcotics, but his fear of gang reprisal was greater than that of the police, so he kept his mouth shut and the Cougars made sure they did nothing overt to attract the attention of The Men. It had been that way for a long time now and the days seemed endlessly plodding in danger to Greaseball. But he did nothing to stop them. Far back, before the Cougars, there had been some trouble with a waitress, and a broken bottle, and a long term inside gray walls. So Greaseball Bolley did nothing, but watch and let them sink into his mind's eye. And if someday the balance shifted he would take as many with him as he could. But till then...

He was well-liked by everyone in the neighborhood.

Rusty passed Greaseball Bolley with all the cool aplomb of the days when he had been Prez. He kept his eyes front and his step assured as he walked past the gigantic heap of doughy flesh. But for the first time since he had met the fat man, on taking over the Cougars, Greaseball spoke to Rusty.

" 'Ey. You, Santori. C'mere."

Rusty stopped and pivoted slowly. His eyes met those of the fat man and for a minute he had trouble deciding what color they were; so deeply buried in caverns of oozing flesh they seemed to be two raisins thumbed into a paste. "The name's Santoro, not Santori," Rusty stated flatly, starting to go

" 'Ey. When I call you, kid, you come, y'hear?"

Rusty walked back to where the hump of Bolley leaned over the showcase. Down on the alleys only two or three people bowled—none of whom Rusty recalled having ever seen in the place before—and it was apparent the rumors of Cherokee trouble had hit the neighborhood hard enough to keep regulars away from the place.

Rusty realized Greaseball was scared. For the first time since he had known him the fat man was afraid of something. Rusty walked over, close enough to smell the odor of garlic and no bathing, and his nostrils quivered. Then he stopped, drew on his cigarette and waited for the fat man to speak.

"You—uh—you hear 'bout trouble, t'night?"

Rusty let his eyes slide tightly closed. The smoke from the cigarette spiraled up past his face and he liked the momentary warmth of it. Cool, that was the angle, play it cool. It goes further, it slides easier.

"Trouble? Like what trouble, man?"

Greaseball felt fire flame in his huge belly. He would not tolerate these kids stooging it out on him. He reached across with one side-of-beef hand and grabbed Rusty about his collar. The sports jacket Rusty wore wrinkled up as the fat man dragged the boy tight to the counter. Rusty reached up to try and jab free, but the hand was a bracelet of soft, spongy, but terribly invulnerable flesh. He was held fast and his breath was jagged as he worked his neck in the grip.

"Lemme go! Goddamn ya, lemme go, ya sleazy crumbum!"

The fat man's other hand came about lazily, almost floatingly (he knew his own strength to the smallest fraction) and landed with a heavy plop on Rusty's face. The boy's eyes glazed over and he staggered in Greaseball's grip.

"Now you maybe gonna talk ta me? Huh? You gonna answer straight like?"

Rusty gurgled and his eyes unfogged. The dim scene of the alley pasted itself back in his vision and he tried to speak. Words would not form. The fat man eased off a bit.

Rusty gagged and coughed. Then, "I heard the Cherokees was comin' over for a rumble tonight. That's all the message I got. I don't get the wire no more. I'm outta the gang."

The fat man's line of conversation altered instantly. His interest was heightened by this new subject, as though he had forgotten the brewing of trouble in his alleys. "Yeah," he wheezed, "I heard that. That cat Candle's got your spot now, don't he?"

Rusty nodded silently. What Greaseball did or did not know about the stand that afternoon was of no concern now.

"How come you ain't the President no more?"

"I got too old for office."

Another slap, not quite so hard. Fear still oozed between the fat man's teeth.

"I wanted out, that's all."

"Then what you doin' here tonight?"

"Lookin' for my sister. I wanna get her home."

The fat man let loose entirely. Rusty shrugged down the wrinkled sports jacket, adjusted the tie and shirt. The fat man gave him the nod. "Watch yaself."

The entire incident was a mystery to Rusty. Why was the fat man so interested? Or was it just that he liked to know everything that went on, whether he could control it or not?

That was the answer and Rusty walked away as the fear submerged itself temporarily in Greaseball Bolley's piggy eyes. He moved his body slightly, and felt the bulk of the ironwood chair leg pressed between his leg and the showcase. If there was going to be trouble tonight he was going to end it before the cops came in to do the job.

Rusty walked past the alleys and the empty racks and made fast for the back door leading to the rooms.

From inside he could hear the beat of music and the sound of girls' laughter. It was as loud as usual and suddenly very necessary. Alone was bad tonight. Stay with the herd and beat the glooms, that was the angle. Cool it!

Margie was just inside the door, in the middle of a group of Cougie Cats—debs—regaling them with the saga of her conception, from start to schoolyard, blow by blow, detailed, painted with adolescent fantasies. Her eyebrows went up as she saw Rusty and the other girls turned too, surprise registering on their faces. This was the first drag Rusty had attended since he quit the gang. If the fuzz found him here, they knew, he would be breaking his custody and back to the can he'd go.

But it was too neat an evening for bombs so they all waved and gave him the eye and Cherry licked her lips hungrily, saying, "Come on back an' see me later, big man."

Rusty smiled vacantly and went deeper into the thick, blue cloud of smoke, catching the telltale muskiness of pot, trying to single out the slim shape of Dolo.

Greek emerged from the smog and stuck out his hand in a heavy salute. "Buddy!" he exclaimed. Greek was the big mouth of the club, and Rusty had great affection for him. The Greek didn't know when to shut up and consequently his outgoing friendliness was a constant warmth in his vicinity. It was good to know a guy like that, every once in a while. An open stud was a relief from all the cool boys.

Greek was fleshy, but not soft. More like a black, curly-haired Buddha than anything else, but with a switchblade, he was nobody's fool.

His face was cheek-marked from a rumble. Another stud had taken a raw potato studded with double-edged razor blades and twisted it on Greek's kisser. It had left raw bloody strips of flesh and the healing had been slow and imperfect. His right cheek looked like a particularly violent case of strip-acne had hit and ravaged it.

"Man, fall down and have a puff with me!" Greek said.

Rusty clapped the big Greek on the shoulder, said, "Not stayin' too long, Greek. Just fell down to find my kid sis—"

"Hey, man, y'know, like your sister's gettin' to be a real knockout. I was gonna try that myself, then I remembered what you told me when she joined up with the debs. That scared me off good."

Rusty started to get mad, then realized he was being spooked and slugged the Greek playfully in the arm. He took the fleshy boy to one side and talked in close.

"Listen, man, I wanna ask you somethin'. See, uh, I'm uh, you know, not in so tight anymore and I don't like to shove my nose in where it don't go, but look, is there anyone who's, uh, well, you know, like—uh—payin' a lotta 'tention to Dolo? You know what I mean?"

Rusty was serious and he could only be serious with this boy, and both knew it. But Greek had a distaste for pigeons and he hesitated.

Rusty added hurriedly, "Look, don't goof yaself with nobody, but if there's anybody out to plank her I'd like ta know so I could warn him friendly to stay off. Ya know what I mean? Hell, Greek, she's onny a kid, and she's my onny sister…"

Greek nodded. "I dig."

Rusty waited, then, "Well?"

Greek looked troubled, then shook his head in the negative. "No, not that I know about. She sticks pretty close to the broads. She asks around once in a while who some guy is, when she don't know, but she acts kinda skitty 'round the men. You know what I mean." Then he changed the subject quickly, "Where's Weezee?"

Rusty waved it away fast. "Oh, she wanted to come, mentioned it this afternoon, but I didn't feel like draggin' no women tonight." Greek understood, and a lecherous quirk of his lips indicated he felt the same way.

"I was out to the dumps this afternoon."

Rusty smiled. "I saw ya, ya bastard. You was yellin' as loud as the rest of them apples."

Greek spread his hands in helplessness. He grinned back. "I don't like a blade in my gut any better'n you do, man. Candle's top dog around here and I like the group. No sense my playin' hard man and gettin' stomped. Read me?"

Rusty smiled back, and a mutual respect flitted between them.

Greek changed the subject again. "Wanna find a nice piece? Some fresh stuff from off Cherokee turf here tonight."

Rusty's brow furrowed, and his gray eyes slitted down. "You let that stuff in, when you know the Cherokees are on the prowl?"

Greek thumbed his nose at the ceiling. "Frayk 'em!"

Rusty wagged his head and pursed his lips with a puff. "That's bad biz, man."

"Ah, hell," Greek said, "they ain't comin' down here. The turf's too hot for 'em since the rumble. They won't show their butts in sight for months. And if they do," he patted his jacket pocket, "we give 'em the way out, put 'em down good."

Rusty chuckled. That's all they ever thought about. Laying and fighting and drinking and sipping the tea. It was all pretty hopeless, but wild in a sort of clockwise way.

"Yeah, point out the fresh stuff. Long as I'm down, I might as well socialize a little." They walked into the crowd together.

The first girl—called herself Goofball, but Rusty heard someone yell to her as Mary, and the broad turned to answer—boxed him into one of the bedrooms and Rusty didn't object too strenuously. It wasn't so good. She was strictly nowhere from style, but it was an interlude and by the time they unlocked and came out the joint was rocking high and heavy and the sticks were passed around free.

Rusty stayed off the pot, the Sneaky Pete, the Sweet Lucy, and the other broads and kept looking for Dolo. From time to time he heard the word that she had been there and leeched out so he stayed, hoping she would come back and he could talk her into going home. But she had come and gone. She didn't come back and an hour after he had arrived, Rusty couldn't leave.

The Cherokees showed on the scene.

He was leaning against a wall with a can of Rheingold in his hand, his tie jerked down to the side, collar open and the heat, body odor, smoke and beer fumes of the rooms closing in. The sweet odor of tea filtered around him. He was talking to little Clipper Adderlee about the Prospect Park war, when the sounds of bowling against the wall stopped. A dead silence from outside, and then they heard Greaseball's high almost-feminine voice shouting something incomprehensible.

Fish emerged from the smoke and Connie's embrace and yelled at Poop, "Shut off that squawker!"

Poop slammed the tone arm of the record player aside and

in the sudden loss of music there was a total absence of voices in the rooms. They stayed quite still and listened. Then they made out what Greaseball was saying, over and over, loud and high, till he was suddenly cut off with a squeak.

"Cherokees!"

Candle showed from a back room where Lockup had gone to fetch him, and stood with his legs wide apart, his eyes blazing for the fight to come. "Okay you guys, get the goddamn lead out!"

Tiger, whose haircut always left him looking like a Fussiwatti, sprinted through the packed mob of kids and reached a big box set against one wall. He pulled a keychain from his pocket and opened the double padlocks. Then the lid went up, and miraculously everyone had a weapon.

The sounds of argument outside grew more violent, and once the crash of a bowling ball going through the showcase split the background down the middle. Rusty felt someone shoving a zip into his hand and a few .22 slugs.

He tried to hand it back, tried to get to the rear door, but his path was blocked by dozens of Cougars and their debs preparing for the rumble.

Braced against his thigh, Fish had a long pole with a jagged piece of glass on its end. He was positioned right in front of the door with the deadly thing angled up to head level.

The others brandished zip guns, switchblades, wrenches, lengths of pipe, homemade knucks, bricks. One girl had a four-foot spike of some sort, stolen from a railroad yard, and she hefted it like an experienced warrior.

"Let 'em come!" Candle screamed, his face swollen with fury and the desire for blood.

Dwarfy Lockup threw open the bolts on the door and before Rusty could help himself, he was being borne forward through the opened door, into the alley proper. The Cherokees were out in strength. The faces of their girls, the Rockettes, were as violent as their own. When the rival gang saw the Cougars streaming out of the back rooms, a wild cry went up and they left the battered shape of Greaseball Bolley—slipping wetly to the linoleum—and charged straight across the polished alleys.

They met head-on in the middle of the twelfth lane.

SIX:
SATURDAY NIGHT

• *rusty santoro*

It was like nothing but hell with screams.

The first bunch of Cherokees came sliding and stomping across the hardwood alleys, their heavy army boots leaving big black marks on the polished wood. The glitter of knife blades and the dull black of revolvers was mixed with the red of faces and the white of staring eyes. They came in fast and the Cougars met them without hesitation. Fish was the first one forward and the glass-end stick came down and jabbed a Cherokee with such impact, the point of the glass entered the boy's right eye, sending him spilling backward.

The boy screamed so shrilly, everyone paused a quarter-instant in mid-step, and then went back to clashing. The boy lay there, feeling the runny wetness that had been his right eye and Fish remained stock-still where the force of the strike had stopped him. Sick, he stared at the mess and started to turn, to run away.

A girl materialized from nowhere with a lead pipe and with a round-cross slam caught Fish alongside the ear. He gurgled something low and pitched over, the side of his head bleeding, the stick and glass dropping to the alley unnoticed.

The blinded Cherokee was lying on his side, crying loudly, running his fingers over his cheeks, feeling his eye socket where nothing but a pulped mass remained. He bit his lips and fainted.

The girl stared at him for a moment, then bent over and began to apply the pipe to Fish with accuracy and ferocity. Rusty watched her for a moment, hardly believing the cool methodicalness with which she was beating him to death. Then he high-leaped over two boys wrestling on the floor before him, and was on her. He grabbed the pipe as it came up and twisted the girl by the shoulder with his free hand.

The girl turned, surprised, and Rusty belted her as hard as he could in the mouth. Her lips tightened back against her teeth, her teeth broke and she fell over gasping.

He turned, to escape, but there was no way out.

A shot rang loud in the place and he knew someone had started with the zip guns. The one in his pocket felt too big, too unhealthy and he tried to get back through the crowd to the club rooms—to escape through the rear exit.

He saw Candle in a clash with a blond knifeman from the Cherokees. Each was slashing at the other with a long Italian switch. Candle eased back, walloped the boy's arm away and caught him dead center in the thigh with the blade. In and out it went quicksilver fast and the boy slumped over. Candle went to work with his stomping boots.

All over the room kids were clubbing each other, working the rubberband-driven zip guns, firing guns, slashing high and hard with warm steel, and he was getting sick again, for the smoothly polished hardwood alleys were starting to become slippery.

A thick-faced Cherokee with a scar over his left eye came at Rusty with a length of chain, and the whip of it was a banshee wail in his ears. Rusty tried to duck away, but he fell toward the assailant.

Rusty fumbled in his pocket, and came up with the zip. He had somehow loaded one of the .22 slugs into the sawed-off car antenna that was the gun's barrel and now he pulled back the firing pin, let it zip into the barrel.

The gun exploded with a slam and the bullet took the Cherokee high in his right arm. A hole as big as a crater opened and bloody cartilage sprayed back, filthying Rusty's shirt and tie. The boy screamed at the pain, dropped the chain and limped back into the mob. Rusty fished in his pocket for the remaining slugs and with the zip threw them from him, under a row of lockers.

The siren wail of police cars broke through the gang screams and the swearing and the sounds of battle, and everyone stopped again, for just a split-second. Then joined in a common bond of hatred for The Men, they started tumbling over one another to get to the exits—occasionally taking a slash or a swipe at an enemy nearby.

But the cops had the place surrounded already. Before anyone could escape—leaving the injured writhing on the floor—the place was crowded with blue-jacketed shapes and the horde began to pull together. Rusty saw one boy try to dive through the front window, saw him leap, saw him nearly grabbed by a fuzz. The kid sailed through the air, his foot was snared by the cop, and the boy went only partially out the window. He landed with a crash, belly-slammed through the glass, the plate window shattering on all sides. When the cop dragged him out, his hands and face were bleeding, shredded meat.

All around him Rusty heard the screams of frightened kids and he wished he had not lingered at the dance. He wished high and hard. This was bad, particularly with him in Pancoast's custody. But there seemed no way out, no way to escape being dragged in. It somehow, terrifyingly, seemed predestined. He was forging his own chains. He never should have come down here tonight where the hell was out.

Then he was ducking past a heavy blue sleeve and a hard face and running for the back way. A path cleared before him miraculously and he dove through, thinking he was free.

Out of the corner of his eye he saw Candle go down under a cop's billy and he spurred himself on. His shoulder was numb from the tire-chain smash he had suffered. The way was blocked by two girls who were still fighting; the one girl clubbing the other in the breasts with a brick.

He elbowed them aside roughly and plunged through the doorway, letting the battered broad's screeches slip past his consciousness. Inside the club rooms things were even worse, if that was possible. The cops had somehow discovered the back way—probably waiting for just something like this to instigate a raid on the Cougars—and the rooms were filled with battling cops, Cherokees and Cougars. The howls of the broads was a wide tapestry of sound and beat almost physically at Rusty.

He tried to get back out, found himself boxed in. He saw a cop fasten his eyes on him, and tried to duck away. But the cop had him and the hand closed tightly about his neck, painfully. He choked and kicked back with his leg, missing the cop, kicking someone else. The cop dragged him by the collar toward the back exit and when Rusty tried to snake away the cop grabbed his arm, twisted it back and up till the socket felt as though it were lined with sand.

The pain was great, so Rusty settled down quietly.

He only tried to kick free once more, as the cop shoved him up the steps of the riot car. But it was no good. And the paddy wagon was dark inside, like somebody's belly, all full of kids…

The squad room was crowded and the kids milled about uncertainly, eyeing the door with a wary craftiness. Once in a while one of the Cherokees would say something guttural to a Cougar and a mild flare-up would start. But circulating cops with ready billies kept the noise to a minimum.

Rusty stood in a corner, by himself, smoking quietly. This was hell on skates! Of all the stupid things to have happen to him, this was the topper. To get himself picked up now, when he was released in Pancoast's custody, when he had gotten away from the gang. He cursed himself for having slipped—so easily, so *goddamned* easily—back into his old ways. Then he realized that the poison was not completely neutralized; it still swirled in his veins and he knew he had to watch himself carefully all the time.

This was going to be rough as banana peels, and he didn't know how he was going to get out of it.

Fish slid over to him from the bench where he sat and spoke from the corner of his mouth, hardly moving his lips, so the cops could not see him speaking. "Hey, man, you got any sticks on you?" His head was completely swathed in bandages.

Rusty shook his head.

Fish nodded satisfaction. "That's your tail if they catch you with pot."

"I know it."

"Man, you shoulda gone home early. Why were you hangin'?"

"My sister, you jerk. I thought she was comin' back and I went to knock off a piece while I waited. She musta come back and left or somethin' while I was with that stupid Goofball, Mary, whatever the hell her name was. So I was a stupe, so I'm here, so I—"

"*Hey! You!*"

A bull-faced desk sergeant, behind the high counter, was motioning through the cigarette smoke and the crowd at Rusty. Rusty played it cool for a minute, looked around, as if to say, who—me? The cop motioned again. "Yeah, you, the one with the butt in his face. C'mere."

Rusty touched Fish with his elbow, and shoved away from the wall, walked forward slowly. A Cherokee gave him the elbow hard as he went past, but Rusty paid no attention.

He walked slowly, and hit the counter with his head high.

"Yessir?"

"Weren't you in here a couple months back, on a rumble rap?"

"I don't know, sir. Maybe."

"Don't ya know?"

"I'm not sure, sir."

"Not sure, huh?" His voice became all-business, hard. "Name?"

"Santoro."

"First name, wise guy."

"Rusty."

"What's your given name? None of that gang crap."

Rusty bit his lip. Oh hell, all right! "Russell."

One of the Cherokees in back said in a falsetto, "Oh, Rawwsull!"

Rusty stiffened, but continued to stare at the plump, dark-eyed sergeant above him. The officer lifted a phone, spoke into it softly and settled back with his arms folded across his chest.

"Can I go back now, sir?" Rusty said bitterly.

"Stay put," the cop replied.

Rusty stayed and waited, knowing they were yanking the book on him. The file, the dossier, the grave-sheet, the record of the sins he had built. He waited and died a little bit inside, knowing he was back on the treadmill, knowing only a minor miracle would save him now.

In a few minutes another officer came in from a side door and tossed the folder to the desk, looking at Rusty with curiosity. "Real juicy," he said, cocking a thumb at the boy.

Silence descended heavily in the squad room as the kids listened to hear the sum total of Rusty's offenses, to see how rough a stud he was.

The sergeant opened the file, and read the make-sheet. "Arrested August 1955, car stripping; first offense. Released into custody of mother. Arrested June 1956, mugging, released on insufficient evidence; arrested March 1957, breaking and entering, assault with a deadly weapon, released in the custody of Carl Pancoast."

He looked down heavily and his dark eyes bored into Rusty's gray ones with rock hardness. Rusty stared back implacably. They weren't gonna make him buckle.

"Nice. Real nice," the cop said with sarcasm. "Good record for a kid your age. This—uh—Pancoast know you were out tonight?"

"I don't know for certain, sir."

"Whaddaya mean, ya don't know?"

Rusty shrugged. "I'm just not sure, sir."

"What were you doing down there in that bowling alley tonight? You go there to fight?"

"No, sir."

The cop leaned heavily forward on his fleshy arms. "Then what were ya doin' there?"

"I was looking for my sister, sir," Rusty said, knowing he would not be believed.

The cop looked quizzical. "Why?"

"I didn't want her to go to the dance. I knew there was gonna be trouble with them," he nodded his head behind him, at the surly Cherokees standing in listening positions.

The cop bit his lower lip. "Anybody know you was goin' there for that?"

Rusty shrugged. "I'm not sure, sir."

"You're not so sure about anything, are you, kid?"

Rusty remained silent. What was the point of answering?

Suddenly, Fish spoke up from the rear. "I knew he was lookin' for his sister."

And Greek stepped out, "Me, too. That's what he said when he come in."

The cop looked up, surprised. This was not standard with the gang kids. Play dumb, that was the rule. And yet here were two of them, sticking their necks out for someone else. The sergeant pursed his lips, thinking.

Rusty knew what it had taken for Fish and Greek to open their mouths. It made them stand out and that just wasn't done in the streets; a stud could get hurt that way.

"Who said that?"

Fish did not answer. To corroborate Rusty's story was one thing, to be singled out and brought forward—that was strictly another. "I asked who said that?" Still no answer.

But another voice—Rusty recognized the heavy voice of the Greek again—chimed in, "That's right, fuzz. He was there for his sister. He told me!"

Then another, Poop it was. "Right, that's right!" They were all following suit, for Rusty had not even spoken to Poop at the dance. But in a moment, all the Cougars were yelling it was so.

The cops started moving through the crowd, uncertain, trying to stop the noise, but the desk sergeant slammed his beefy hand on the desktop, yelled, "Okay! Okay! No more of that, shut up or you all go into the tank for the night." He looked down at Rusty uncertainly.

Rusty stood with his hands deep in his pants' pockets, not saying anything, neither recognizing the comments nor denying them. But a thin, satisfied look crept over his lips. They weren't bad kids—good guys when they had the chance. Except who the hell ever gave them half a chance?

The cop motioned to the officer who had brought in the dossier and the man came up closer to the counter, stood on tiptoe and leaned in. The sergeant leaned across and they spoke together for a few moments.

Then the sergeant nodded, said, "I don't know," and the other said, "So give him a ring. It's early. Maybe he can do something."

The sergeant nodded again and picked up the phone. He spoke into it, waited a moment, then looked down for something in the dossier. Rusty had a good idea what was happening and he wanted to croak.

The cop was going to call Pancoast. What a bitch of a deal! There went all the teacher's confidence in him.

The cop started dialing and Rusty moved to stop him. The cop looked up and Rusty had an abrupt, terribly vivid impression of bars, between himself and the cop, and he said nothing.

The cop got the number and listened. It rang. Again. Finally, after perhaps a minute, he hung up.

He stared at Rusty for a moment, then leaned over, said, "You're out on custody, you know."

There was no point to answering, so Rusty didn't.

"I said something to you, kid—Santoro."

Rusty nodded, "Yessir."

"You knew there was gonna be a rumble tonight?"

Rusty spread his hands eloquently. "That's why I went after my sister. I heard there was gonna be trouble."

"You know you're skatin' pretty thin ice, Santoro."

"Yessir."

"Go on home and we're gonna call this Pancoast. He's not answering now so we'll call him tomorrow, and we're gonna give him a report on this, let him decide if he still wants you under his custody. If not, you'll sail into the pokey so fast it'll make your butt ache. Be at home when we want you."

Rusty was amazed. Go home? Just like that? What was this? What was the catch?

The boy turned and started toward the door.

The Cherokees set up a howl.

"Hey, man! That ain't no fair!"

"You gonna let him go like that?"

"You let *him* go, you gotta let us *all* go!"

"Lousy fuzz-lover!"

The sergeant bit his lower lip, regretting his decision. Then, "Hey, you. Santoro. Wait a minute."

The cop tapped a pencil against the desktop, then said resignedly, "Wiswell, put him in a cell, by himself, till tomorrow. Protective, call it. We'll call this Pancoast tonight again and if he doesn't answer, then tomorrow morning. Can't just let him go without some word, y'know." His voice was apologetic, to no one but himself.

"Tomorrow's Sunday," said Wiswell.

"I know it," the desk sergeant snapped back. "Do like I told you."

The officer named Wiswell took Rusty by the arm and led him from the squad room, down the corridor.

They opened the cell block and Wiswell walked Rusty down the broad aisle between the cubicles. In the center of the room was a heavy wooden table and benches joined together like a picnic table, and bolted to the floor. Either wall was the barred face of a cell.

Wiswell stopped before one of the empty ones and motioned to the end of the line. The turnkey there threw the bar and the cell door slid into the wall. Wiswell motioned Rusty forward and the boy walked into the cell.

"Wait a minute," said the cop. "We didn't book you in because you're not charged. But you better let me have your tie and belt. Any weapons hidden?"

Rusty shook his head, and slipped off his tie. He pulled the belt loose with a swishhh and handed it over, too. Wiswell took them, said, "Ask the guard in the morning…I'm not going to bother with a receipt tonight. Too late.

"Take it easy," he added and left the cell.

Once outside, he motioned again and the cell door slid to with a clump. Rusty looked around: a metal trough without a mattress suspended by clamps from the wall (bowed in the center, and smelling faintly of urine and the last man who had slept there); a toilet without seat or paper (a wall button for flushing); a sink with one hold-in button (cold water only); a wire-shielded naked bulb in the ceiling.

Even as he stared at it, the light went out, throwing the cell into striped duskiness.

From a cell across the block, a Negro voice called out to him. "Ay, man."

Rusty moved to the bars, hooked his fingers through, and tried to stare across, to discern who was speaking. Finally, through the darkness, he got a dim picture of the big, ebony shape in the other cell. The man repeated his first greeting.

"Whaddaya want?" Rusty answered, wary, though separated by two thicknesses of steel bar.

"Ay, man, you got a cigarette there for me? I ain't had one in fo' hours."

Rusty fished in his pocket, came out with the deck and pulled one loose, then he realized they were beyond flipping distance and if he chanced it the cigarette would lay in the aisle till morning when they were turned loose into the tank.

"How'm I supposed to get it over to you?" Rusty asked.

The big Negro pressed up against the bars, instructed, "You lay it down on the floor, man, and then like you snap yo'r finger aside it, and it should roll right in here sweet-like. Okay?"

Rusty did as he had been told, and snapped his finger against the tube, sending it spinning straight across. It rolled, and for a second he thought he had not tapped it hard enough, but the years playing "knuckles-down" in the streets had done their work. It skittered across and the man reached out, snaring it.

"I got no matches, man."

Rusty threw him the matches. They struck the cell door, and rebounded, but not out of reach, and in a few moments he saw a firefly tail winking in the blackness across from him. He watched the dim shape silently, then heard the soft, "Thanks, man," and grunted an acknowledgement.

After a little while, Rusty realized he had been standing at the bars, his fingers hooked through, without movement, and though he knew no one could see him, he was aware that this was the traditional melodramatic pose of the prisoner and he stepped away from the cell door.

There was a barred window far down at the end of the tank. Through it he could see the night sky. It was as though he were in a well, looking at the stars. But there were no stars. And no moon. And no clouds. And nothing up there but what should be there; the sky. Somehow it meant something to him. He wasn't quite sure what, but he thought it meant something like inevitability. It was a cinch the sky was there and it was a cinch he was down here in the cell. That was the way it was and the way it would wind up. You'd never find the sky being used as a rug and you'd never find Rusty Santoro living the good life. Didn't figure.

He sat down on the trough, then remembered the last prisoner had peed in it and got up before he felt moisture. He slouched against the wall and then decided he, too, wanted a smoke. He had the cigarette in his mouth before he remembered he had no matches.

"You wanna send them matches back?" he asked.

For a second he saw relationships all too clearly, and was sure the Negro would say, "Go screw yaself. I got 'em, they're mine."

The Negro said, "Sure 'nuff, man," and they skittered across the floor, sliding up against the cell door. Rusty reached down in the darkness and found them.

As he was lighting up, the other prisoner remarked, "A real bitch, man." As though they were not in jail, merely neighbors. A casual remark, so incongruous.

Rusty looked up. "What's that?"

"They get you in here and they let you have butts, but no matches; so we got to keep one butt goin' all night or nobody smoke. You know?"

Rusty grunted understanding.

"I 'member one night they's about six of us in here and all with butts, none with matches. One guy was lit-up when he got in, an' we hadda roll them butts back an' forth all night, till we was near shook, man, we got so nervous."

Silence for a while. Then, "They take your shoelaces and belt, jack?"

Rusty leaned his head against the wall. "Not my laces. Took my belt an' tie, though. Yours?"

"Mmm. Took mine." The Negro laughed deeply, it rumbled. "But then, I'm a veteran. I'm tank bait, man."

"Why they take that stuff?"

"You know, like some cat gets the lows. Tries to cool hisself with his belt. Ties it up to that screen 'round the light thing in the ceilin', and hangs hisself with it. That makes a bad smell for the coppers, somebody goes out the hangin' way overnight. So they takes the stuff. They must not of booked you if you still got your laces an' matches."

Rusty grunted agreement. "No, they didn't."

The Negro went on. "That explains it. They can't take ya stuff they just holdin' ya, in procoo or like that."

"What's procoo?"

"Man, you sure 'nuff new to this, ain'tcha?"

"I been in the cooler a couple times. With some other guys. I been around."

The Negro chuckled wryly. The calf trying to be the bull. "Yeah, sure, jack. Didn't mean no harm. Sure you been around, you say so, it's so."

"What's procoo?"

"Protective cust'idy, man. Like they's holdin' you for your own good. A crock. You know, so they know where you are overnight."

Rusty stood up. He leaned his head against the thin, cool metal of the bars. "What you in for?"

The Negro laughed cheerily. "Sheet, man. Nothin' much. They makin' a big thing outta nothin'."

"Oh? What?"

"Sheet, man. I just cut someone, thass all."

"Who'd you cut?"

The prisoner hesitated, and Rusty heard a deep drag on the cigarette. The Negro's voice came in a deeper, more strained, more worried tone, belying his words. "Oh, no one much. I just cut my old lady a little. She peed me off and I took the blade to her, is all."

Rusty slid back along the wall, staring up at the ceiling, staring at nothing. He didn't want to talk to the guy; that was nowhere. He had to think. He had to give it a long, long think.

Was Pancoast going to come down tomorrow and bail him loose? Was he going to sit in the can till his tail turned blue? He thought of Moms and he thought of Dolo and the last thought worried him.

Where was she? She had been at the dance, he was certain of that, but she had gone and not come back. For some reason he worried the thought about and found it singularly unpleasant. He wanted to get out, fast—to check home with Moms.

That had been a rough time and anything could have happened. Rusty realized he was foolish to be worrying about Dolores when he was so deep in trouble himself, but he could not help himself.

The darkness of the cell did nothing to reassure him.

He took his handkerchief out and moved in the cell till his thighs hit the trough-bunk. He struck a light and swabbed out the troughload of puke as best he could. It wasn't much to sleep on, but he had to try.

He loosed a flood of cursing at the sight; but did the best he could with it. He prepared to lie down, finally. A deep tone sounded from the cell across the way.

"What *you* in for, man?"

Rusty turned, and tried to make out the face of the man in the cell opposite. For some strange reason, he wanted to see his face, to engrave it with bitterness in his mind. He never wanted to come back here again.

"Nothing, mac. Just—nothing at all," the boy answered.

He lay down in the shallow trough and the hard, unyielding metal seemed right, somehow. He knew it was foolish, the same as Moms' religion kick every now and then, but he wanted the bunk to be hard; he had done wrong tonight, very wrong. He had let himself slip back a little, thinking release from everything he had been and done was so easy to come by. He knew better now. It was a constant thing, a steady thing. He had to work at it and keep himself clean and away from it. It was like pot or liquor. It got to you and sucked you down every time, if you weren't careful.

He closed his eyes. But sleep would not come.

Finally, the lights behind his eyes dimmed away to a darkness deeper than that of the tank and he slipped away to weird, disquieting, running dreams.

Just before the curtain slid down completely, he thought he heard the fuzzy, indistinct, deep voice from nowhere saying, "You got to be good, man, or they set you in the jailhouse. An' that's so bad, man, so bad…"

It registered. Rusty slept.

❀

The morning dawned muggy and gray. Rusty slipped out of the trough, and his back was a mass of aches. His neck was stiff and he had a chill that ran through his bones. It wasn't the most pleasant awakening of his life, but somehow things seemed all clear now, all clean, all fresh and ready for a start.

The turnkey came to open the cell doors at nine o'clock, and as the bars slid into the wall with a thump, Rusty turned away from the sink, his face wet, his eyes feeling strange and gritty in their sockets, even with the cold water doused in them.

He stood there and watched the other man come out of the cell across the way.

Rusty knew he would remember what the big Negro looked like. Not the color of his skin or the range of his arms or the skew of his nose, but the lines of the face, the meaning in the eyes, the whole composite thing. The whole, damned-forever thing. And it wasn't nice, but he knew he would keep it close and any time he might need it there would be no trouble getting it out where he could look at it tightly.

The man did not speak and Rusty did not come out of the cell. But when the big man went down to the far end of the tank to rattle the bars and scream for breakfast Rusty knelt down on the sandpapery floor and shut his eyes.

"Hail Mary, full of grace, blessed—"

Later, the turnkey came to get him. The officer walked Rusty back down the corridor and into the squad room. The beefy sergeant from the night before was gone. In his place was a sallow-faced officer with a Madison Avenue haircut and large ears. Rusty had seen this man around the neighborhood from time to time. His name was Bedzyk. It seemed right, for this morning.

No matter what happened, Rusty felt very, very clean.

The desk officer looked up as he came in and his eyes frosted over quickly. No emotion before these street punks. Bedzyk hated the gangs. A group of hoods one afternoon had followed his bride of eight months, calling filthy suggestions after her as she walked down the street to her apartment. But there was nothing he could do to rough it on them this time. He examined the notation.

"You Santoro, Russell?"

Rusty nodded.

"Answer when I speak to you!" Bedzyk's voice was hard and deadly. Rusty felt himself averting the man's snake-like gaze.

"Yessir."

Bedzyk grudgingly acknowledged the boy's thumbing-under. "I got a release order here for you, left by Sergeant Dohrmann. Says some man named Pancoast okayed your release. You're supposed to report to his place this evening. You know where to go to see him?"

Rusty answered sharply, "Yessir."

"Okay. Then remember this, kid. I ever see you in here again, I'm going to personally see that the book's tossed at you. Understand me, *comprende*?"

Rusty bristled at the offhand remark, but answered humbly, "Yessir."

"Okay then, get the devil out of here. I can't stomach looking at your ugly face."

Rusty felt anger frying the insides of his gut, but he held it back. He needed some information. " 'Scuse me, sir."

Bedzyk looked up blackly. "You still there?"

" 'Scuse me, sir, but can you tell me like if they let out the other guys?" He thought of the blood in the bowling alley.

The cop stared the boy down for a long instant, then his neck cords began to stand out, and in a terribly soft slow voice he said, "Get the hell out of here."

Rusty left as quickly as possible.

Outside, Boy-O was slouching against a wall, an ordinary cigarette dangling from his unshaven face. He smelled even stronger than usual and the wild, junkie-stare was so bad Rusty could have sworn a pair of diamonds were screwed into the sockets, blazing out.

Boy-O took a shove away from the wall, approached Rusty. The other tried to swerve around him, but the junkie said, "Hey, Rusty, hold up a second."

Rusty stopped and looked at the hophead. "Whaddayou want?"

"I been waitin' till they let the gang out. Some of the guys needed carfare like. They're holdin' three or four of the guys."

So that explained what had happened to the Cherokees and the Cougars, but Rusty was impatient to be away from the great gray hulk of the police building. "So? Why you stoppin' me?"

"I just wanted to tell ya I was sorry ta hear what happened."

Rusty was puzzled. Boy-O never had been a good friend. What did he care if Rusty Santoro spent the night in a cell on a metal trough?

"For what? I'm out, ain't I?"

Boy-O looked surprised, then shocked, then partial understanding filtered through to his dreamy brain. "Oh, hey, man, then you don't know. Hey, that's right, they didn't find her till this mornin', so you didn't get the word yet."

A chill slipped up Rusty's neck and he grabbed the junkie by his filthy lapels. "What? What are you talkin' about? Come on, you sonofabitch, open up or I'll cream ya!"

He knew, somehow, horribly; even before Boy-O spoke.

"Your sister, man. They found her this mornin'. Somebody— uh—raped her and left her in an alley behind Tom-Tom's joint."

Rusty felt the anchors of his jaws tighten and he thought for a moment he would drop into the street. He had to know. *He had to know—*

"Tell me! Talk, you dustie, talk! How is she?"

Boy-O looked terrified, as though he were face to face with something alien. He wanted to run away, but Rusty had him fast and was choking him without knowing it.

He stammered and Rusty hit him across the mouth. "Talk! *Talk!*" He bit his lips in fury and screamed loud so the whole clean, fine, nice start-all-over day would know, "Tell me—how is she?"

"Gee, man, I'm sorry…She's dead like. Somebody stuck a knife inta her."

The past screamed and Rusty heard.

SEVEN:
SUNDAY AFTERNOON

- *rusty santoro*
- *moms*

Somehow, the walk home, partially through quiet Cherokee turf, passed without his knowing it. His feet moved and his arms swung and he stopped for traffic lights when he stopped. But he saw nothing and no sounds or smells came through to him.

He was a five-foot nine-inch moving statue. He was on a trek through nowhere at all and he walked with steady persistence. Where thoughts had been, where the clean reach of the day had lain, nothing but a swirl of color remained. It was a wild mélange of heaving, surging dull orange, wisps of light gray almost blue, streaks sudden and painful of red and heavy black. It was impossible for anything to get in and nothing trapped inside could find its way free.

Shock!

The steady movement of feet that was completely unnoticed.

He opened the door to the apartment and walked in. No sound. No movement of air. A stillness and a softness almost oppressive in its totality. And yes, of course, the clock had stopped. He knew it would be like that, like a dream he had once had, and forgotten, now rushing back like the night wind to fill his mind. The clock had stopped, the unity was gone, Dolores was—

The word came then: *Dead.*

No, not dead. He said it once aloud to hear it, "No, not

dead," then added as though the word meant something for the first time, "murdered."

No gang rumble where a nameless boy who held a switch-blade lay with his belly split wide; no stomping of a Greenwich Village queer, so his head was mashed potatoes; no technicolor, CinemaScope, stereophonic daydream in an RKO shadow-house. This was real and it was the thing in itself. This was his sister, the last one, the lost one, and she was gone. And that was *not* just that. That was the end of a bit of the world that meant something, that had a way to the light, that moved and talked and swayed prettily to the phonograph's noise, that tapped the fork at dinner, and that was too young—yes, goddamn it—too *young* to die.

The clock had stopped. Someone had let it waste its time to stillness. It meant something, but Rusty did not know what or why, or even if he should care about it. He wanted to cry. Why couldn't he cry?

There was a vague noise from the kitchen. Moms.

He walked through the long railroad flat and into the kitchen where she prowled like a warm, soft gray animal.

He saw her as though he were looking through the wrong end of a telescope. Very far away and moving with terribly ex-aggerated actions—first at the vegetable bin, then at the sink, then carefully peeling the potatoes. Were they the only things in the world for her? Didn't she know?

"Ma," he spoke softly, and was surprised to hear how loud and unpleasant his voice sounded in the mausoleum stillness of the apartment. She turned to him, blank eyes that were luster-less and face devoid of expression. He knew her, then; knew her as she was inside, stripped as bare as the potatoes in the sink, with only the blank eyes left.

She turned back to her work without a word and began sys-tematically to gouge out the potato eyes.

He repeated the single word. "Ma?"

She slumped a bit more from the shoulders and he thought he saw her shiver slightly. The trembling carried itself and he felt a weakness in the back of his own knees. "I was downtown, Ma," he added.

She did not respond and he wondered if she had suddenly gone deaf. It was an odd feeling, all at once, and he thought of Rip Van Winkle. Had he been away more than one night in jail? Had he been shut up behind steel for, say, fifty years, and had now come back to a stranger who no longer knew him? It passed in an instant, but for that instant he was standing on a cold, empty highway, watching the Last Car Ever tooling away in dust.

"I said, I was downtown, Ma. I got picked up last night when I went after—" He stopped himself short. Dolores. He didn't want to say her name like that. He wanted to build to it. At first, when he had come up the three flights of steps to the apartment, he had thought he would burst in and yell *Where's Dolo? Ma, Dolo's dead!* but the silence of the place had smoothed over the inferno within him.

The fire was still there, and he could feel it building, but he knew he must be careful. She had had it bad, and if she knew—

If she knew.

"Ma," he hesitated. The words were like taffy in his mouth. "I talked to somebody, Ma. He t-told me Dolo was—Dolo's—"

It would have to lie there. He was not going to say it.

She saved him the trouble.

"I know."

The voice came from the other side of the universe and barely made the journey. Soft. Soft.

"Is it true? She was—she was—I mean, like he said?"

Then she turned and the blank oval spaces that should have

been her eyes grayed out at him and her mouth moved like a pencil line that had somehow been endowed with life. *"Raped,"* she said and twisted the word once. "She was on her face, in a dirty alley with a garbage can tipped over on her, to hide her. Empty ice-cream containers was dripped all over her, I don't know. She was. There. I saw her face. She was wet. It rained last night. I don't know. Her blouse was black where he did it with the thing, with I guess he did it with a knife, it was black…"

Her words were confused, the agony ramblings of a woman in shock. Rusty listened, knowing he should remember all this. This was the death of his sister and perhaps the death of his mother. But it all went by rapidly and he saw her only as hysterical. He had to stop her talking that way.

"Mom! Stop it, you gotta stop it, please, stop it!"

But she went on, talking more to herself than to him. "I went there. I don't know why they let her lay there like that. Why was that? I don't know. There was a policeman who said, 'Look there lady and tell us if that's your daughter,' so I looked. I thought you had to go downtown to that there, I don't know, what do they call it? Why was I called down to the street? Why was she there in the…the…there? Why was she killed?"

Her hands had twined soundlessly together. Two lost things searching for peace. Her face had turned half away, and the wall received her words. Rusty could not move to her, could do nothing, for a long century of pain in his chest. Then he walked slowly and put his arms around her.

She seemed to melt, then, and she was a child who had lost a dear loved thing. She did not cry, because that would have been easy, that would have been a release. She was numb and trembled under dry, wracking shakes that were a product of disbelief, of confusion, of searching. Rusty realized how much he needed his mother, how much she needed him, and he lay her head on his chest, said to her softly, "Mom, Mom, please.

It's okay, you'll see, it'll be okay, we'll be all right, just take it easy, Mom; and it'll be okay." He said it again and again, in endless strings of words that started nowhere, ended nowhere, and soothed himself alone. He knew they did not reach her, but he said them more and more, hoping.

"Do, do you remember, she was ten then, just ten, and she come home, said the other kids wouldn't play with her 'cause she was Puerto Rican and slammed the screen door on her knee. You remember, just ten, and she cried, god how she cried, and I wanted to tell her it don't matter honey, 'cause you're good too and prettier than any of them whites…You remember that?"

Rusty remembered. He remembered all the stupid people who had hated the Santoro family, the trouble they had had getting squared away in the new neighborhood, the way Pops had done them so low with his drinking and all, and the way Dolores had grown beautiful and ripe like a flower, just the same. A spot of pretty in the gray of the streets.

Moms stiffened in his embrace and suddenly she shoved against him, threw him back with hatred. Her face was transformed. It was like a scream in the night. Bright red flash in the gray. He felt attacked, he countered with fright. Why that expression?

Her eyes were livid pits of slag and her mouth was a raw, wounded gash that opened and snapped closed with hatred and vehemence. "*You!* You did it! You made her join that gang. You killed her. Like the knife was yours, you killed her. You're the one. Oh, god!" She tore at her breasts, at her belly, screaming, her hair wild and streaming. "Oh, god! I gave birth to you, you filth. You scum, you bastard son of mine! Oh, god, I wish you'd died in my womb, died, god, died! If you'd never touched her with your filth—if you'd never touched her she'd be alive now, she'd be alive!"

Rusty could not speak. What could he say? Was she hysterical or was it the truth? Was he to blame, indirectly?

"I wish you was dead, dead and in the grave and buried under six feet, and she was here, and God I'd make it up to her, I'd treat her fine and damn her father for his wild ways...

"But it was you, you that killed her as sure as if you put that knife in her breast! Get out, get out of my house. I don't want you here. I don't want you sleeping in the same house where she slept or ate off the table—or—*get out! Get out!*"

Her face was livid, her hands claws that tore at the air. She came toward him haltingly, with that loathing burning in her face. Her hands moved out for him and Rusty was frightened at the abrupt change the space of a minute had brought. Her mouth opened and no words came this time, but a spatter of drool oozed from one corner of her thin gray lips. No words came out, though the fire burned high and bright in her cheeks, but Rusty knew what was being said.

You killed your sister. You did it. You're responsible.

Rusty stared unmoving as his mother came toward him and suddenly she lashed out with both hands doubled. Her fists thundered against his face and he felt pain that rocked his head. All her fury went into those blows, as she mumbled over and over, "*You! You* made 'er join that gang! If you'd of left her alone, she'd be alive! You did it to her! Murderer! Murderer murderer murderer..."

Rusty turned and fled.

The street was filled with Sunday crowds of housewives, slobbering dogs, sweating trucks. There was a steady beat in the streets and sidewalks—the sort of beat that makes you fall asleep over tiresome desk jobs; the kind of beat that makes the loners in the pool hall toss down their cues, gather up their winnings and slump against the Coke machine. The sort of beat that makes the old men lounging on the stoops in front of the buildings think they're catching a tan. The sort of beat that brought euphoria to Rusty. He walked aimlessly.

He remembered having seen Pancoast sometime that afternoon. He remembered having seen Pops, too, but that was a memory he wanted to slip away and he did not dwell on it.

Pancoast had been annoyed at him. Sullenly annoyed, and he had not come right out and called Rusty a turncoat. The boy remembered the red-haired teacher, the way he had sat in the modern contour chair—an inexpensive replica of a Paul McCobb original—and sucked on the dry, split end of a metal-stemmed pipe. He remembered the dark gray eyes as they turned up to him and the worry lines about the man's mouth and eyes.

The voices that had been there came back as they had been; strong, clear and filled with hidden emotions.

"You let me down, Rusty." It was a statement.

"No."

"What were you doing there if you weren't waiting for the rumble?"

"My sister...I was...was looking for her."

"I know. I heard a while ago over the radio. It made the papers."

Rusty knew the conversation had gone on from there, with his position strengthening and the teacher's calm trust flowing back. He had been glad about that. It had helped him a little and for a few minutes he saw a clearing in the fog. But the teacher had been a shadow, really, and the recurring image of Dolores, so small and pretty, kept returning to eat at his mind. He had assured Pancoast nothing more would happen, and had left, with the teacher making a gun of thumb and forefinger, aiming it and saying heavily, "Be good, son. They'll find the bastard."

Rusty had left and walked some more and the afternoon had softened into evening without notice. He recalled seeing Pops, slouching in a doorway, a bottle empty beside him. His eyes wandered away quickly. His steps carried him to the opposite side of the street, for fear the old man would see him, and in a few moments he had passed the spot.

He still saw the man's eyes, however; rimmed with black and deep pools of red that beat at him ferociously. He remembered one night the old man had come home from a drunk and found him sleeping on the sofa. In his besotted state he had clubbed Rusty with a rolled-up magazine and sent him reeling. That had been one of the last times Rusty had allowed himself to get close enough to his father for the man to strike him. That had been a long, long time ago, and Rusty tried to exclude Pops from his world, as much as possible.

It was three or four days, sometimes, before the old man impinged on his consciousness. Then it was a shock and a sharp wrench to blank out the old man again.

That had been hours before and Pops was far behind, far uptown, and Rusty walked Times Square like a hungry animal. His feet marked the paving blocks, ticking them away, one after another till he was sure the next would mark the end of the world, and he would step off into quiet oblivion.

His mind was tormented; he had to do something.

The walk downtown had taken a long time, and Times Square —the cesspool of 42nd Street between Seventh and Eighth Avenues—drew him like a quicksand bog. He stumbled into the neon and blare of the area hardly knowing he had been unerringly aiming at it all day. The Strip was crowded, as only a Sunday night crowd in New York can be a crowd. One gigantic, pulsing, living mass, moving, surging, pressing, hot and sweating, carrying along with it the fever of lechery and the stink of bad hot dogs, good papaya juice, tired feet. Rusty joined the tide and let it carry him along.

He paused before an open-air restaurant where bright cards hung above the soiled counters, enticing Rusty to dishes of fish and salad. He turned in and passed the bar. No beer now. He knew instinctively that his stomach would not take it. He passed down the counter to the hot table, and got in line. He stood silently waiting for the people before him to get their meals, and as the swarthy, muscled cook looked across tiredly, Rusty said, "Shrimp plate."

He watched the stocky man smoothly gather up the shrimp from the grease bucket, the salad, the potatoes from the deep, snapping fat and empty them all into the paper plate. It was a remarkable thing, Rusty thought, the way the cook could handle all those things, so fast, so agilely. It was very much like the way a man handled his own life. Some men better than others. Some men not at all.

He paid across the counter, received his change and carried the plate to a table. Beside him a fat man in a dirty white shirt, open at the neck and showing curling strands of wet hair, watched as he set the plate down.

The fat man turned back to his own nearly empty plate, and concentrated a piece of bread on a puddle of gravy. He licked his lips with a tongue-tip, and leaned across as Rusty settled into his food. "You, uh, you wanna pass the salt, please?" he asked. His eyes were tiny and very white at the outer edges.

Rusty hardly glanced at the man and passed the salt shaker across. The man tried desperately to touch Rusty's hand as the shaker passed between them, but he failed.

Rusty concentrated on eating, and the fat man toyed with the scraps on his plate, finally leaning over, breathing warmly into Rusty's neck, and saying, "You, uh, you like movies? Huh, kid?"

Rusty turned, seemed to notice the man for the first time. He saw the plump, moist hands, the greasy folds of skin that wattled the neck, the tiny, piggish eyes and the movement,

movement, movement of the lips. The man's crew-cut, Prussian look startled the boy. At once he knew the fat man for what he was.

"No. I don't dig movies. Never go." Rusty started to move to another table.

The fat man's pudgy hand snaked out and touched the boy's. A sharp intake of breath came from the man, and he wet his lips again. "You don't wanna go to a movie with me, huh?"

Rusty shook his head, tried to get away. The man held fast, like some sort of porous plaster. Rusty grew panicky, and he received a clear memory picture of the day a snapping turtle had fastened on his finger and not let go till he had mashed it between two rocks. He grew more frightened as the seconds grew and finally he jerked at the grip.

The man slid closer. His free hand went beneath the table, as though trying to escape the revealing light. It came to rest on Rusty's knee, and the boy's face went gray.

"Leggo!" Rusty snarled, and his hand found the handle of the fork. The fat man was immersed in technicolored fantasies of his own; his fingers clenched the boy's flesh. Rusty struggled, but was blocked by the man's terrible hold and angle of chair and table. He grasped the fork tightly and before he knew what he was doing, swung the utensil overhand with ferocity.

The fork caught the fat man in the hand, and the four prongs went into the soft, flabbed skin with a ripping and scraping. The fat man's eyes unfilmed and a gurgle rose up in his mouth. He bellowed something unintelligible, and struggled back up out of the chair.

The fork still hung from his hand, loosely, but imbedded and surrounded by spraying blood. He clenched his teeth, bit his lip and pulled the fork loose. He threw it from himself, and went back, back, back, as though an innocent and delicate child had attacked him.

He did not look at Rusty, but though he looked elsewhere, his surprise and horror were directed at the boy. Rusty slid his chair away from the table and as the fat man cried and moaned he ducked out of the restaurant, and quickly lost himself in the tide that flowed toward Eighth Avenue.

The movie houses all looked run-down and too glossy for any fun. He caught a disjointed view of a million neon words wriggling across marquees, and decided he did not want a movie now. Perhaps later, but not now. Now he would try the shooting gallery. Yeah, that was it. The shooting gallery.

Playland was open—always open, never closed, always open—and through the big front glass windows, he could see all the tourists and hangers-on, spending their dimes and nickels on Pokerino and skeet ball.

He walked in, and leaned against the counter, watching the bald, ugly man behind the printing press making fake newspaper headlines in the white empty spaces on dummy papers.

BEN AND WALLY HIT TOWN
GIRLS RUN FOR COVER!!

ARMY LETS GEORGE LIPPOLIS OUT
U.S. FRIGHTENED

MARGIE AND FRANCINE AVAILABLE,
BOYS STORM N.Y.

He read the samples upon the walls, and chuckled dryly. It was all a bad dream. There was no forgetting. He turned to the balding, ugly man and said, "How much?"

"What?"

"I said, how much for one of them papers?"

"Fifty cents. Anything ya wanna say, I'll put it on."

Rusty knew he was doing something he shouldn't…knew he

was sinking himself deeper into his own misery, but he told the man, "Put, 'Dolores Santoro murdered.' Then, uh, write, 'Her brother killed her. He'll get his.' "

The balding, ugly man looked at the boy strangely, and said hesitatingly, "That's more'n I can get on two lines."

Rusty shoved off, walked away, the man behind him yelling across the floor, "Hey! You! Don'choo want that paper? Hey, c'mon, I'll figger some way to get it on—aw hell!"

Rusty stopped at the booth and changed a dollar into nickels and dimes. The attendant fished a fistful from a dirty white hip apron, and two-finger counted them into Rusty's palm. The boy turned away and considered the machines. Instinctively, he went to one of the target machines and fingered the metal barrel of the rifle. The background behind the glass showed a forest with levels in which a few scattered rabbits and turkeys stood, a b-b shoot center in each. He slid a dime from the heap in his hand and put it into the slot. The machine clicked, banged and lights went on in the forest. Bunnies popped up, turkeys popped up, a white-goateed farmer with a corn-cob pipe popped up, clutching a straw hat, a bear peered from behind a tree, weaving left to right, and out of sight around the trunk. A timer began snapping off the seconds.

Rusty plunked the change onto the wooden frame of the rifle machine, fitted the weapon to his shoulder and took aim.

The first shot knocked down a rabbit. The second did the same. The third and fourth shots missed. Then the shapes began to waver and shimmer and run like hot tar on a July street. The rabbits were no longer rabbits. The turkeys had no resemblance to turkeys. The farmer with the white goatee was not the farmer with the white goatee.

The farmer was Pops. The bear was Carl Pancoast, weaving back and forth, trying to stay in sight, but failing miserably. There somewhere, lost in the forest, trying to get out, trying to find a path through the trees and the snarling roots, was Rusty himself. There was Rusty, plunging through the foliage with his scarred forearms crossed before his eyes, his feet piston-pumping, the shadows trailing behind, the tree branches reaching for him. The wind rising in a keening whistle. The moon diving for cover behind cotton-batting clouds, the sky dark and gloating. There was Rusty running like hell, knowing he wasn't gonna make it, goddammit, not even a little.

There was Pops, coming out of the woods with that stink smile on his jaw and his hands big as catcher's mitts, ready to whack. There was Pancoast making imploring gestures, making sneaking, requesting, prodding gestures from behind the big old trees and Rusty running past, 'cause that was the way of it.

And there was Dolores.

It had to be. Crap yes. It had as hell to be. There she was swingin' from a tree limb by her neck, with her tongue stuck out of the corner of her crooked mouth, black and swollen. There were her eyes, bugged huge and starting to water and all the flies on her. The flies that looked like Candle and Boy-O and Fish and Poop and all the rest. There was even a bunch of girl flies that looked like Cherry and Caroline and Weezee. And a big horsefly that was the Beast. She was swingin' in the wind, with the fraykin' night beatin' on her and a scream coming out of her throat but how could that be if she was lynched and dead and swingin'? But it was. It was a scream. And it came up from the bottoms of her feet, high over Rusty's head, and it rose through her twisted body, and it came out of her mouth, past that lump of charcoal that was her tongue, and it sounded like...

TILT TILT TILT TILT TILT TILT TILT TILT

"Looks like I shoved too damned hard," the kid at the pinball beside him said lackadaisically.

Rusty moved his head slightly, shaking his brains back into

shape. It had been so real, so deep, so interesting. He was there and he was here. The machine had already clicked off all his seconds and he noted a ridiculously low score. He leaned against the machine for a moment, steadying himself, feeling a strangeness inside himself, where the sorrow dripped into his blood stream.

Dolores gone. It didn't seem possible. It was all a big joke, and soon someone would give him the clue-in, and he would laugh. But now, now, it was real, too real, and he had to get away from thinking.

He moved on down the line to the next machine, ignoring the kid at the pinball game who had slid another nickel in.

It was an hour before they palled on him and he felt the tugging inside. He had to move on. Move fast and run far. He left the Playland, not in the slightest satiated, the terror of emptiness and loneliness haunting him. Times Square was no better. At eye level it was a rippling obscenity of crowd motion and neon emergencies. Above the glare, the buildings rose in dirty spires. And above that—as though it had wandered into a private party and was too shy to make itself known—the night sky swirled past impregnated with dust and smoke.

New York has no stars.

Rusty walked carefully. The sidewalk was peanut butter. The movie loomed up overhead and reflex took over. It was a Jayne Mansfield picture and he realized that he wanted to see it... before what had happened had happened. He saw two girls getting tickets. His thoughts were not his own. The same crazy emotions that had drawn him here were drawing him into actions he knew he did not want to commit. He bought a ticket and followed the girls into the lobby.

One was brunette, her hair worn in the frowzy pageboy style of the Forties, unkempt and straggling about her face. She had pimples and her legs were very heavy. She wore her sweater and skirt badly; her breasts were monstrous under the pink argyle. The other was prettier, in a mousey way. At first glance she had seemed about eighteen, but a closer look, as they stopped before the candy counter, showed Rusty the other girl was over twenty. Some indeterminate age between high school anxiety and the frenzy of pre-marriage. They were on the loose and Rusty made the same sort of mental note he always made when he was stalking broads.

The mousey one was not as hot a job as the fat slob, but she had a round little po-po on her and she seemed to be at least moderately clean. He decided to make the pitch there.

The psychology of the streets had already been put into effect: never buy a ticket for a broad when she can buy her own. Pick the piece up inside, it's cheaper.

Rusty moved in. His feet carried him without his knowing their direction. This was escape, goddammit, this was a way out—for the time being.

He moved in behind and his arm lightly brushed the smaller girl's back. She turned and her face was just below his own. He stared at her boldly and the ritual began.

A slight, rakish grin spread across his even features, and he bounced the change in his hand. "Want some candy?"

The fat one looked interested from the first. That was no score and Rusty knew it. He'd had her pegged as warm drawers from the outset. He ignored the twin signal beacons that screamed CLARK BAR BABY RUTH RAISINETS from her tiny eyes, and looked squarely at the smaller girl. He was rewarded. Obviously they had not come to the movie for the movie. There would be none of the shallow fencing and double entendre he hated so much in boy-girl byplay.

She looked at him and said, "Popcorn is all, thanks." Her tones were Bronx. Lower Bronx. He bought an open-topped box of hot buttered stuff and walked beside the girls into the theater, keeping hold of the popcorn. The investment had not been cinched yet.

They went up to the balcony and found three seats amid the smoke curtain. Rusty sat between the two girls and was annoyed when the fat one wasted not a moment, placing her warm thigh close to his leg even as he sat down. The smaller one settled herself, adjusted her skirt primly, and thoughtfully chewed her gum. After a moment she leaned over, put her hand on Rusty's and said sweetly, "C'n I have the popcorn please?"

He handed the box over and slipped toward her slightly. His hand went around the back of the seat and dropped low on the front of her shoulder, just above one of her small breasts. She made no move to remove it.

It wasn't a very good movie. But that didn't matter.

After the show, Teresa took Patty aside and talked to her very low and excited for a few minutes. Rusty leaned against a poster of the coming attraction and lit a cigarette. He heard Patty say, "Like hell. I saw 'im first." Then the voices of the two girls sank into a low monotone again and Patty shook her head a few times. Teresa finally took a bill from her little clutch-purse and slipped it into the fat girl's hand. Then she gave her a shove, and an imperative nod of the head, and Patty moved out into the street, with a belligerent and semi-hungry stare back at Rusty and the girl.

"Okay," Teresa said, coming across the lobby to Rusty. "Now if you wanna go get somethin' ta eat, I'll go with ya."

Rusty nodded his head at the retreating back and wobbling buttocks of Patty, heading toward Eighth Avenue. "Won't she tell your folks?"

Teresa unfurled a fresh stick of gum, popped it into her mouth, rolling it up as she did it, and waved away his comment. "*My* folks? My old lady's dead and my old man wouldn't care what happened to me as long as I kept bringin' in that twenty a week for rent."

They walked out onto the sidewalk and he started to steer her up the street to Romeo's where the thirty-five-cent plate of spaghetti seemed about right for this date. "Whaddaya do for a livin'," Rusty asked.

She cocked an eyebrow at him and a little half-titter escaped her small mouth. "I work in a office down on Nineteenth Street. Accountin' an' like that, y'know." Rusty knew. He knew many young guys and broads who had been forced out of the streets into these treadmill jobs. If she cleared forty-five dollars a week she was lucky. Twenty to her old man for rent...no wonder she was looking for a pickup come Sunday nights. She was past kid age when she could scream over Eddie Fisher and Elvis without being self-conscious. She had reached the age when she was worried about the future and knew she was not pretty enough to make a good match. She had reached the age when comic books no longer appealed to her. She was a lost one, too—a transition person—stuck in a groove and too confused to find her way out.

Sunday night pickup. Just out of the jailbait class. And raring to romp.

They ate their spaghetti in relative silence. She liked Fats Domino. She did not like the movie they had seen—wasn't that Jayne Mansfield just too cheap in them tight red dresses why hell *I'd* never wear a dress like that. True, thought Rusty, all too damned true. She did not like New York mugginess. She did like Rusty. She would not at all mind the idea of going to a hotel with him.

She was old enough to buy a bottle at the state store, but it was closed. Rusty knew a place where Sunday did not matter. She only hesitated a moment when Rusty suggested a fifty-fifty split on it. She bought a bottle of good Scotch from the man and

Rusty wondered how she knew good from bad. She didn't seem to have the brains.

They had no trouble at the Southern Hotel—Rusty had been there before and knew the system. Two bucks extra and they weren't disturbed all night.

She wasn't very good in bed and later in the night, when the sounds from the airshaft had diminished, she cried against his unresponsive shoulder. She cried about the trouble she had curling her hair, and the way her nose swelled with allergies in the summer, and the way she loved him, and the sorrows that only the city and the night and life can bring. Rusty hardly heard. He was sunk in his own black thoughts.

It did no good; Dolores was dead, Moms was dying inside, there was no thought at all of Pops, and he was garbage from top to bottom. Everything was sliding downhill again. It did no good to make the attempt. It did no good. What the hell, it did no good.

Everything was rotten. Everything stunk. He hit her and she crept closer to him in the sticky sheets. He reached over and took the nearly empty bottle. If it ran out before the thoughts were drowned, he'd send her out for another.

She'd go. He'd make sure she went.

He finished the bottle.

It was a bad night all around.

EIGHT:
MONDAY MORNING,
MONDAY NIGHT

- *rusty santoro*
- *the cougars*
- *the beast*

Beside him in the dirty, rumpled, sweat-reeking sheets, the slim body of a strange girl lay humped and sleeping. He stared across and down at her for a long moment, trying to place her—then it all came back in sequence and his hatred for himself became even greater. She had cried and he had hit her in the face. She had not left him. He recalled dimly that he, too, had cried, and that was the reason she had stayed, clinging close to him in binding misery.

But the stench of sour liquor pervaded the cheap hotel room, seeping in and out of the cracked yellow paint, rolling around the rusty shank of the fire extinguisher pipe jutting from one wall at ceiling level.

The place was hot and muggy. He stumbled from the bed, dragging a sheet with him and stamped furiously at it, finally disengaging its cloying weight. He threw up the water-stained blind and the dim light of the gray airshaft poured across the bed. He turned in the face of it and stared at her naked body, sprawled sidewise across the mattress. It had been a lousy night. Poor slob of a broad. He slumped down in the seedy, over-stuffed armchair near the silent radiator.

The picture of Dolores came back and he could hardly help comparing her with this girl in the bed. It was not a flattering comparison, and then he remembered this girl had one thing his sister had lost.

Her life.

He twisted in the chair, and bit his fist. He beat at the arm of the chair and golden spores of dust rose twistingly in the weak shafts of light from the window. He could feel the tears coming, he could feel his heart breaking. God, he could feel the edge of the Earth up-ending to send him screaming into the Pit. Rusty had never known such a pain, worse than switch, and worse than zip, and worse than broken bottle. It was the worst. It was so low, it crawled.

Moms was all alone. He had to get home. That had been bad yesterday. Real bad. Leaving her like that. He must be crazy, he must of been out of his skull. He had to get back.

He moved rapidly, then, and paused in his dressing for only a moment, considering whether he should waken the girl and say goodbye, take her to breakfast. He decided not to do it. The nights were one thing, but the days were another. For a minute he stood watching her deep, even breathing, watching her small breasts rise and fall, half covered by the not-quite-clean sheet. He felt terribly sorry for her, and for himself as well. He started to reach for his wallet—perhaps a dollar would help her out—then stopped his hand. She wasn't a whore, he berated himself sharply. She wasn't cheap although she was lonely. She wasn't a slut just because she was afraid.

He reached into his hip pocket and took out his wallet.

In an inner pocket he found the souvenir Spanish coin he had been given by his mother, many years before, to keep as a good luck piece. ("Keep this in your pocket, and you'll never be broke.") The boy stared at it intently for a long second.

He laid it down on the soiled towel that lay across the bureau top as a doily.

He closed the door quietly behind himself.

The subway was nearly deserted. As he sped uptown, he could see trains zipping past in the opposite direction, laden with early morning office workers, their faces blank with half-sleep, their eyes directed to their newspapers, folded lengthwise for column-reading, and to avoid jostling the riders on either side. But Rusty's train was nearly empty.

The train roared clankingly through the tunnels, the stanchions zipping by outside the window till they became one vertical blur. An old woman sat huddled against the far wall, beneath a spaghetti ad, looking as though the sauce was dropping on her, weighing her down. A young man with a tweed topcoat lounged across and up a few feet from Rusty, reading the day-old book review section of the *Times*. Every few minutes he would rub the bridge of his nose.

The constant machine thrummmm of the train somehow soothed Rusty. He thought of the million times he had ridden the underground, and it was a familiar thing. It made his thoughts easier, his thoughts clearer.

He thought of the times he had ridden this subway with his sister. She had been so gentle and slim beside him. Her face the playground of a thousand smiles. Her eyes the lights that lit the darkness. She was gone now. Dead. The family had two dead ones now—Dolores and Pops. He was as good as dead. He was no use to anyone and she was cold and gone.

Then his mind shifted, a camera playing across a landscape. He thought of the night before while the train lulled him. He had come to face his past again, last night, and though he had allowed himself to sink lower than he could ever remember, he now saw it all as clearly as in a crystal, and he knew there was a direction to everything.

He might never get to be the industrial designer he sometimes thought of himself as being, sometime in the future. He might never get free of the scum and filth of the streets

But he knew one thing. He knew it sharp and clear and brightly shining the way a switch brightly shines. He was going to find the bastard who had killed his sister.

No heroics. No big man stuff. No fancy movie acrobatics. He was going to do it because it had to be done and because he knew he was the one to do it. The cops'd never find the guy. They didn't know where to look. The cops'd never find him. They didn't know who to ask. But Rusty knew. Rusty was part of it. He had helped Dolores along. He had fought with her that night, driven her into the waiting streets. He knew who to look for to give him the straight words and he knew how to make those people talk. He had the way and he had the drive. So it had to be him. He knew this as surely as he knew he would kill that man when he found him.

This time the apartment wasn't dead stone quiet. This time Mrs. Ramirez and Mrs. Givens and Mrs. Guzman-Rolon from the building were there. This time a white-jacketed interne from the Charity Hospital was writing out a prescription and handing it to Mrs. Marroquin, who accepted it with furrowed brow and a pinched expression on her little brown, wrinkled face. This time Moms was down for an awful long count.

Collapse, he heard the interne say, before the man picked up his black bag and shouldered past, looking about with distaste at the shabby surroundings—not at all like the home of his parents on Central Park West.

This time it was bad. When it couldn't get worse, it got lousy and lousier.

Rusty came through the open door with stark bewilderment shining dully in his eyes. The women turned as he came forward. Three of them sniffed the air, said something soft in Spanish, and slipped past, carefully, avoiding touching him. Rusty was alone with Mrs. Givens. He stared at her in mute appeal. She stared back with contempt on her dark face.

"You been away." She said it so distinctly, even the accent was muffled. She said it with venomous undertones. Rusty was bewildered. Another shock right now was more than he could take and keep his balance.

"I—I stayed with a friend…overnight," he stumbled. Her eyes mocked him. Her mouth twisted. She looked away, and her head tilted in a slight, peculiar movement.

"*Su madre,*" and he knew Moms was lying in there, where the sunlight was cut to nothing by the drawn blinds. He knew she would be pale and gaunt between the white, white sheets, and he did want to go in to see her.

"How…how is she…" He could not finish.

"*Sinverguenza!*" she cursed him. "She is sick. She will die if she does not find some love. You live here, you don't know her, you never know her! Now you all she got—and that *borrachon* —you don't deserve to see her ever!"

Rusty flinched at mention of his father, but knew the woman was right. Pops was a drunkard, and a waste, and a bastard! He turned away, and wanted to run. She stopped him with a word, softly.

He turned back and she was bobbing her head in solemn understanding. There was no malice in her, just pity for the children of Angelita Santoro. She continued the up and down movement, her little head nodding evenly. Rusty felt the need to touch someone, to seek comfort somewhere. He moved toward the bedroom door, and she stepped back out of his way. She had been left by the protecting women of the building as a watchdog. She relinquished her guard only in crisis. She moved back for Rusty.

He looked down at her with a film over his eyes, as he passed, and his heart was very tight and very dry within him. *"Muchisimas gracias,"* he said softly, and watched his hand as it touched briefly at the thin fabric covering her shoulder. She bowed away without a word, and as he turned by the door, he saw only her back. She stared down from the window at the bedlam street outside. It was good to have friends.

He went into the room.

When he came out, when the sun had ceased its mechanical baking of the streets, when the night sky had rolled in across Manhattan, he was determined. Moms had come awake for a little while. She had slept deeply and it seemed to be nothing more than weariness that had felled her, but when she slowly rose up on her elbows—as he kneeled beside the bed, touching the edge of the sheet—he saw reason flood into her eyes. Then she looked at him and the message passed so clearly, so completely, so finally, there was no need for words. She put her white hand across his own tanned one and he kissed it fiercely. It was the message, and for the first time, really, the meaning to everything. There was a drive and a purpose and a goal. It might not have been the finest goal in the world, nor the most uplifting, but it was a real one. It was not something built in the mind; it was the stuff of blood and bone and flesh. Dolores' bone and blood and flesh.

Moms had said it silently.

He had heard, and he would act on her words.

He would find the man. And when he did, that would be the end. Perhaps to his own life, perhaps, but definitely, it would be the end of the man's life. Whoever he was.

Mrs. Givens was still at the window. He had no idea whether she had moved from that spot or stood there the whole long time. He closed the door, making certain the loose knob did not clank, and she turned half-around, cocking her head to one side. He came across the room and stopped near the outer door.

"Missus Givens?" She faced him slowly and he saw that the angled planes of shadow had changed her from a little nut-brown image to a pixie. Her eyes shone brightly by the lone lamp's shine from the table.

"Watch her for me," he said. She nodded briefly. She knew what he felt and she knew what had to be done. He was being given his freedom, to do what had to be done.

She turned back to the window and he left silently.

Monday night. Quiet out and an occasional cat in a back alley, battling it with another tom for a fish head. Cars mostly away for the night, and the office crowd preparing themselves for the sweaty day ahead. Hot and sticky. The T-shirts snug up under the armpits and the body heat melts you. The sound of TV sets filters dimly, like voices from another world, and snatches of beer commercials hit between the ball game patter. Natural night. Quiet night. Night to stay home and out of trouble.

Trouble night for Rusty Santoro.

The fuzzes rolling the streets in prowl cars, watching for auto strippers and sneak thieves. The beat cops carrying their billies with the wrist thongs dangling. Too hot to wind the stick. Everybody too weak and wet to move much.

Rusty walked past the bowling alley. Boarded up. The beat cop came around the corner as Rusty stopped before the nailed-up door. Rusty caught the flicker of T-shirt white at the cop's open shirt neck, the shine of brass buttons, and he moved on slowly. That meant the Cougars were meeting somewhere else, if they were meeting tonight. And after what had happened to their drag, a definite rumble would be in the planning stages. He knew how they thought, and right now their thoughts were completely tied up with evening the score to the Cherokees.

He had to figure where they would go. To Tom-Tom's? Not likely. The baby-faced soda clerk would probably close early, having heard about the trouble Friday night. He would want no difficulty so soon after a hot period like that. To someone's home? Possibly, if the kid could get his parents out of the apartment. But that was still dubious, because a war council usually turned into an orgy—as did most club gatherings. The garage? Not again. Fedakowski who owned it had taken to carrying a Stillson wrench since the kids had been coming around. And he was too big and Polish to be screwing around with.

Rusty slumped down on a standpipe for a minute, and let his mind kick the ideas around. Where would they be? Finally he had two possible answers.

They were either on the roof at Fish's building, which faced on an empty lot and was pretty well secluded or they were in the condemned warehouse on Wharton Street.

He checked the first out, and it was silent, black, with the silhouettes of pigeon coops among the TV antenna tendrils. The Cougars were not "high" on the roof tonight.

But they *were* in the warehouse.

They had put blankets up around the broken windows on the third floor, but Rusty was not a cop walking the beat and ignoring a warehouse about to be torn down. He was a member of that select clan of delinquents who knew what he was looking for and where to go to find it. They were having a war council in the guts of what had been a toy factory—till the building was done dirty by the man who owned it, who had it planted for arson, who had the insides fire-gutted and then got nabbed for the job—and they were after Cherokee hide. They were gonna get it too, sure as lights light and breath goes in and out. Rusty made it by the back way, up the stairs, close to the wall, so the steps didn't creak and let on he was upcoming.

Halfway up, the stairs just quit and charred planks ran across. He went back down a ways, and climbed into a hole burnt through the wall. The structural boards were somehow still there, and he walked inside the wall, past the spot where the stairs were gone, though he almost took a header three times.

Finally he made the right floor, and climbed back out through another hole, just below the door level. He stopped on the stairs, and saw a thin wash of dim yellow light under the ajar door. Another gloss of yellow watered down the right-hand wall, where the door was partways open.

He crouched down, and stuck his ear close to the opening, to listen.

He could hear them, clear and smooth, and right down the line, the way it had been when he had been Prez.

"Now, who wants to be War Councilor?" It was Candle, being the big wheel, as per usual.

A mumbled jumbling of high and medium voices, and finally Boy-O's watery piping. "Hey, Jack! Lemme go, I wanna be a hero this time." Laughter filled the room.

Then Candle Shaster's voice rose up above the babble, annoyed and peremptory. "Shaddup. You just wanna go up there to peddle your snuff. They'd cut you up and drop ya down a manhole. Shaddup!"

Boy-O said something frail and the laughter rose again. Someone chimed in with another remark and the noise grew. Then Candle said, "Okay, wise guy. You so smart, *you* can be War Councilor. *You* go on up there with the white rag."

Rusty heard Poop's voice, querulous and angry. "Hey, why the hell me? Lotta other guys goofed off. Don't toss that crap at me, man."

Candle said something low, barely distinguishable in the rising clamor, and for a moment Rusty thought there would be a fight. But Poop backed down and the rumble discussion went on.

Rusty decided now was the time to make his play.

He stood up and threw the door open wide. It banged against the wall of the stairwell, sounding like the report of a pistol in the shallow confines of the passage. For a moment, while his eyes were adjusted to the gloom of the stairwell, he did not see those inside in sharp focus. Then the light flooded in, and Candle came through nasty-looking and a little frightened at who was before him.

Beside the new Cougar Prez was Weezee.

Her eyes banged open wide till the blue of them was a color contrast with the white of her painted face. Her hand flew to her mouth and for a moment she looked to Rusty as though she would faint. Everyone else remained motionless.

They were all there. The Greek, Poop, Johnny Slice, Tiger and the broads. But most of all, and it hurt on top of all the rest, there was Weezee, sitting beside Candle. He had his big, hairy spade of a hand on her knee. She didn't mind. Times change, people change. Maybe. Not down inside. What's there is there, and you're screwed if you think what's there is what you want it to be. She was here, now, and that was what counted. There were no excuses in the jungle. Live or die was all that counted. Rusty had long since decided he would live.

The guy who had killed Dolores… *He* would die.

The room was silent for a long minute and then there was lots of movement. Rusty wished in that instant he had borrowed a gun from somewhere, but there had been no place, and all he had was the stuff he was born with. He knew it was bluff or get stomped. He was no longer a Cougar, so he had to make a fast place for himself here, right this instant.

"Okay, knock it off!" he yelled. And stepped into the room.

The place was rotting away. Fire had consumed one entire

wall, leaving the skeleton structure of old wood and plaster showing through. Metal, small-holed sheeting was peeled away within the walls, as though a giant hand had crumpled it up. The floor sagged noticeably. The ceiling was shrouded in darkness and the three kerosene lamps they had brought with them cast a fitful wavering glare across the room, down the now-empty stairwell.

They were stopped by his command for a moment. He had burst in and the time was not that far past that they had looked up to him as Prez of the club. He seemed to have momentary authority, for he had found them in an illegal place. Rusty came through the door, pulling it closed behind him. He walked across the room, staring straight into Weezee's wide, frightened eyes. She had begun to nervously twist her ponytail.

Candle stood up, dropping his hand from her, and advanced a short step. Rusty bawled at him, "Sit down! I wanna talk to ya for a minute, and you'd damn well better feed me straight…"

Three of the club members moved in toward Rusty. He edged to the side, closer to Candle. The Prez of the Cougars had not sat down. He had moved a step further away from the girl, but he had not sat down. Rusty came on straight, and in one sharp movement had the Prez by the arm. He whipped it back so fast and he yanked it so hard, Candle screamed sharply in pain, and then the arm was up behind in the ridge of his back, and the knife from the sleeve was in Rusty's hand.

The hand moved a fraction of an inch, the blade snicked open, and the point was indenting the cloth just between the fifth and sixth ribs on the right side of Candle's body.

"Now," Rusty forced his bluff, "now, if you wanna see how hot I am to get to know what I wanna know, then you brace me, all you fraykin' rocks, and I'll slide this so easy he won't know it's in till it's out."

His false bravado rang like tin on his ears, but the knife was in Candle's side, and he had come bursting in suddenly, and he did look like he wasn't playing around. The three members backed off. Candle struggled.

"My sister got it last night. You know that. You all know it. You guys're sittin' here and my kid sister's downtown in the chill house. Now I'm gonna know who did it like, or so help me god like I'm standin' here, I'll scream fuzz so loud, you'll all stay pokey till you drop.

"I know enough to get ya all canned in the Home for five years, and you," he drove the point of the knife a little deeper into Candle's side, "ya sonofabitch, I'll cut out ya gut if ya don't open up."

Candle Shaster's mouth opened wet and wide. He wanted to speak, but there was sharp, tiny pressure alongside his ribs, and the fright was big in him, so damned big. He squirmed in Rusty's grip, but the boy was a rock, and held the knife tight to the cloth. It was the only thing between him and the violence the Cougars could unleash in a second, if they overcame the cold sweat of the switch in his hand.

"Talk, damn ya!" Rusty said tightly, edging the point of the knife in more sharply.

Candle could not speak. He could only squirm, and he did that with abruptness that threw Rusty off-balance. In a moment he had a wedge with his hip against the boy's side, and an imperfect lunge tossed Rusty away from him. Rusty went side-wise, into the crate on which Weezee sat, frightened and still toying unknowingly with her ponytail. He slammed into her and she went over, her legs flashing brown and slim as she tumbled to the dirty floor. Then Rusty had his hand under him for steadying and was coming erect. The gang moved in fast.

The first three who had attempted to take him when he had

entered the room came at him again and Candle was right alongside. The blades flashed wickedly in the glare of the kerosene
lamps, but Rusty was on his feet and backing away.

This was it, so this was it, damn it this was it.

Close, but not nearly close enough. He knew there was something here, but now he was stopped. He was going to be stopped
good and proper in a minute. How much blood could three
switches draw?

He saw a flash of big movement from the corner of his eye
and then the three Cougars were being elbowed aside. One of
them turned to the newcomer, his blade rising, and a thick hand
came down from the darkness, plucked the knife from the boy's
fingers and it leaped upward, was stuck far above in the ceiling.
The thunk of the knife sticking into the charred wood of the
exposed ceiling stopped the others. All but Candle.

He kept coming, not quite realizing he was alone again, and
facing Rusty's knife. The activity to his left had been so swift, so
complete, he had not realized what it meant.

Rusty saw it all. He saw the gigantic hulk that was the Beast
come out of the shadows where he had lain slumped against
the wall. He saw the huge idiot face contort in anger and violence as the Beast shouldered aside the three Cougars, and he
saw the dummy rip the knife from the boy's hand, and with a
movement more agile than any Rusty had believed the Beast
could employ, had seen him throw the knife, quivering, into
the ceiling.

Now Rusty bent forward at the knees and the knife came out
before him, like the head of a snake, swaying, swaying, deadly
and waiting. Candle came on solid and then he realized he was
alone. He brought up short and started to turn, but a hairy arm
went around his chest and he was lifted clear of the floor. He
hung there, thrashing for a long instant, and then another hand
caught him under the crotch. Candle went up, up, over the

matted, caked filth of the Beast's hair, went up bubbling and trembling and the Beast pitched him forward heavily.

Rusty watched as Candle Shaster swung through the air and fell heavily. The boy hit, and then flopped onto his belly. He lay there for a moment, then heaved and lay still. He was not unconscious, but the sharp, tiny exclamations of pain that escaped him showed he was not going to get up soon.

Rusty stood staring into the round, idiot eyes of the Beast. The eyes that said nothing at all. The eyes that were filled with a great void, a great sadness, a great uncaring, unknowing nothingness. They were windows to the house of his soul and they were dead windows. Rusty saw the great face in its rigid immobility, nearly incapable of expression with meaning. The putty wart of a nose sucked air in, quivered as the air sped back on its outward journey. Rusty watched the Beast's face for a moment, letting the full, unpleasant picture register clearly.

He had seen the Beast around the neighborhood for years. He was a traditional joke, taunted by the younger punkies around Tom-Tom's place, avoided by women and snapped at by the fuzz. He was always in some alley, or under a pile of newspapers in an apartment building's basement. What he did to keep himself alive was a mystery, though from time to time rumors flashed about him. Robbery, breaking and entering, assault, mugging. Lord knew he was capable of any of them— but there was never any real inquiry into his affairs.

He was just the thing called the Beast. And he was there. That was all.

Now he had made a definite step. He had done something concrete and had saved Rusty's life. Why? The boy could not recall ever having done anything to acquire the huge man's good will and friendship. Why?

The Beast looked down at Rusty and put out his hand. For a moment Rusty had no idea what he wanted, then he realized he was still gripping the switch, underhand. He rubbed a finger along the green plastic of the handle and then closed it reluctantly. The knife clicked as he lifted the lock at the back and he awkwardly handed it to the big man. The Beast shoved the knife into a side pocket of his rumpled, dirt-streaked slacks and turned away with a nod to Rusty.

The Beast walked back into the shadows and slumped down once more, his back edging down the wall till he lay in the angle of the charred walls.

Rusty pursed his lips. There seemed no sense to it. The Beast had never spoken more than three words to him and suddenly he had become Rusty's protector. The boy was confused, but sensed his advantage now. He took three short steps to the barely stirring body of Candle and hoisted the boy to his feet roughly. He shoved the squat Cougar leader to the wall that was bathed in the yellow light of the kerosene lamp, and systematically brought him to.

The almost-Mongoloid features of the Prez began to flicker out of grogginess and he batted his eyes several times as Rusty shook and slapped him.

The Cougars watched in transfixed helplessness, knowing if they moved the Beast would move; and though fat and filthy, the dummy could crush any one of them easily. They stayed put and watched Rusty work Candle over thoroughly.

"Now, I wanna know," Rusty said, each word accentuated by a sharp, stinging slap of his palm. Candle's face was becoming flame red along one cheek, as Rusty tried to drag information from him by the only sure method he knew.

"Talk!"

The hand came out, flashed and cracked briefly against skin. Candle's head jerked. His eyes opened wide and he twitched as though he wanted to retaliate. From the shadows the red coals of the Beast's eyes, staring straight at the Prez, kept his hands at his sides, limply.

"Talk!"

Candle jerked his head away and Rusty's next slap landed against the shoulder. It went that way for ten minutes, as Weezee sat biting her fist, her eyes wide. Violence was loose and there was no telling when it would come her way.

"Who killed my sister?"

No answer. The bond of silence was tight. Candle could no more speak, if he knew anything, than he could throw himself off the Staten Island Ferry. He was tied to silence. Rusty grew furious with frustration. His blows became more violent, and the Cougars knew this was not the fake rah-rah they usually saw in fights and rumbles. This was serious, this was the next thing to slow death. Rusty Santoro was on the edge and he wanted the word. The straight stuff, and they knew he would work each of them over till he got it.

Then their silence was no longer challenged, for the one who had stopped them before spoke from the shadows.

The Beast's hoarse, unsteady voice came up in the room and he said, "I seen who took ya sister…"

Rusty was holding Candle against the wall with one white-knuckled hand, the other poised for a sidearm whack at the squat boy's face. The hand never landed. Rusty stepped away slowly, letting his grip loosen on Candle, and the boy slid in a bumbling shuffle, before he fell again and lay panting, angled against the wall.

Rusty turned to the dummy, and there was a strange luster to the boy's glare. This was what he wanted, this was all of it. This was the beginning of the trail that would end with a dead man in a gutter or hallway or alley, a Santoro-driven knife in his gut. This was it on skates and Rusty wanted it all.

"I seen her come in, an' then I seen her go out, before you come to th' dance." The Beast mumbled scratchily. His voice was like a rusted saw laboring through tough wood. He stumbled over words and many of his sounds were mere suggestion. But the words were the right words.

" 'N' then she come back again, y'know, an' when she left, I was outside lookin' fer some beer what they might've left inna cans they t'rew outside, y'know, an' I saw'r with a guy inna long coat…"

And then the dummy gave a remarkably lucid description of a camel's hair coat.

NINE:
TUESDAY

- *rusty santoro*
- *mirsky*
- *miss clements*
- *pops santoro*

Rusty had not been to bed. The week's sweat had dried on him and he felt filthy inside and out. The memories of the weekend were a jumbled, kaleidoscopic horror. The stand with Candle, the dance and the drag back to the old ways, the rumble and jail overnight—staggeringly terrible in terrible gray and steel—and then Dolores. The terrible wallop in the head of her death, like that, that way, in an alley. Then Moms and the trouble with the Cougars. And the first word about what had happened in the darkness back there, behind Tom-Tom's malt shop. The word about the man in the camel's hair coat. It was all too much.

Rusty had gone home and Mrs. Givens had still been there, hunched over in the big armchair, shrouded in darkness, only the black, scuffed tips of her shoes showing from shadow, in the reflected light from a streetlamp outside.

He had sent her away, telling her he would watch. She had asked him nothing, not where he had been, or what he had found out, nothing about Dolores or the word from the street. She merely nodded at his words and left silently, like some velvet-furred animal.

Rusty had sunk down into the armchair and summer night

had gone by in remote noise from crosstown, and mugginess. Now with the faint gray wash of dawn slipping down the buildings, he met the day with a desperation and determination to find that man in the camel's hair coat. Somehow, some way. And kill him.

The past had forged strong chains, not easily broken.

The buses ground past downstairs, and the sounds of the city awakening climbed higher and higher, like a generator warming up. Rusty sat immobile, thinking.

No one in Cougar turf wore a camel's hair coat. That wasn't sharp; black leather jackets, chino slacks, stomping boots, Sam Browne belts with razor-sharp buckles, duck-fanny haircuts, but no camel's hair coats.

That was downtown stuff. Straight down the main line.

Rusty could not quite grasp the sense of that. What was a downtown hooker doing here in Cougar turf and why should someone like that kill his sister? Why should she be raped like that? The answer popped in sickeningly. Dolores had been an attractive girl, that was reason enough.

Rusty had seen enough of the streets to know the score. Sense, there was none. The blood that filled the manholes to the tops came from sick minds and fast action. There was no reason and no end to it, of course, so Dolores was dead, and there was nothing more to say after that. Except the man in the camel's hair coat would die, naturally. That was the way of it.

But how to go about it?

There were still two problems, or rather, two untied ends, aside from the one final end that would be tied with a knife. What was the camel's hair coat doing in Cougar turf and why had the gang clammed up so tightly? It had become apparent after a few minutes with them that the Cougars were quiet for a good reason and one a lot stronger than merely "the code." There was something back there, but Rusty did not know what it was, what it meant, how it tied in. This was far out of his depth. He had no idea where to start, how to begin to find a murderer.

It was a far different thing, this hollow hungry killing need to find the man and punish him. A far different thing than bludgeoning his way through a rumble, or knife-gutting a rock who had offended him. They were in two different classes, and Rusty felt like a fly on flypaper, trapped and helpless.

But there had to be a way. There *had* to be a way because more than God, or Earth, or Life, or any goddamn thing he wanted his hands soaked in the blood of the man who had raped Dolores. Rusty Santoro, seventeen years old, and crying warm inside, sat tensed in the big armchair and swore he would find the man. There was nothing, nothing at all, for him, if that was not done. He sat back and started to figure—hard.

Mrs. Givens came in at eight o'clock and prepared a hot breakfast for Rusty. He slapped his spoon at the thick oatmeal. He toyed with and broke the toast. He ran a finger around the moist, beaded lip of the glass of milk. He did not touch a thing and when Mrs. Givens went into the bedroom to see how Moms was resting, he slipped out the front door.

He carried the big switchblade in his jacket pocket.

School was where he headed, down the street to the subway. But he never made it. Somehow, his feet led him away, far away from the subway and toward the line dividing Cougar turf from Cherokee territory. Rusty had decided something. Somewhere in their silence, in the fact of the Cherokee rumble at the dance, in the whole tangled web of it all, there was a hookup between the Cougars, the Cherokees, Dolores' death and the man he sought. What it was, he did not know, nor how it was constructed, but there was a dragging in him that led him toward Cherokee turf. There was a hookup and it seemed he would

have to knuckle down in enemy turf to find the answer; to find
the next bit of path that led to the man in the camel's hair coat.

He invaded Cherokee turf shortly before nine o'clock Tuesday
morning, cold-eyed and searching. It was quiet, gang quiet,
with the kids in school, but there was always the subterranean
murmur of rumbles. The whispers were there, if you listened
closely enough and if you could decipher the animal intensities
that gave them meaning. Rusty was looking for a pigeon.

Looking that way, looking that hard, he was bound to suc-
ceed. It was like looking for trouble. Look long enough, turn
over enough rocks with a rude kick and eventually a trouble
came forth. That was the way of it. Seek and you shall find. A
pigeon.

Finally, he got the word from a tailor deep in Cherokee turf
—a little man with a hare lip who wore a satin-backed vest and
who feared for his front window. He gave Rusty the second
clue to the track. He directed the boy to a garage it was healthy
for citizens to avoid, where the Cherokees spent their evenings
shearing down cams, trimming away chrome, souping up their
heaps.

Rusty asked the little tailor where a gun could be purchased
in Cherokee land. The tailor did not know. He was lying, but
Rusty had no stomach for the tactics which would persuade the
man to tell him.

He hit for the garage.

It was a gaping hole in a line of apartment buildings. The
street was run-down. The houses had once been stately brown-
stones, but refugee owners had divided each apartment into
dozens of minor one-room closets and had rented them to
Puerto Ricans, fresh to New York. It was a dirty, noisy street
with cardboard milk cartons crushed flat in the gutters, battered garbage cans on the sidewalks and obscenities chalked

on pavements and walls. Laundry hung from windows. The smell was oregano and some sweet, the odor of cigarettes and pine cleanser fighting a losing battle with dirt-caked corners. It was a depressing street. It was all too familiar to Rusty. It was typical.

The garage was open-faced amid these buildings, with a big red sign announcing rates per hour, day and week, and the name TINY'S GARAGE STORAGE. Rusty walked up the sloping walk into the dimmer, cooler interior and almost immediately saw the rodent.

He was perhaps five feet seven, with no chin whatsoever and eyes slitted to fine lines. He wore sloppy sports clothes, and his hair was cut in a severe crew-cut, so a bald spot showed at the center of his scalp. But there was more than just a mousiness and furtiveness to him. He looked more like a twitching gray rat than a human being. As he chewed a piece of gum, his aquiline nose twitched, accentuating the resemblance.

"Yeah. What c'n I do ya?" the rodent squeaked as Rusty came in from the street.

Rusty walked toward him, watching the boy as he leaned against the front end of a Buick. The boy seemed loose-jointed and nervous and he grew even more so as Rusty approached without speaking.

"You—uh—you know where I can find some'a the Chero-kees?" Rusty started.

The rodent watched in silence for a minute, then swirled the gum to the other side of his mouth. He plucked at his nose tentatively, then nodded his head. "Yeah. I know where ya c'n find the Cherks. So what? Whaddaya want with 'em?"

Rusty walked slowly, coming abreast of the boy without alarming him. "What's ya name?" Rusty asked.

The boy stared back as though uncomprehending.

Rusty reached into his pocket. The opening of the knife was sharp in the silence of the garage. "I—I just watch the joint for Tiny Sacher when he goes up fer a sanwich. I—uh—got no connection with them, like ya know…"

"I asked you what was your name," Rusty repeated.

"Mirsky," the boy answered slowly, with pain. "M-Mirsky."

"Well, now, M-Mirsky," Rusty accented each word with harshness, "how's about you telling me what you know about the rumble up in Cougar turf Friday night."

Mirsky slid around the side of the car. His face had turned ashen. His eyes were almost closed in fear. He struggled to deny all knowledge of the fight, the party-crashing.

"Who you, to ask sump'n like that? Huh, who are ya? I don't know you. You got somethin' round here? If y'don't then scram. I got work t'do." He continued sliding around the dusty surface of the car. His charcoal slacks picked up a thick coat of filth from the movement.

Rusty took a quick step and his hand wound in Mirsky's jacket lapels.

"The name is Santoro, kid. You know the name?"

Mirsky shook his head violently. His little rat eyes that had been buried deep in the creases of his face were now hanging out, wide and awake with a slippery fear. "I n-never h-heard that name. Whachoo hangin' onta me for? Lemme go!"

Rusty backed him into the angle of the car and wall.

He held him tightly, twisting the fabric till Mirsky was breathing with difficulty. The boy was shaking terribly. "Please, man, lemme go. L-like I don't know a thing. I just work here. I ain't inna Cherks…"

"Kid, you're sweatin' too much not to know somethin'. And I got a hunch you know who I am, that maybe even you was told to expect me around here. That so?"

The kid refused to speak. His little aquiline nose twitched, rodentlike, and Rusty felt a straining within himself. He spoke quietly, quickly. "Look, Mirsky. I want you to dig somethin'. I got to find out what happened the other night. I got to, you read me?"

Mirsky would not answer, and Rusty forced the boy's head to nod yes, by pulling at his collar.

"So get this, fella. I'm gonna find out if you tell me your way, or if you tell me my way. Now I ain't such a gentle stud and I c'n cut ya if ya make me." His voice was almost pleading. "Look, kid, don't make me. Please, I'm askin' ya, don't make me!"

But Mirsky was adamant. He was terrified and quaking, but more frightened of something else. What it might be, Rusty did not know, but he was certain whatever it was, that was part of the story behind the Cougars' refusal to talk and the mystery surrounding the death of Dolo.

"You're all I got to give me some poop, man," Rusty begged him, tears starting. "Please, don't make me do this." He was crying now, from sheer frustration, and the knowledge that what was to come was inevitable. "Please!"

No sound. Then he had to do it, crying all the while.

The knife was effective. In the dimness of the garage Rusty Santoro drew a thin red line across the boy's right cheek, and found the next bit of the trail.

I don't wanna do it this way, Rusty cried to himself, methodically doing what had to be done. His stomach wobbled within him as he applied the screws to the boy. He saw the same methods he had always used before, being used again. He saw the punch being thrown, instead of the logic being applied. But it had to be done this way. This was the way they knew, the way they feared. This was the way to get what he wanted. "Please!" he cried aloud once more, in the darkness.

Finally, "Stop! Y' gotta stop! I'll tell ya! Stop on me, stop now, stop stop…"

Rusty let the boy loose and Mirsky slid down in the darkness. He lay back and his tears were tears of pain. As painful as Rusty's had been all through it and were still. "Tell me what you know, goddamn it, tell me."

Mirsky put a hand to his cheek and when it came away slippery, he started to faint. His face went dead white again, and he started to slip back under the car. Rusty grabbed for the jacket again and hauled Mirsky erect.

"Th-they came d-down last night," he said softly. His eyes went around the garage fearfully. "They came down an' said somebody'd be lookin' for word. They said I wasn't ta say anything or they'd get me. You gotta promise me ya won't s-say nothin'. Please, y'gotta make me a promise or I'll get it. I'm tellin' ya."

Rusty stooped down and broke the knife. He looked around him, found a grease-spattered rag and wiped off the blade. He put the weapon in his pocket. "Don't think I can't bring it out again. Talk."

"Y'gotta promise!"

"Talk!"

Mirsky wet his lips. "They came down and said I wasn't to say nothin' about the tea and the Cherks bein' hopped-up when they went on that rumble. I wasn't ta say nothin' or they'd get me. Y'unnerstand that? Ya gotta promise me!"

Rusty stood up. "Who was it told ya?"

Mirsky thought a moment. "There was three Cherks and one guy from off-turf, like I didn't know him. I think he was a Cougar."

Rusty stopped breathing for a second. That was it.

"What was his name?"

"They didn't call him by name."

"Well then, dammit, what'd he look like."

"I didn't see him, man, he —"

Rusty hit him. Fury and frustration swollen in his brain. He drew back to slug him again.

"No, man, stop, hold it! I ain't lyin', they had him back where it was dark. I couldn't see him, 'cept he was short, was all. They just called him kid, or boy, or somethin' like they din't want me to know his name."

Inside, Rusty was twisted and beaten. It was always a dead end. He met a wall of silence, even where the wall was not too solid. He turned away from Mirsky.

When Rusty left the garage, Mirsky was sitting on the grease-spattered floor, his slacks filthy, the thin line of blood dripping down onto his shirt, like watercolor, running. He would be all right. The scar would heal to a faint white line and soon he would be filing the motorblock serial numbers from more stolen heaps. But right now he lay panting deeply, running his tongue-tip around the corners of his tiny mouth, his eyes closed in shock and pain. He would be all right, soon, if it never got out that he had talked to a Cougar. If it never got out that he had spilled the cherries on what had prompted the Cherokee raid that night. Dope.

There was a part of it. There was a section of it. Down near the bottom some place, dope figured in. But how? The kids had been using pot for a long time, what could that mean in the death of Dolores? It was all fuzzy, all screwed up. This was more than Rusty had bargained for.

Dope.

The Cherokees had been hopped-up. More so than they usually got on a rumble night. Someone had come across with a big packet of pretty decent white-cut, and the raid had followed naturally in the wake of the sky-flight. Almost as though someone had wanted that raid to come off, almost as though someone had needed that raid to cover up Dolores' murder. Or maybe it was backwards. Maybe whoever had peddled the tea wanted to keep the passing of it quiet, even though the killing was bringing notice to the rumble, almost as though the Cougars and Cherokees were in on it together. The silence of the gangs was oppressive. Too tight for the mere rules of the Code. There was something deeper in this, much deeper. It had to be dope.

Tuesday was a day of warnings. Tuesday was a day of caution and wondering. Why? Why—because of three things that happened after Rusty left Cherokee turf, with the word "narcotics" festering in his mind. Three things, that happened too quickly and too closely together to be mere coincidence or idle interest.

The first incident happened when Rusty went home. He wanted to go out, but where could he go? There was no more information to be had, anywhere. Mirsky had not recognized the boy who had been with the Cherokees when they had warned him to be silent and the Cougars had dispersed effectively. He would have to bide his time, wait, watch. He went home.

Miss Clements was waiting at home. She was sitting straight and stark—a stuffed bird, gathering dust, rigid with death, in the window of a taxidermist. Her nose was a long, thin and sharp projection that dominated her bone-thin face. Deep hollows accentuated the stark outlines of her almost-cruel face. She was, in fact, the perfect representation of a Grimm's witch, minus the broomstick and the black, peaked hat. Her face was pasty white under her imperfectly applied powder coating. She watched Rusty come through the door. Quick, sharp needle-pointed movements of little brown eyes. The deathly paleness of her face was made all the more remarkable and disturbing by the abundance of freckles that covered her cheekbones, fore-head and nose. Rusty despised her.

He had closed the door and taken three steps into the living room before he saw her. But as he did his own body stiffened up, equally as rigid as her own. She sat forward, clutching her little rectangular purse to her lap, the indefinite fabric of her skirt stretched tight across her thin legs.

She cleared her throat with awkwardness and self-consciousness. It was a close sound in the silent living room, against the sealed-out background of New York street noises. Rusty tried to force himself to untwist, to relax before her. This was his home now, not her blackboard-bordered stamping-ground. He was on top here, not her. Now he could call the trick and line up the attitude.

But still the residue of fear and hate from the days in her classes stopped him. He was the pupil, she was the teacher. And that hard, unyielding sharpness was Miss Clements.

"I din't know you was here…" he began.

She nodded rapidly, as though nervous herself at being in this strange, unfamiliar place, with its Spanish smells and its pictures of Jesus on the wall. Its squalor.

"I came over to—to see you," she started, her lips barely moving. "You weren't in class yesterday."

Rusty realized he had missed the entire day of school. It came to him with an abrupt sense of loss. He had skipped, he had done just what he had promised Pancoast he would not do. He was getting into trouble. Loss, also, for it was a day taken from him, a day in which he might have learned something vital for his new future—the future he had planned for, before Dolores' death. The future now was a short, red thing that would end suddenly at knife-point or zip-blast. The future now had no need nor room for school or architecture.

He heard her speaking. She had been speaking for the last few seconds. "…And there was a Spanish woman here, she told me about—about your mother, I'm sorry." She said it all in one fluid run-on, as though it had been rehearsed. She did not mention Dolores. "I wanted to talk to —"

She cut off and her head turned as the brown, wrinkled face of Mrs. Givens peered from the bedroom. The door had opened silently and Rusty had no way of knowing how long the woman had been listening.

"Ey," she called softly, sharply, nodding back with her head, "*ven aca.*"

Rusty looked to Miss Clements, worriedly, for a moment, then shrugged within himself, and walked to the bedroom door. Mrs. Givens motioned him inside.

Inside, the room was dim and faintly moist, as before, with the late morning sunlight coming through a rip in the drawn window shade. Resting-place.

Rusty leaned over the edge of the bed to see his mother's face and felt no emotion at all that she was sleeping once more. Time had lost all meaning for Angelita Santoro. Not as time had stopped for Dolores, but as it stopped when it did not matter.

"She's all right," Mrs. Givens said softly, then, "That woman there." Her tone was one of dislike and distrust. Her words were whispered, but carried the force of a scream.

"She come in a little bit ago, like *una mujer loca*, a—a crazy woman! All scream and bang on door and she want you to talk, an'—an'—" She trailed off into a quavering silence, her hands flapping. "What's wrong with her?"

Rusty's brow furrowed. What was this all about? It was the truant deputy who came around when a kid cut school, not a teacher. Unless it was someone like Carl Pancoast, and Miss Clements had never taken that sort of interest in her pupils. Why was she so interested in him? Rusty bit his lower lip in thought and worried.

"I come in here, make sure she din't wake Angelita; what she wants with you?" Mrs. Givens' face was drawn in concern.

Rusty was at a loss to answer. Whatever the woman wanted,

it seemed she was going to a lot more trouble than one day of missed schoolwork demanded. "Don't worry, Miz Givens," Rusty smoothed her concern, "it's about school. I missed a couple classes. It'll be okay, so now don't worry."

The little woman nodded her head as though she was reluctant to believe such mad actions could have a basis so slight. But her nod finally changed to one of acceptance. She frowned so two tiny dimples fell in her cheeks, and she said, very, very softly, "Mama is very sick. Very sick. Not so good, but maybe tomorrow she'll be fine. We'll see." Her words had ceased to be conversation. She talked to herself now, the old people way, the old country way. She walked back across the room to the window and stood staring out through the rip in the shade. It cut in sections the silver falling across the room.

Rusty took another look at Moms and renewed his promise. It would be kept, that promise. Finally.

He went back into the living room.

Miss Clements was testing for dust along the top of one low cornice, with a long, white finger. She brought her hand down self-consciously as Rusty came into the room.

Somehow, that meant something. That and the fact that her eyes were very odd looking and her manner was high-strung and her complexion was fish-belly white. All that meant there was more to Rusty's side of this than she wanted him to know. He felt a new strength in her presence invade his manner, his voice.

"What'd you want, Miss Clements?"

She took a long moment to begin and her hesitation was coupled with a turning of the little handbag. "You shouldn't miss classes, Rusty," she said. It wasn't what she had wanted to say at all.

Rusty did not answer. It was her hoop, let her roll it.

"What I mean is," she went into her frigid classroom tone, "there are ways and means of making you people attend school when you are required to do so. If you persist in cutting classes, I will be forced to go to the Prin—"

Rusty cut her off with a half-cough, half-chuckle that had been waiting to emerge for two semesters. It stopped her. She licked her thin, icy lips.

She started again. "I'm, I'm very sorry to hear about your sister. I've seen her many times in the halls and she seemed like an intelligent little girl with a remarkable capacity of learning."

It died. It just fell down and croaked. Rusty stared at her with hatred bubbling in his eyes. Bull! That was what she was spitting, just plain bull!

"Whaddaya want from me, Miss Clements?"

Her look became one of huntedness. To Rusty it was sadistically fascinating to make her squirm, as she made him squirm in class. She hated Puerto Ricans. She had often spoken of them as "You People" as though they were untouchables, and now one of Those People had her wiggling on the end of the rod.

She tried to start several times, then gave it up and murmured a good-bye. She started for the door, but Rusty stopped her with a word. She turned and the real reason for her appearance here came out in a flooding rush.

"You've got to stop this running around and—and looking for people, Santoro!" She spat out his name as though it were coated with alum. It typified her attitude in class; bitter, nasty, tactless. "You've got to buckle down and stop this senseless, this stupid…" She waggled her hands for emphasis, came up with another thought entirely. "Do you want to flunk History?"

Rusty eyed her coldly. It was apparent, she was threatening him with the one weapon at her disposal. She would lay the skids to him in school. Well, then, okay, lady. Do your sleazy damnedest!

He shrugged. "Don't care."

She bit her lip. Desperation rang in her voice. "I'm warning you, Santoro," her voice rose sharply, "if you don't cease this childish melodramatic detective business, I'm going to take you to the Principal. You wouldn't like that. You listen to me!" she was almost screaming, for Rusty had half-turned away in restrained fury.

The bedroom door popped open and Mrs. Givens emerged, her plump little hands twitching in brown circles. "Go 'way! Go on, go 'way! You making more sickness here! G'wan, get out!" She lapsed into deep Spanish, and the force of her tirade drove the bone-thin teacher before her, as though whiplashed.

Miss Clements cast a frantic look at Rusty who had turned his back and was clutching the fabric of the easy chair with unbelievable tenseness. He was deaf to her, his eyes were closed to her. School? Nothing, next to finding the man in the camel's hair coat. No matter how much she warned him, and cajoled and threatened, he was on his way somewhere, and no one would stop him. No failure meant anything, next to that final failure.

Mrs. Givens' low but furious words sent the teacher to the door. Miss Clements tried to hurl one last threat at the boy, but the little Puerto Rican woman had the door open and the teacher was outside before she could stop herself.

The door slammed in her face, softly.

Rusty was alone with Mrs. Givens. She knew enough to say nothing. She went back to the bedroom, to resume her vigil, and as she passed within, the trembling words, "So much trouble…" trailed like smoke behind her.

Rusty stood clutching the fabric of the easy chair till it ripped with the intensity of his grip. Then he dropped his hands free, and sank into the chair, despair choking him.

That was the first incident.

❖

The second incident was much less complicated, affected Rusty less violently and promised much more trouble.

He had left the apartment, again pacing the street in search of an answer. Several times he left the beaten track of the neighborhood, and sought nothing at all on the rooftops, in the big weed-high lot between a deserted dry cleaning plant and the back of a row of apartment buildings, in the alleys. He searched and found nothing. The city had drawn in its lines to him. He was seeking and they wanted no part of him as he trudged that road.

He received the warning as he entered Tom-Tom's joint. The baby-fat sphere that was the soda jerk came out of the back room, the shine of sweat across his forehead. Nipping at the Tokay again. Well, that was okay, too. Everybody had a skeleton. Tom-Tom's didn't rattle as much as some.

"I got a message for you," the fat little man said, coming up behind the counter.

Rusty had swung up automatically on a stool. It was the way he did it when he came in, and reflex carried him. "From who?"

Tom-Tom shook his head in an indefinite bobble. "Don't know, y'know. Some kid, one of these kids that hang with the little kids around the stoop up the street, y'know, he brought it around, said to give it to you."

He reached up onto the mirror and from behind a stud that held the mirror in place he withdrew a folded envelope. Dirty and frayed. He handed it to Rusty, and moved away.

Rusty tore it open sloppily, and drew out the single sheet of notepaper. It was from a three-ring notebook such as the type used in his high school.

In a painstaking print that tried valiantly to be anonymous, the note said, STAY OUT OF CHEROKEE TURF AND STOP TRYING TO STICK YOUR BASTARD NOSE IN WHERE IT DON'T BELONG. COUGARS.

So that was the second warning, was it? Now the gang was afraid he was getting too close to something. What the hell *was* all this? So far Rusty had found out nothing, really. He had two bits of information that were valuable and a round cipher of nothing for the rest. He sought a man in a camel's hair coat, and somehow that man was tied up with dope. Other than that— nothing.

He read the note again. The Cougars had changed a lot since he had been Prez. They were wilder now, though they had never been chicken-gut while he was top man, and there seemed to be something about them they did not want known, even to the gutter-runners who knew them so well.

Rusty tapped the note against his fingernail for a moment. Then he laid it down on the counter. A wet ring, left from a Coke bottle, darkened through, and the paper lay flat to the micarta surface. He stared at it for a long time, and then folded it up, put it in his pocket. Bull! It meant nothing, except that someone was putting the screws to the neighborhood. Whoever had shuffled the Cougars onto him was not going to stop with anything as simple as this. He wondered for a moment why they hadn't just taken him into the alley and leaned on him heavily. Then he remembered the Beast and the night before, and he knew they were not going to fool around any more than they were forced to.

Rusty had a silent, hulking protector there and that bothered him, too.

For a minute he contemplated going after the gang, trying to wring out of them the names of the persons who had made them send this note. It was obvious there was a line of communication between that Mirsky kid and the Cougars, or the gang would never have known he had been looking. The tie-up between such live enemies as the Cherokees and the Cougars brought the first faint tingle of tenseness to him. It had to be a strong tie, and one that put the fear of something into those knife-happy tenement kids. Rusty grew worried, and almost immediately discarded the idea of going looking for the gang.

First, they were probably well gone by now. Second, he did not want to press his luck with shoving them. Once he had beaten Candle fairly. The second time he had been saved by the Beast, but a third time might shove the juvies a little too far.

Tom-Tom walked back up, stopped in front of Rusty, and leaned a plump, pink arm on the counter. "Bad news?"

Rusty looked up, and the natural belligerence he felt at being so helpless emerged. "Good news. They got a special on, down at the undertakers. They'll let me have you embalmed for half-price. Special on all busybodies."

Tom-Tom edged away, a lingering fear of the kids in his eyes. He busied himself with non-essentials.

It was a dead bit, all the way around. Rusty slid off the stool, ambled toward the door. He stopped with one hand on the glass and turned to the little soda jerk with a stark expression on his face. "You see 'em, you give 'em the word. I don't scare easy, man."

Then he hit the street. That was the second incident and it didn't really matter.

The third did. It was bad.

If there was a tie-up between the Cougars and the Cherokees, if there was something in common, something already stated as important, it was the dope. The weed. The H. The white powder that had invaded the club since Rusty had left. Rusty had fought against the encroachment of dope since he had won the presidency of the gang from the previous leader in a fight. But after he had left, and Candle had come to power, he had heard many rumors.

The kids were on. They were real high. Sky.

Now the Cherokees had been hyped to a rumble and the Cougars were warning him away from that turf and the kid, Mirsky, had indicated a tie-up somewhere. So he had to find the source of dope in the neighborhood. Obvious. The pusher.

But that would not be as easy as it looked.

The pusher was Boy-O, naturally. Everyone knew that. But where did the scumbag get it from? The Horse didn't come up out of the sidewalk and it didn't fall from the sky like manna. It had to come in from Mexico, or it had to come ashore down at the docks. But it sure as hell didn't spring full-blown into Boy-O's reeky fingers. So just finding the little scumbag wasn't enough. He had to find the hands that put the stuff into Boy-O's hands and the hands that were behind those. And on, and on, until maybe even downtown was involved, and that was way the hell out of Rusty's territory.

What the hell had he fallen into? Or rather, what had the death of Dolores dragged him into? He had to find Boy-O. Then it hit him...

Boy-O! That was part of the answer. The tie-up he had been seeking was now quite clear to him. He should have realized it when Mirsky said, "They kept callin' him kid, or boy, or somethin'—"

Boy-O, who ran tea in the Cougar turf—and now it was apparent he had a similar route in Cherokee turf—had been the other person Mirsky had not seen in the darkness of the garage. He had persuaded some of his addicts to warn everyone in the Cherokee turf that Rusty was around and not to spill anything. It had to be. Sure they had called the half-seen person "boy." But it had been Boy-O, not just boy. The tie-up was there. Dope and Boy-O and the rumble and the silence of the gangs. Now Rusty knew why the Cherokees and the Cougars were silent to him. If they spilled anything, they would get their pot cut away from them and that was the worst that could happen to a bunch of junkies.

But whether Boy-O had wanted silence simply because he was afraid Rusty would find out who had peddled the stuff that had gotten the Cherks high enough to rumble, or whether there was another tie-up between Boy-O and the death of Dolores he didn't know. But he would find out.

It was fairly obvious why Boy-O wanted so much silence. At best, peddling the snuff was a risky bit and with Rusty so hot to find out who had done his sister, there was always the chance Rusty might reveal the snuff-peddler's name to the cops, either out of hatred (for the rumble had been taking place while Rusty might have stopped whoever raped his sister) or just out of spite. So the silence curtain had fallen.

But now Rusty knew the score. He had to find Boy-O. He might be the key—the key to the man in the camel's hair coat.

But where was Boy-O? He had gone underground. Would the neighborhood help Rusty find him?

The neighborhood was cool and deadly these days. They were waiting, like a driver on a dynamite truck, waiting for the big boom that had to come. The word had filtered all through the turf and everyone knew the big trouble was brewing. When one of the gang turned on his fellows, when the club went after a lone stud, there was bound to be trouble. Worse than a rumble. There would be running and shooting and one morning the Department of Public Sanitation would find something messy in one of the gutters.

Then the fuzz would start prowling and a lot of families would be broken up as kids were hauled away to the line-up. This was going to be a bad time and anyone who felt the chill wind of trouble in the neighborhood was clamming up, staying as far from the boom as possible.

Doors were closed to Rusty.

Duke Ferreira might have helped, but—

"Look, kid, it's not I don't wanna give you the word. It's not you ain't a good kid. But I got a business here, an' I can't take the chance on goofin' out. Y'know what I mean?"

Rusty knew what he meant and left the horse parlor with the blare of the loudspeakers from Santa Anita, Belmont and Hialeah ringing in his ears. The next time Duke needed a runner in a hurry Rusty was going to be unavailable.

Whitey Savest might also have helped, but—

"Geddouda here. You're a jinx. I don't need no more fraykin' trouble. You promised me protection when you was with them kids and when you got the boot that stinkin' Shaster kid put the screws to me good. I got ten machines out of whack 'cause of them kids. So beat it. Now!"

Rusty left the pinball joint with his ears stinging. He would see that Whitey had more trouble, if he could. But, hell, why bother? He didn't care for revenge. Not on Whitey, at any rate.

Weissenborn couldn't help. Wouldn't help. Mae Franco wouldn't help. Swart wouldn't help—he was out cold and snoring in a rear seat of the Tivoli, anyhow.

So Rusty walked the streets till the evening closed down again, and Boy-O had laid out some place where he was unavailable.

Then the third incident occurred.

Rusty passed the black mouth of the alley separating two nameless apartment buildings and his mind was a welter of worry and indecision. So far, everything he had done had come to a blind end. He had been threatened, not very hard, but enough to warn him that he was treading dangerous ground. He passed the alley without pausing to steer away from it as he usually did at such empty holes.

The arm came out and grabbed him around the neck. He slipped and fell, and the hand at the arm's end grasped his collar, dragged him, sitting, into the darkness.

He knew the odor instantly. He tried to blank it off, tried to pretend it was not happening. It was Pops.

He could smell the odor of the sewers. The smell of doorways with copies of the *Post* beneath the man's dirty suit jacket. The smell of desperation and over it all, stinking god, smelling like the slop it was, cheap wine.

Tokay. California White. Sneaky Pete. Sweet Lucy. Rubbing alky. Radiator anti-freeze, filtered down through a three-day-old loaf of bread. High and smelling, a palpable aura around him, reeking, rising into the garbage odor of the alley. Rusty choked and his throat clogged and his eyes screwed tight-shut and he tried to get away, twisting on the pavement. He was dragged quickly, backward, the seat of his pants burning cement. In a moment the hand tightened, slung him forward against the brick wall of the building and Rusty scuttled around till he could see the dark shadow of his father, hulking before him.

"You stay home an' don't go botherin' nobody no more," the man said. His breath was the foul stink of decayed teeth and rotten food. The air was filled with it and Rusty gagged again. He wanted to hunker over, pull his knees up and lay his head down, eyes closed. He wanted to get away from here.

The man before him was a dimness, yet Rusty knew every inch and plane of his face. It was strange. He had spent years forgetting that face, blanking it so that each time he saw it, it passed out of his mind instantly. Yet now, so close to that face, but unable to see it, he knew it far better than anything in the universe—the puffy eyes with the black, humped rings beneath them, the flattened, putty blob of a nose, the fleshed pads of the lips, it was all there, so clearly, so real.

"You hear me?" he snarled, his voice thick and syrupy.

Rusty tried to move sidewise, tried to get away, but though the boy could not see in the dark of the alley, the standing man could and Rusty heard the swish of fabric against legs an instant before the feet struck him in the stomach. A ball of pain exploded outward in his gut, sending tracers of agony up into his chest and down into his groin and he slumped over with a moan. He was not out, he was not even graying, but the shock of it was so great, he lay still, motionless—yet quivering inside.

"I asked ya hear me?" his father repeated. He bent over to see if he had hurt the boy, but more to see if he had ruined his chances of communication than in concern over injuries. He bent down, slumped onto his haunches and Rusty acted by reflex. The compulsion was not there, nor the confidence, but the streets had done their work, and his leg—bent at the knee in front of him—came up whip-fast and caught the man in the groin.

Pops Santoro screamed with the querulous screech of a confused animal and doubled over, his mouth wide, his eyes fully open, and Rusty took the opportunity to move. He started to his feet and the pain in his side sent a sharp cramp through him. He could barely walk and his hand scratched across the rough brick surface of the building as he tried to get away.

The little moans of agony that had been coming from his father ceased and Rusty felt a hand, tentatively, on the back of his neck. The man was trying to stop him. Rusty spun, using the hand that held him as a pivot, and shoved his elbow into his father's chest. The hand let loose and Pops Santoro stumbled back. Pain continued to blanket them both.

The spoor of conquest was high in Rusty now and he thought of this man before him not as his father—no, it had been a *long* time since he had considered him that, anyhow—but as an opponent. Another obstacle the gutters had thrown up to confound him. His hand went to his pocket and the switchblade he had put there for no one but the man in the camel's hair coat came out.

Even in the darkness of the alley, with only the faintest light from a street lamp down the block casting a lighter shadow over the building, the knife seemed to draw all brilliance to itself. It was up straight in the boy's hand, and its pointed head was aimed at Pops Santoro's throat.

Rusty dragged for breath, came up with enough to gasp, "Y-you hear me, I don't know who set ya on me, but you stay the frayk away from me, far away from me. Cause I hate you, you sonofabitch, I hate you all over, and you come near me again, I swear to God I'll kill you. I'll kill you and that's it!"

The man stumbled back again, seeing the line of steel that extended out from Rusty's fist. He put a hand to his stubbled chin and his voice was too thick with liquor to be forceful.

"You stay home, an' stop interferin' with people's business."

Rusty backed away and as he passed out of the line of faint light that came in through the alley's mouth, he saw his father's face in a half-light. At that instant, it all tied together and he knew he had been right. Something he had seen in the man's face told him he was right.

And after he had left the alley at a dead run, after he had scrambled over a fence and run through a dozen other alleys, after he was on the roof of his own building, with the night a hood over him, he sat down and thought. And knew he was right, that he had stumbled onto the answer long before and was going about it in the right way.

No wonder they were all scared. No wonder they were all trying to get him to lay off. Boy-O was the key right now. What he had seen in his father's face was the same thing—he now realized with shock—that he had seen in Miss Clements' face.

The eyes had been the same. Very white and no pupil at all but a pin-prick of black. Eyes that were made by the Devil, eyes that were made by one thing. The dream-dust. The narcotics habit.

His old man was on it, too. Miss Clements had been on it.

That was why he was being warned away. Now all he had to do was find Boy-O. After Boy-O, if he could make the pusher talk, the next link, and on up, till he found the one he wanted.

Hell yes. The man in the camel's hair coat.

TEN:
SATURDAY, A WEEK LATER

- *rusty santoro*
- *boy-o*

Boy-O didn't come out of his hole for almost a week.

It was a bad week; one of attending classes and having to bite his nails while waiting for a break. He had considered cutting school and spending his time looking, but a stern warning from Carl Pancoast bit the end off that idea. Also, Rusty was certain whoever had put Miss Clements on him would do his damnedest to make sure he was stopped from looking too hard —though how they could know he was looking for Boy-O was something Rusty could not imagine—even if they had to send the police after him, to arrest him as a truant.

Moms lay still in her bed, though now she was well enough to take a little clear chicken broth from either his hands or Mrs. Givens'. The kids in school avoided him. Cougars passed him in the halls with softly murmured catcalls and Weezee was a total stranger now. Only Carl Pancoast was any help. Rusty spoke to him several times, and though the older man harped endlessly on staying away from this business—allowing the police to solve the murder in their own time and way—he was a reassuring factor and Rusty knew he had at least one friend.

Then, the following Saturday, Boy-O crept out of hiding and Rusty went for him.

The boy had obviously known Rusty was looking for him. Rusty no longer trusted anyone in the neighborhood, and had carried on his efforts surreptitiously. Yet the neighborhood, with that unspoken instinct, like the mute communication of jungle vines, knew there was something going on, something tense, lying in wait. Rusty had not for a moment given up hope of trapping Dolores' murderer, and the low plant sense of the neighborhood may have felt it. But they wanted to stay out of the line of fire, and almost no one would help him.

So when Boy-O left his pad—a room in a cheap flophouse outside Cougar turf—and wandered back to Tom-Tom's for his dope-peddling run, Rusty knew it and he was there.

No planes to the face. Just a floating hunger, with no bones to support it. A starving animal, with eyes that never rested, never closed. Boy-O lived where he was supposed to live—in the gutter. His clothes reeked of the street and his face was always marred by patches of dirt or soot. A high-water mark ringed his thick neck. He had quick, scarred hands; filthy, untrustworthy hands.

He was passing a bundle to a Cougar named Clipper when Rusty came into the malt shop. He was removing the little white packets from the slit inside-edge of his pants-top, as the boy came through the open door. He looked up, started, then dragged himself into a semblance of nonchalance. It was instantly apparent to Rusty that whoever had been warning him off the finding of Dolores' killer had also warned Boy-O that Rusty was on the scent.

A thought flashed through Rusty's mind: *why don't they just put me down and stop this bullshit?* The thought flickered and was gone. Along with the fear. He was doing what had to be done, just as he had had Giulio, the butcher, watching Tom-Tom's place from his shop across the street, watching for Boy-O, forewarning Rusty.

Just as he had crossed into Cherokee turf. Just as he would

find that last man, and do him the way he should have been done.

Just as he was going to make Boy-O talk today.

Boy-O saw him and a film of craftiness clouded his eyes. He turned his head slightly, continued talking to Clipper. But he knew every step Rusty took and as the Puerto Rican came up behind him, Boy-O did not move, but said quietly, "Anything I c'n do for ya, Santoro?"

Rusty paused and wet his lips. He had to handle Boy-O delicately till he got him someplace where no one would interfere with the question-and-answer game he wanted to play with the pusher.

"Yeah. I wanna talk to ya about somethin'."

Still with his back to Rusty, Boy-O handed the little packets from his pants to Clipper, and accepted the two five-dollar bills with the other hand. It was all one fluid movement without pause or fumbling. Clipper looked up at Rusty and the boy saw the nerve-jumping tension in the Cougar. Clipper was on it hard and he needed a fast mainline to get rid of the monkey. Even as Rusty thought it, Clipper pushed up from the booth and left the shop hurriedly, the packets in his pocket, his hand jammed tight down on them in protective adoration.

Boy-O turned then. He faced around and leaned against the table. He was the biggest junkie of all, bigger than his customers, bigger than any Rusty had ever seen. The scumbag was constantly broke, though he raked in a staggering amount of money, just from the neighborhood kids and junkies such as Finkel, the barber, and the boys who worked on the docks…

…and Miss Clements

…and Pops Santoro.

Yet he was always broke and filthy and sleeping in fifty-cent pads. He spent all he made on more of his own product. The face that looked up into Rusty's was a lost one. It was devoid of purpose and strength, contained only the driving hunger for the dream-dust, the stuff that made a man temporarily twelve feet tall, and all trouble six miles away.

"Like what ya wanna talk about?" Boy-O said. "I don't know we got anythin' to talk about?"

"Sit down," Rusty instructed him, with a friendly tone to the words. He waved his hand to the booth and then half-turned to call to Tom-Tom. "Hey! Tom-Tom! What'll ya have, Boy-O?"

Boy-O shrugged his shoulders, surprised at this sudden friendliness on Rusty's part, suspecting it, but philosophically deciding a free soda was a good deal anyhow. He slid into the booth, said, "A black an' white, heavy onna syrup."

"Tom-Tom, a Coke an' a black an' white shake, heavy on the syrup." He slid down across from Boy-O and let a friendly smile play across his hard young face. "Hey, man, I haven't seen much of ya lately."

Suspicion flickered across Boy-O's face, but he replied, "Oh, yeah, well, I been busy. You know." Rusty knew all right. Busy getting the stuff to peddle and lying on his back in his pad with the light pastel dreams flitting by overhead and the holes like a million mosquito bites in his arms and thighs. Yeah, sure, busy. Hiding out!

"So? Whaddaya want?" Boy-O was too anxious to terminate the conversation. It showed nervousness and that he had something to be afraid about. That was good. For an instant Rusty felt bothered that he was going to have to use force again, but realized immediately there was no other way to get through to this hophead. The street called its own rules and a stud was a fool to play a kill-game by gentlemen's rules. If it was going to be rough, then it was going to be rough. But was there no end of it, finally? Was the web always getting stickier, dragging him back always?

"Well," Rusty began, feigning nervousness, twining his fingers, looking down at his hands, "I—uh—well, I didn't wanna say anything *here*, y'know…" he nodded his head at Tom-Tom, busily fixing the milk shake. "But, I—uh—I gotta have some stuff. I been gettin' kinda nervous, an' I need a fix…"

Boy-O's face jumped sharply and his eyes narrowed. Rusty was not a hophead. What did he want with the dust? Boy-O knew it was all wrong, right from the first sentence. This was some sort of trap, some sort of tie-in with Rusty's sister and the hunt that had been going on the past weeks.

"What're you tryin' to pull?" the pusher said softly, his filthy face tense under the imperfect light of the malt shop. "You tryin' to pull me into your trouble? You got some idea I was in that rumble with your sister?"

Rusty had to fight to hold back his desire to grab the junkie and throttle him. He held back and let an expression of hope-lessness and doom cross his features. He shook his head sadly, lost, needing solace. "No, man, no, no…" His voice was a thready whisper, dripping with remorse and unhappiness. "I—I been sniffin' a little and when my sister Dolores got it, I—I don't know what happened to me, man. I just started hittin' it like mad, y'know, an' n-now I gotta have more. I been gettin' it from—"

Tom-Tom came around the counter, bringing the Coke and the milk shake, and Rusty cut himself off. He did it only partially because the soda jerk was within earshot. The other part of his reason was that he had to quickly figure out a source for the stuff he was supposed to have been mainlining. Where could he get it, that Boy-O would not doubt, could not check on?

The baby-fat hand of Tom-Tom came into sight with the milk shake gripped in the fist and Rusty took a dollar from the pocket of his jeans. He laid it out alongside the glass, and kept his eyes on the light brown surface of the shake as he heard Tom-Tom clinking change. When the coins were down, Tom-Tom was gone and he saw the wet ring on the table where Boy-O had lifted his shake, he began again.

"I been gettin' some stuff from a friend of mine crosstown in Harlem, but it's all g-gone now, an' ya gotta help me out, man."

Boy-O did not reply. He sucked on the lip of the glass and his little feral eyes stared across the dark milky fluid and at Rusty. He knew the kid was lying. It was obvious. But he couldn't refuse and not get himself creamed. Boy-O wanted out of this mess. There was no way to stay out of Santoro's path, it seemed, without giving him what he wanted to know.

Rusty Santoro had changed. He was no longer a gutter fighter. He had changed. He was a steam roller now and that roller was bent on crushing anything—or anyone—that got in the way. Boy-O was wary of this kid. There was no sense tangling with him if it could be avoided.

"What you wanna know, Rusty?"

Rusty's eyebrows went up. Startled, he said, "I dunno what you mean, man. Like all I want is some dust, and we're wheelin' an' dealin', y'know."

Boy-O went back to his drink. He wasn't getting through. "Come on," Rusty urged, a heavy edge to his words, "let's fall up to your pad and find a pack. I need a shot right now."

Boy-O looked up through half-slitted eyes and did not have the stomach to refuse. He slid out of the booth. He had snuff with him, Rusty knew that. Rusty wanted him away from here. To talk, it had to be!

Well, get the talk over and then he was free and clear. He preceded Rusty out of the malt shop, as Tom-Tom tried valiantly to raise Glazounov or Bach on the tiny radio behind the counter. As they hit the sidewalk, the radio let fly with—"Ohohoh, *yes!* I'm the grayyyte pre-ten-en-der..."

"Why din't we go to my place?" Boy-O asked. Fear rippled deeply in his voice, and his face was white beneath the dirt film.

The basement was cool and dark and from somewhere behind

stacks of old newspapers, rats moved in search of food. A bulb burned low, swinging at the end of a thick cord, its shadow-image here then there then back then there then back again as the bulb described an irregular arc. The ruined furniture that had been stored down here lay jumbled like strange burial mounds, chair legs and table extensions sticking up like the snarled, clutching arms of half-buried corpses. The ceiling was low and covered by softly rippling coverlets of cobwebs.

Boy-O looked around in open fear. Maybe Rusty didn't just want to talk. Maybe—

"Siddown," Rusty ordered the junkie. He pointed to a crate and when Boy-O hesitated, he shoved. Boy-O stumbled backward, tangled his scrawny legs and fell in a clattering heap, knocking aside the crate. He stared up from the floor, his eyes large and white with terror. He never should have humored this stud! Now he was solid trapped.

"Now, look, man, I don't want no trouble, ya dig? I mean, I don't know what kinda business you got goin' and all, but I had nothin' to do with it. I'm just a guy minds his own—"

Rusty brought out the knife.

It had come to be more important to him than the pencils and pens and inks which he had used for mechanical drawings, with which he had thought he would build a future. It had slowly come to mean more to him than his brain, or his eyes, or anything. It was the only tool that seemed to work in the streets. The only one they understood, and the only one they respected. He had not wanted to use it ever again—he had wanted to throw it away, but they had forced him to resort to it, again and again. It was his lone companion against them all. It was the only mouth-opener in the world. The only thing that could find for him the things he needed and the information so vital to the location of Dolores' murderer.

"Now I wanna know where you get your dream-dust from,

scummie. I wanna know right now." He stood silent, then, letting the shaft of the shank talk for him.

Boy-O lay there and his mouth remained closed. His life was the dust. It was the only thing he had, as Rusty had the knife, and if he lost it, he was less than nothing. The neighborhood despised him. They would put up with him only so long as he brought them the vital narcotics. Rusty could never make him speak.

The next hour was short for Rusty, terribly long for Boy-O. But they reached a stalemate.

Rusty stood over Boy-O, and what he saw was the end of all the violence he had known. He knew now that he could never raise his hands to another person. It had all been futile, of course. Boy-O lay flat on his back, his chest heaving up and sucking in with great effort. His eyes were closed and his face was a mass of broken veins, welts, sticky blobs of blood and stripped flesh. A gash had been opened along the right side of his neck, and a warm pulse of blood pumped steadily. He was not deeply hurt, but the pain that filled him was a living thing. Yet he had not uttered a word. Moans and screams, perhaps, but not a word.

Rusty sank down against the wall of a coal bin. He could no longer hold his fists up. They were black with blood, and he was certain he had broken his thumb—or at least thrown it far out of joint. Desperation and futility and horror at what he had done mingled in his brain, and he laid an arm across his eyes to block out the sight of Boy-O, lying in the dirt and the dim one-bulb light. He had to make the junkie talk. He had to find out the next link.

"Who d'you get your dope from?" he asked for the hundredth time, really expecting no answer. There was only silence.

How to make the pusher talk? How to get that name from him? Rusty was up against a steel wall. But whatever happened, he was not going to hit Boy-O again. He gagged on a rueful chuckle, as he realized he was too late. He had sunk all the way back to his former level. He was nothing but a street bum again. The web had claimed its own.

What a stinking mess he had made of things. His sister was dead, all because he had gotten her into the Cougie Cats, and his mother was sick. He had alienated everyone in the neighborhood. His record at school was ruined and Carl Pancoast would be perfectly justified in having nothing further to do with him. He had beaten up strangers, that Mirsky kid, and people he knew. And where was he? Nowhere.

"G-give—up—bas…bastard…?" Boy-O croaked from the floor. His face was pale, still, and his eyes, despite their junkie weirdness, were filled with pain. Rusty dug his hands into the fabric of his jeans, pulling at the flesh of his thighs. Damn it, damn it, damn it! He had to make Boy-O talk.

He rose, to start again, and the terror-filled eyes of the junkie filled his world. They filled his world and they gave him an idea, a new idea, a payoff idea that had to mean success. Because if it didn't, he was finished.

He bent down, slapped away the feebly moving arm of Boy-O, offered in resistance, and began searching the junkie. After he had found three dozen little white packets of dust in pockets, and another half dozen in hidden flaps in the clothing, he realized that he would have to strip the junkie down.

It took him longer than he thought it would, for the pusher dredged up a supply of strength from somewhere, and caused him trouble in removing the filthy rags that were pants and shirt and jacket. But finally, Rusty had the junkie lying naked to the flesh on the basement floor. He took the dope and the clothes and put them high up on a pile of furniture in the farthest corner of the basement.

Boy-O watched it all with mounting fear. Every few seconds his eyes strayed to the dead-silent furnace. It was summer, and no one would come down here to the basement, but if Rusty tried to shove him in there—

"Wh-what're ya g-gonna…do…?"

Rusty sat down again, back to the coal bin and crossed his arms. He shook his head. "Nothing Not a goddamn thing. I'm gonna sit and wait."

Boy-O was bewildered. What was Rusty talking about? He was confused and in pain and bewildered, but he knew one thing: he would never talk. Because if he talked, just as sure as the street was hell, he would lose his junk, and that would be the end of him.

He had to have his junk to live.

And Rusty knew that, too. Unfortunately.

Cold had come crawling. It was bitter. Not only the cold of the moist basement floor, but the cold from within. Boy-O was shivering, lying huddled like a foetus, knees drawn up and hands thrust into armpits for what little warmth there might be. His face, beneath the grime, was strained and peaked, and his lips quivered. Nerves in his upper arms and temples jerked spastically, giving him a constantly moving, restless appearance. He moaned softly from time to time and every few minutes a shudder would run down his body.

He was not cold from the air. He was junkie cold. He was dream-dust miserable. He was cut off from the dirt that counted and Rusty watched as he got worse. Much worse. The first hour it hadn't been so bad, till Boy-O had realized what Rusty was trying to do. Then he had started to crave it more than he would have ordinarily. He had hungered deeper than ever. It had been a long time since that spoon had been out, that dust had been soaked down, that needle had hit the big vein on the inside of his arm. He wanted!

"Gimme! Gimme!" Boy-O half-rose up from the floor, his

mouth stretched flat on his face, in a weird grimace. His scream rattled across the hollow basement and Rusty got up himself from the floor as Boy-O tried to rise, tried to fall to the pile of furniture where the dope was secreted. He grasped the junkie by his forearm and thrust him back. Boy-O's flesh was clammy with sweat, his limbs quivered. He was a ghost human, warped out of shape and sanity. Rusty quivered as much, inside. But he let the feelings within him wither. Boy-O would sweat away the monkey till he squawked and gave out the poop Rusty needed.

The junkie fell back, lay in a sweating heap, his head buried in his thin arms. His black hair was tumbled out of its crude duck's-tail, and lay in a triangular shape over him. His body shook, his sobs climbed in intensity. "Oh god, god, gimme, don't be a b-bastard, gimme some, gimme a shot, g-gimme a pop. Please, I swear to god I don't kn-know nothin', please ya gotta, ya g-gotta *help me*, HELP ME—" his voice rose out again, ending in a high, womanlike screech. He clawed at his face, dragged bloody furrows down his cheeks. He was going insane from lack of the stuff.

But he was not ready to talk. Rusty waited, his mind closed to the screams, his eyes shut to the hideous sight that had been Boy-O, writhing in the dirt.

It took only four hours.

Rusty had to club the junkie twice, both times when Boy-O had struggled erect and tried to grab a packet from the furniture pile. The second time he almost made it, grasping a broken chair in his hands and swinging it full at Rusty. The chair connected with Rusty's head and for a long minute everything fuzzed out gray at the edges of his sight. He stumbled in and clinched with the suddenly strong junkie and by sheer weight forced him back.

The chair came up again and grazed off Rusty's shoulder, sending a bright lancet of pain down through his left side. The pain in his head was growing. He could see infinitely brilliant pinwheels of fire cascading down and down and then suddenly it ebbed away, and he brought up a knee straight to the junkie's groin.

Boy-O went down, slobbering, crying, begging for a mainline pop. Rusty sank back, drawing grateful lungfuls of air, fighting away the nausea the pain brought him. He shoved all furniture up out of reach then, and waited.

It took only four hours.

Finally, Boy-O dragged himself across the floor and a crooked finger touched Rusty's shoe. "Help me." His voice was weak, a catch in the throat, a mere whisper, a pleading.

Then, "Okay. Okay, I'll t-tell ya. I'll let ya know, just gimme a shot, man, please, just one…" he sagged off into a gasp and his teeth chattered. His body shook with the effort to stay on one elbow.

"First talk. Then we'll see," Rusty said. He despised himself. Boy-O was a wreck.

"M-Morlan's his name. Emil Morlan. He lives uptown. I get it through a feeder—guy supplies me an' a pusher in Cherokee country. I n-never met this Morlan, but I f-followed the feeder once." His mouth was a black line and the sweat was big as grapes on his upper lip. The dirt ran streakily on his face. It mixed with the blood and smelled.

"Where's he live? What's the address?"

"You're killin' me, please a shot! A shot, for Christ's sake, I'm beggin', beggin' ya!"

"The address. Now. Quick!"

"Y-yeah, yeah. He lives up on Central Park West." The junkie gave a fashionable address. "Fifteenth floor."

Rusty moved closer. "Now you tell me, man, all this runnin' around I been doin', and everybody no-talk, and them threats I got to shut up—all that came from you. Right?"

Boy-O did not, could not, possibly would not answer.

Rusty waited. The shakes claimed Boy-O once more.

Trembling, he answered, finally, "Yes, god it's s-s-so bad, so bad, help me! Gimme a pop, p-please."

Rusty plowed forward inexorably, "You were behind it."

"Yes, yes, I said yes, what ya want from me?"

"Why? Tell me why—"

Boy-O's eyes rolled up and his filth-caked fingernails bit into his palms. He bit his tongue, for the snakes had come…in a moment the screams, if he didn't get a pop.

"Answer me," Rusty said.

Boy-O sucked air and said, "That night the Cherokees were high on tea, I'd b-brought 'em a big bundle and they got high an' went to crash the dance. We was afraid after it was over that you was gonna tell the cops they was on pot, and throw me in the can, an' Mr. Morlan, too. So they told me to get some p-people to keep you away. We din't know, *you* know, we was a-afraid you was gonna go ta the cops, cause you was sad or somethin'."

It was just as Rusty had supposed. Rusty repeated the address on Central Park West and Boy-O nodded. "Fifteenth floor?" Again, Boy-O agreed, then his eyes closed.

Rusty threw the pusher his clothes and the packets. He watched as Boy-O dug in a pocket for his spoon, cigarette lighter, needle. He watched for a while, and as Boy-O sank back with tight lips, a god-living expression of peace passing over his planeless face, he said softly, "If you're lying to me, I'll kill you, junkie. S'help me god, you'll die."

Then he took a length of rope from around a pile of newspapers, and bound the junkie to the furnace pipe that ran across the floor. He shoved a portion of a furniture-covering rag into the junkie's mouth, and left him there. Along with the switch-blade. Buried in the arm of an old chair—

—broken at the shank.

Forever.

A gelatinous sky, quivering with indignation at having been left to shimmer above the city. Dark as a muddy river, but moving, with storm clouds that would burst before morning, with stars that disdainfully denied all knowledge of Earth or city or the boy huddled in the bushes watching the glass and stone front of an apartment building. A city almost on the verge of sleep, with the smell of gasoline fumes in the nostrils of its inhabitants, with the clamor of late-evening beer hall denizens, with the transient swoosh of cars and buses tooling the streets to a hundred thousand destinations.

Rest and peace, of a sort, to all the inhabitants of the city, but not to Rusty Santoro. He crouched watching, waiting for a break, a nameless something to happen that would allow him to bolt across the street and gain access to the building. In his path lay a bush, a street, a door and a toady doorman, pledged with wages, steeped in snobbery, dedicated to keeping "the riff-raff" away from the door.

Over the door, on a plate glass as clear as the light of the stars, in black script, the words SAXONY HOUSE sprawled contentedly. It was money, this place. And on the fifteenth floor, where no light showed, lived a man named Emil Morlan, a man who made his living not at stocks, or insurance, or services of a general nature, but by the dissemination of death.

Rusty Santoro waited, a leather-jacketed, blue-jeaned fury, waiting for that goddamned break so he could go up and talk to Mr. Morlan.

Oh, he wanted to talk so badly. He wanted to talk about the city Morlan did not know, about the gutters and the fat women and beer-bloated husbands, and kids in the streets, and a girl who had died in a nasty way. He wanted to talk, and he prayed to god he would not have to use his fists, because all that was through, please dear Lord, let it be through at last. But he knew it would come to that. It had to because if it wasn't Morlan, then it was another link along the way, and when he needed the way to find the link, the only help he had lay at the ends of his arms.

He studied the front of the building, the way the architect had fused the beauty of granite with the flamboyant extremes of glass to make a wonderful façade. He studied it and thought of the future he had left behind, trailed into the slush of the gutter. Was it only a few weeks ago he had been so eager to learn the potentialities of a slide rule and protractor? Too late now. All gone like the fog of a Manhattan morning. All gone, but the man in the camel's hair coat was still alive.

This building. A camel's hair coat fitted this place just right. Was this the end of the trail? Seemed like.

A fat woman with a fur coat thrown over a pale blue silk nightgown, her feet thrust into mules, came clattering out of the elevator inside the building, in Rusty's sight, and the doorman opened the glass door for her.

Rusty could not hear what they said to one another, but the woman reached into a pocket of the coat, brought out a bill and handed it to the doorman. She pointed off in the direction of lights far down at the corner, and Rusty saw a drugstore's sign glowing. The doorman nodded, touched the brim of his cap reverently and strode off in the drugstore's direction. The fat woman stared after him for a moment, then went back inside. The elevator door was just closing on her as Rusty got to his feet—ignoring the cramp in his legs—and strode quickly across to the building.

He was inside in a moment and looking around the lobby for

a stairway. The door was a shiny metal one, and before it had sighed pneumatically closed, he had three-stepped to the third floor. He paused there to catch his breath.

The climb to the fifteenth seemed much longer than he had imagined it would be. But once there, a great calm came stealing in through his nostrils and he sank down on the top step. He lay back, feeling the cold of the stone landing against his neck and hands.

He had reached the top. He was sure of that. This was the place where he would finish the tragedy that had begun with Dolores in the alley behind Tom-Tom's shop. He felt certain, deep inside him, that when he left this building, it would be between cops, his hands manacled, his life ended. Because— clear as hell, no doubt at all, sure as god made little green apples—he was going to beat the man in the camel's hair coat to death. Now, if Emil Morlan wore such a coat, that was it. A stupid way to figure it, he knew. A stupid way to arrive at con- clusions, and no damned motive for this Morlan to kill his sister (hell, with his money any broad in the city was available, what did he want with Dolores?), but the search had been a long one, and the word was that she had been killed by a man in a camel's hair coat, and the track had led here, so that was the way it would be.

Why?

It all seemed so stupid, suddenly. He had only one man's word about it. The Beast. He had tracked a path of dope-peddling from Mirsky to his father to Boy-O and now to Morlan. But what did one have to do with the other? Anything? Sure, it had to, but why? There was no coherency here at all.

Thoughts swirled darkly and his mind tumbled them back and forth as he tried to discover some rationale. But it always ended up with Morlan and the need to end it all.

The elevator sighed open and he heard heavy footsteps

beyond the metal door to the fifteenth floor. He pushed himself up and took a long step to the door. It opened a crack at his
pull, and he saw the tastefully decorated hall. He saw the single
door to the apartment that covered the fifteenth floor, and he
saw the man who applied the key to the ornate lock.

The man wore what Rusty had come to hope he would not
wear.

In the summer, a man would be crazy to wear a camel's hair
coat.

ELEVEN:
SATURDAY NIGHT

- *rusty santoro*
- *morlan*

Rusty caught him low in the small of the back, just as the door swung inward. He hit him with his bad shoulder—the one Boy-O had injured with the chair—and the pain washed Rusty anew. But the force of his drive from the back stairway sent the man spinning forward, to crash into the wall of the apartment's hall. Rusty stumbled forward after him, grasping the door by the huge center-set brass doorknob and thrust it closed. It was pitch dark and Rusty fumbled for a switch, found it, clicked it on.

The man had fallen over and was just starting to rise, supporting himself on the wall, as Rusty clipped him again. The man caught it behind the ear and lost his balance. His short, sharp exclamation of agony was cut off as his face hit the polished tile of the hallway floor. He rolled a few inches and lay on his stomach, the camel's hair coat bunched around him. He struggled on palms to rise. He could not make it and slumped down, breathing heavily. One hand went to his head, feeling the spot where Rusty had hit him.

Rusty used his foot to roll the man over.

He had a thin, pale face, with deep hollows under the eyes. His hair was thinning and brushed straight back from his high forehead. A birthmark purpled his cheek almost at the left corner of his lips. His eyes were green and smoked with pain.

Rusty had seen the expression in those eyes in other eyes, too often lately, for it to escape him. He bent down and brought the man to his feet with difficulty. The man struggled in Rusty's grip, but Rusty was as tall as the other, and held him fiercely.

"You don't give me no trouble, Mr. Morlan, an' we'll be okay." He hauled him across the hall, into the darkness of the living room. As Rusty struggled across the room, he knocked against a floor lamp and quickly switched it on with one hand, regaining his hold before the gray-haired man could break away. All the way across the room he maintained a precarious grip on his companion.

The strength was flowing back into the man's body, and suddenly he shoved Rusty from him, at the same moment hurling himself sidewise.

Rusty tried to grab him, but the gray-haired man eluded the boy's attack, and ran into a bedroom off the living room. He slammed the door and Rusty heard it lock.

Suddenly Rusty realized how scared he was and what he was doing. If this man—and it was certain this was Morlan—called the police, they would arrest Rusty for housebreaking and assault. He went to the door of the bedroom and put his ear against it. He could hear vague sounds of movement from within.

There was no keyhole in the door.

He didn't know if he could do it, but he had to try breaking in that door, before Morlan could use the phone. He stepped back and took a run at the door. He hit it with his good shoulder, and even so felt the pain down his side. The door held and he was thrown back violently.

He tried it again.

He hit it from closer up, harder, and this time he felt pressure ease as the door strained on its hinges.

Again, and this time he heard the faint crackle of wood

preparing to splinter as the center panel of the door began to buckle. Still nothing from the man within.

He smashed against the door for the fourth time and it crashed inward before him, slamming against the inner wall. The brittle metal of the lock itself had snapped. Pieces of metal hit the floor with soft clatters, and Rusty was shot through into the center of the bedroom.

He had been wrong. The man within was not calling the police. The phone stood unattended on the nightstand. The gray-haired man was standing half-turned toward Rusty, trying to extricate something from a messy tangle of papers and stray objects in a wall safe.

A picture had been revolved upward on the wall, and now hung upside down, grotesquely framing the gray-haired man who yanked at something in the safe, and abruptly spun full-face to Rusty—a gun in his hand.

Without thinking Rusty threw himself forward. He hit the bed just as the revolver went off and behind him he heard the bullet smash into the wall. He bounced off the bed and came at the gray-haired man from the side. Tackling him as he would have brought down a man on the football field at a pick-up game, Rusty caught Morlan around the knees and dug in.

They fell backward and Morlan crashed to the floor, still holding onto the revolver. He tried to bring it down on Rusty's head, but the boy threw up a protecting arm and caught the other's wrist as it came down.

Rusty swung over his head at the older man's face. He could not see, but he felt and heard the blow land. The other slumped back on the floor, and the hand that held the revolver opened. Rusty took the weapon, and got to his feet. The bedroom was a wreck.

For a moment Rusty considered using the gun to beat what he wanted from this man, but the memory of Boy-O was still tonight-fresh, and he turned and thrust it back into the wall safe. He slammed the circular plug and spun the tumbler knob. He revolved the picture back into place.

Behind him on the floor, the man said levelly, "If I hadn't been so nervous and forgot the combo to my own safe, I'd have gotten that gun sooner—and I'd of killed you!"

Rusty did not smile. He dragged the man to his feet and pushed him ahead, back into the living room. "But you didn't get it in time, so we're right back where we started from."

He shoved the man into a deep wine-colored armchair. Rusty stood watching him carefully for a second. "You Morlan?"

The gray-haired man looked up with a surly, confused, frightened expression on his face. "I have no money on me. It's all locked in my office downtown. You're wasting your time. I have a few dollars…" he contradicted himself, "you can have that if you get out right now—"

"What about your safe in there, where we were?" Rusty asked sarcastically, indicating the bedroom with a jerk of his head.

"You little whelp bastard!" the man's voice was rough and angry, but lit with fear. He studied the boy before him with an intense wariness.

"No dough. That ain't what I'm here for. I want some talk with you, mister. That's all I want." Rusty marveled to himself how calmly he was talking to this animal who had murdered and defiled his sister and whom he was about to kill.

A change of expression came over the man's face and he sat forward, massaging the back of his head. "Who the hell are you?"

"You Morlan?"

"Yes, goddamnit! I'm Emil Morlan, now what do you want?"

Rusty took a deep breath. He had known it, of course, but to hear him say it, was something else entirely. The end of the road. All screwed up and confused and no reason for suspecting this man—except here was the camel's hair coat—but here he was. He'd forced his way into a swanky apartment and he was about to commit a murder. Not a switch stand or a zip duel or a brick in the head in an alley—but cold, sharp murder. He would stomp this man to dust beneath his boots.

"Why'd you kill my sister?"

Morlan's face went back into shadow. His eyes opened wider. He let his mouth move and his hand came away from the bruise on the back of his head. "You're that kid from way downtown. What's your name—"

"Santoro," Rusty tossed it at him, hard. "Russell Santoro, an' my sister's name was Dolores. Remember now?"

He started forward and had his hand wrapped in the full, thick cloth of the camel's hair coat before Morlan yelled, "Wait a minute! Hold it! For Christ's sake, hold it, not me, not me! I didn't touch her! I wasn't anywhere near her! I can prove it. Stop!"

Rusty was close to him, bending over the chair, half-dragging Morlan erect. "Then talk mister, talk so fast, 'cause I'm gonna do something, one way or the other. Talk now and make it good, or Jeezus I'll k-kill ya…" Rusty's voice broke, and he found himself trembling with fury. The shaking concentrated in a tic and it battered hot and fast in his cheek, and the pain hit him in the gut again when he thought of Dolores and the days of looking, and now it was almost finished. Everything was almost finished.

Morlan tried to talk, but Rusty had him too close under the chin with the coat wrapped in his fist. He motioned futilely and struggled to speak. Rusty backed off a little, letting loose of the coat.

Morlan started to talk fast and he did not stumble or hesitate. He could not afford to be slow or inarticulate. His life hung on his glibness. He tumbled it all out in one wild rush of words.

"I didn't do it. I had nothing to do with it. I heard from one of my contacts all about it and that someone had given you my name, or what I looked like. I tell you I was nowhere near there that night. I was down in your neighborhood, but I was nowhere near your sister. You've got to believe me. I was down there— because—because—"

Rusty tried to stop the trembling with an abrupt movement and nodded his head sharply. "I know you push the stuff into my turf—an' Cherokee turf, too—so stop the crappin' around. Gimme the scoop, or I'll put you down final, right now."

Morlan continued, anxiously spilling it all out. "I went down there with a couple of friends to see a man who's been cutting in on our trade. He's been raising his own stuff in a deserted lot behind this dry cleaning place. He's got it in the middle of a thick patch of weeds. Nobody would recognize what it is, even if they should stumble on it. Just some pretty flowers—"

Rusty tried to remember: he had gone through that empty lot a hundred times. In fact, he had been through it just the last week, looking for Boy-O. So someone was raising tea in that field. He turned his attention back to Morlan.

"This guy's been supplying a few people and for a time it didn't bother us, he was on such a small scale. But he's been branching out, starting to grind up more snuff. Then a few weeks ago he tried to put the scare into my pusher down there—" Rusty knew he must mean Boy-O, "—so my pusher told my contact man to put a scare into this creep. I went down there with a pair of buddies who used to box a little, to scare him off our territory. We don't kill people. I'm a businessman. I got interests all over town, I can't afford that kind of stuff."

Rusty found himself believing Morlan, though he knew with each bit of belief his solution to Dolo's murder was dissolving.

But he could not bring himself to kill that easily. He wanted a passage out.

"When I got down there, I saw the guy, and he wouldn't be scared off. He was pretty big and it would have been a bad fight if my friends had jumped him. Anyhow, he ran away when my two friends tried talking to him. I saw my pusher down there and told him we'd handle this guy and not to worry about it.

"That was when this affair at the bowling alley occurred. My pusher told me they were high on my snuff and I warned him that I didn't want to be involved.

"Then my two friends and I came back. I went on to a party—I can prove it—and the next day I got word that a girl had been killed, and one of my sources down there—" again Rusty knew Morlan meant Boy-O, "—told me this big guy that has been cutting in on us, he had given you a description of me and told you I did it."

Rusty stopped him. "What proof you got that you was at this party, and not down in Cougar turf?"

Morlan started to rise. Rusty made to stop him, then let him get up. Morlan went to an ornate Oriental-engraved breakfront and pulled open a drawer. Rusty moved over to make certain it was not another gun the gray-haired man was getting. Morlan pulled out a folder and opened it. The folder was an eight-by-ten nightclub photograph in a white cardboard frame. It showed Morlan at a table with several brassy-looking women and a half dozen other men all of his approximate age, all wealthy and shifty looking. A newspaper clipping was tucked into one corner of the photo.

He picked it out and showed it to Rusty. It was a replica of the larger photograph, with a gossip columnist's story attached, giving the date the party had occurred, and noting that in the background could be seen on the stage the remarkable new comedian—it gave a name Rusty did not know—in his first show.

Morlan went to the phone, dialed a number and said, "Is this the Golden Sparrow?" That was the name of the nightclub where the picture had been taken. "Let me speak to the manager." A pause, then Morlan said, "I'd like you to tell a friend of mine at what times the show goes on at your club." He said hold it a second and handed Rusty the receiver. Rusty took it and listened. The cultured voice of a man told him the hours of the two regular shows each night. In the background he could hear music and the noise of a crowd. Morlan was leveling.

He hung up, and handed Morlan the photo and clipping. Morlan put them away. Rusty was convinced. The first show, the show at which Morlan had been seen and photographed, had been on at almost precisely the time Dolores had been attacked in the alley. Morlan was plainly not the man.

Rusty had almost killed an innocent man.

Then why had he been after this Morlan and his camel's hair coat? Why? He knew, of course, but Morlan was speaking again.

"I never thought you'd get this far. I had a few feelers put out, to keep you away. I told my pusher down there to keep you off the scent, to get those kids to keep their mouths shut or we'd cut off their supply. I told him to find some other people to warn you away—" Rusty thought of Miss Clements and his own father and his stomach heaved, "—and they did it because they were afraid we'd stop their snuff if they didn't. The cops got nothing, so I figured *you* wouldn't get to me."

Rusty realized how lucky he had been. By bulling his way through to Mirsky—strictly by chance—and finding out the Cherokees had been doped up, he had traced it back to Boy-O, who had cracked and revealed his boss by the only possible torture method that would have worked. Then he had found Morlan, and though the police had found nothing, and Morlan did not suspect, Rusty knew one thing neither of them knew. The connecting link.

"Who is this guy that's been raising tea?" Rusty asked.

"I don't know his name. He's a big man, very big, with a face like an animal." Morlan seemed over-anxious to explain why he had tried to stop Rusty's search. "We were afraid with all the notoriety that fight had, it would come out that the kids were hopped-up. We paid to have it kept quiet, but with you running around, stirring up trouble, there was no way of telling how far you'd go. We had to keep you away, but we couldn't take a chance on hurting you. That would have started the rumors all over again, twice as loud."

"So why didn't you cool this guy since the rumble?"

Morlan spread his hands. "We couldn't do anything in that territory. Another killing would have really made it so hot we couldn't have covered it if we'd put all the money in the world into it. He's been cutting into our concession, but for now we have to let him have his way. We supply a lot of the city—you don't think we make our dough off school kids do you?—but we can't afford anyone cutting in, or pretty soon we'd have nothing left. You understand, don't you?"

Rusty let Morlan finish, a note of apology in his voice.

He took a step backward and turned. "S-sorry. Sorry I bothered ya. I'm...I'll be goin' now." He was dazed. It had dawned on him suddenly, a mixture of his own information and Morlan's description. It all fitted in now and it fitted properly. Except there was still no sense to it, down at the bottom. He should have known from the first. There had only been one link between Dolores and this man in the camel's hair coat. The rumble and the dope, they had been one thing, and Dolo's murder had been another. Two separate tracks, joined at only one place.

One link, and that link without verification. He had been going on the word of one man. And that man had been leading a double life. That man had lied to him, to create the link, so Rusty would come here and kill Morlan—who stood in the way.

It had been chance that the rumble had occurred the same night as Dolo's murder. Or perhaps Dolores' murder had been accomplished with the rumble as a distraction. If he had not driven Dolores out that night, if she had not gone to the dance to spite him, if he had not surrendered himself to his old vices when he had gone after her—he might have saved her.

But the murderer had used the hopped-up rumble as a club to get Rusty to do his dirty work. He had used Rusty as a tool, with one simple lie.

All birds with one stone.

So damned, completely obvious now and he had stumbled about like a blind man. Now he knew. Finally, he knew. You can't trust anyone. No one is a friend. It's a jungle and it's a web and it's quicksand, and you can't trust anyone.

He made his way to the door, somehow, and behind him he heard the now-indignant voice of Morlan telling him he was going to let him go free, this time, but Rusty had been damned lucky the cops weren't called in. He was bluffing and Rusty knew it. Morlan could no more afford the fuzz than he could.

Rusty heard nothing more because he was thinking of one ending, one person, one job, one final goal. He had to get back to the deadly streets he knew. Back to the gutters, for that was where his ending lay waiting, somewhere. He had to get back to the old neighborhood.

He had to find the Beast.

TWELVE:
SATURDAY NIGHT

- *rusty santoro*
- *the beast*
- *the death*

Rain had come and gone so swiftly, it had hardly been at all. The streets were slick-shined from it and small galaxies of oil made rainbow auras on the black tar landscape. Darkness was a live thing that walked with terrible softness through the city. The air was clean and cool, but there was a tautness in every-thing that overlay the calm, making the city a waiting animal, hungry for what was to come. It breathed in and out quietly, hunkered down on black haunches, its million-window glit-tering eyes aware of every scene, every life, every conclusion. It waited.

Rusty made it back to the neighborhood in a cab. It had been the second time in his life he had squandered money so reck-lessly. The first time had been when he and two Cougars had taken a cabbie over the rocks. They had made the hackie drive them all the way from West One Hundred Fourteenth Street and Broadway deep into Cougar turf and the meter had read three bucks and fifty. Then they had jumped the cab and started to run away. But the cabbie had caught Rusty and taken a five-dollar bill for his trouble. Then he had booted Rusty into the gutter. That had been the first time. This time was something entirely different.

His nerves were ticking. He had St. Vitus Dance of the innards. He couldn't stand still and a subway did not seem as fast as a cab. So he laid out the money, the last of his money, and hit Cougar turf just after the bars had begun to close. He got off near the apartment building where Boy-O lay bound in the basement, and paid the cabbie with a ten-cent tip.

"Thanks," the cabbie sneered. He held the change in his hand and snorted an obscenity about late-night non-tippers. As the cab's taillights winked off around the corner, Rusty stood undecided. How was he going to get the Beast?

In any event, he had to let Boy-O go.

He hit for the basement, and found the junkie sleeping, still tied up. Boy-O's back was up against the furnace pipe, his wrists raw and bloody from trying to break the rope. Rusty found a piece of glass from a broken window-fronted cabinet and slashed the ropes off Boy-O's arms. The pusher woke almost immediately and the fear returned. Rusty pulled the gag from his mouth, and Boy-O started whimpering. "Don't kill me, man. D-don't kill me. I marked for ya, I to'dja what ya wanted to know, din't I? Let me 'lone…"

Rusty settled back on his haunches and ran a hand through his hair. An infinite weariness passed up his body and he wanted to lie down there and sleep. But he held the weariness off, because sleep was something he couldn't afford—not just yet. He had to find someone first.

"Look, Boy-O," he began, his eyes closed for a moment. Silent for another moment, then, staring at the ceiling because he could not look at the dried blood on the junkie's face, the condition of the junkie's body, "I wanna find the Beast. You know where I can locate him?"

Boy-O shook his head rapidly, fear driving it back and forth. "Uh-uh. I don't know where he hangs, man. I got nothin' ta do with that stud. He's mean. I don't know nothin' about him—" He added with hurried fright, "An' that's the god's truth, Rusty, man, s'help me, honest!"

Rusty nodded slowly, understanding and futility in his movements. "Okay," he said softly, as though talking to himself because no one else was left. "Okay. I know. That's okay."

He got to his feet, and started for the stairs. He stopped with one hand on the bannister and looked back into the darkness of the basement, lit by only that one swinging bulb.

"I'm—I'm sorry, man," he said. Then he was gone.

How to find the Beast? Rusty sat on the roof of his building with the summer chilliness enfolding him and he wanted to know, worse than anything else. How was he going to smoke the Beast out, smoke him out so he could get his hands on him? Not for a moment did Rusty consider how he was going to kill a giant of the Beast's size. Not for a moment did he worry about what happened to him if he did. All he wanted to do was smoke the Beast out.

Smoke…

He got up, and stood staring off across the city. He saw the broken black line that was the building tops against the lighter dark of the sky. The strange angles and spires of TV antennas, the towers that were chimneys, the box-shapes and chicken-wire of pigeon roosts. He saw it all and knew what would smoke the Beast out.

He went downstairs, into the apartment and Mrs. Givens was there. She had not left for more than fifteen minutes since Moms got sick. Who was watching after her kids, Rusty did not know. But there she was, in the big chair, almost asleep. She woke as he came through the door and a quizzical expression lit her face. It was very, very late.

"Miz Givens," he said, not closing the door, "keep the shades down, an' keep the windows closed. Don't let nothin' bother ya t'night, an'—an' don't let Moms hear the noise." He started to close the door, but she motioned him back with a pudgy, brown hand.

"What noise? What you mean?" He waved her off.

"You'll know real soon."

He smiled at her and her face was so strained he wondered if she was not sick herself. "Don't worry," he said. Then he closed the door and went downstairs and over to the corner, and found the fire-box, and pulled the lever down. Then he went back up to the roof to wait for the fire engines.

He had known it would be just this way. The sirens, the red, winking lights, the long engines with their ladders tucked down and all the noise. Noise! That was it. If there was anything that could drag the neighborhood from its beds at this hour, if there was anything that could bring the blackjack players out of the back room, if there was anything that would smoke the Beast from whatever warren he was using tonight, it would be the complete pandemonium of a false alarm fire. The engines pulled in to the curb near the alarm box and the firemen climbed down, looking for the blaze.

In a few moments they would realize it was a false alarm, then they would tear off again, leaving the neighborhood for the cops to comb for the alarm setter. Leaving the crowds to disperse, asking each other, "What happened, what went on, what was that all about?"

Before then, the Beast had to come out of his hole, had to come into the crowd to see what was happening. He had to.

Rusty watched carefully, straining his eyes to make out the faces of everyone down there, in the streetlamp light, and the glare of the engine's headlights. He saw the women, in their nightgowns, with the terrycloth bathrobes pulled across their fat stomachs. He saw the balding men, their heels red and bare in bedroom slippers. He saw the young girls and some of them reminded him of Weezee and some reminded him of Dolores, but that was too long ago to think about. But he did not see the gigantic hulk that was the Beast. He saw nothing like that.

Then the firemen were cursing loudly and they were piling back onto the engines, and scream-roaring away. Then the street faded into silence and the crowd milled around for a few minutes asking what had happened and then they started to disperse, as Rusty had known they would.

He had failed. He had fouled up again.

Then he saw the Beast.

The big man was standing in the alley across the street. The fire engine's headlights had blinded Rusty before, but now he could see the monstrous slovenly shape angled against the brick wall, watching everything, taking it all in, the gaping mouth wet and wide, those little eyes, like two spots of hell, ripped free and thrust into a doughy face, the two meat-chunk hands, those fingers, each as big as a sausage.

This had raped Dolores?

Rusty felt nausea grip him. He leaned his face against the cold brick of the roof's ledge and he prayed. He said to the sky and the night and the god he was so sure no longer knew him, "Please oh dear god above hear me hear what I'm saying tonight and forgive me for what I'm gonna do."

Then he stood up and lit a cigarette.

He saw the Beast's face swivel upward and he saw the eyes cold and deadly staring into his own, across that space. He raised his hand against the sky and motioned the Beast to come up. "I set it," he said. He said it loud enough to carry to the street and hoped a cop did not hear it, too.

The Beast hesitated a moment, then looked both ways on the street and started across. He disappeared from Rusty's sight under the angle of the building, and Rusty knew he was on his way up. Neat. The sonofabitch still thought Rusty didn't know. He still thought Rusty was looking for the man in the camel's hair coat. Neat. The sonofabitch. Sure he had given Rusty the tip. So Rusty would look the other way and find Morlan and take care of him, the Beast hoped, before Rusty could find out Morlan had been nowhere near Dolores when she had been killed. That would get Morlan out of the Beast's way and get Rusty cooled permanently, too.

Neat. So neat Rusty had run around like a chicken with its head detached, following up a trail that meant nothing. No wonder there had been no connection between the dope and the death of Dolores. How could there be?

The only connection had been there all along and Rusty had been too dumb to see it. Now the connecting link was on its way upstairs.

The door to the stairwell banged open and the huge shape of the Beast was there.

He came across the tarpaper roof and he grew monstrous in Rusty's eyes. His arms swung to his knees and below, and he seemed more a gigantic parody of some pithecanthropoid than a human. Rusty stared at the man who walked toward him and all the cold fury, all the hatred, all the brutality he had been driven to in the name of his sister, washed over him. He was going to kill this cold-blooded sonofabitch without remorse and without compunction. He was going to tear out his tongue and tear off his manhood, and stomp what was left into a runny pulp, and then—

And then he was going to give himself up. The future was dead, but so was the Beast. He didn't know it, but he was already dead.

"Hi," he said. Rusty did not answer, just watched.

"I say, Hi."

The Beast stopped, uncertainty in his face. "You ever hear anything 'bout that guy I told ya I saw?" He licked his fat, gross lips.

Rusty wished he had the knife. But his hands would do.

"Whutsa matter? I ain't seen ya in a while. Where ya been stayin', huh?" Rusty looked around for a weapon. He needed something. Those arms of the Beast's could crush him in a second. He saw nothing.

"Whutsa matter with you? Can'cha talk?"

Rusty got up, moved to the side. He rested his hand on the aluminum stalk of a TV antenna, knowing he could not pull it loose from its moorings to use as a weapon. But at least he was touching something. The antenna was right at the edge of the roof, where the ledge rose up. He wanted a weapon, desperately. Something to beat this giant to his knees with. Something with which to pound in that ape-face.

"I saw Morlan tonight," Rusty threw at him in the silence. For a moment the Beast's face was lax, devoid of expression, then the name must have registered, for his eyes narrowed and the stare left his face.

It was miraculous. Rusty watched as the imbecile light left him, and a look of craft and cunning came over the coarse features. This was no idiot. This was a man who had played the part for a long, long time, but was not a moron at all.

"You killed my sister…" Rusty said.

The Beast stared back in silence. His eyes never left Rusty's face and his jaw worked slowly. "Oh? Makes you think that?"

"You told me about Morlan. Morlan says he wasn't near her. Says he came down here to stop you from cutting in on his dust route. Where you raise the poppies? In that weedy lot behind the dry cleaner's place?"

The Beast stood still, framed against the stars and no moon at all. The night seemed part of him, like something from the dawn of time. He was a caveman out bravely in the night, looking for meat. But this was no strong, brave man of pre-dawn. This was a filthy, butchering bastard who had killed an innocent girl.

"You haven't said a thing yet, Santoro," the Beast said. "The only thing you're saying is you don't know nothing."

Rusty found himself marveling. "You ain't a dummy at all. You ain't stupid. You been pretendin'."

The Beast's face crinkled in a hideous grin, a travesty of a grin. "Oh," he said sarcastically, "you finally figured it out, huh?"

"You been two people all along," Rusty said in amazement.

"You was sayin'—" The Beast took a step forward.

Rusty moved back an equal step, toward the edge of the roof. "Th-the only thing I knew about Morlan was what you told me. That he was down here, in a camel's hair coat. You knew I'd finally get to Boy-O and find out who was pushing through him and then check back. You were hoping I'd kill him, weren't you, you sonofabitch? You were hoping I'd kill off your competition—then that would put me away, too. Then you'd have the whole turf for your own dust."

"I saved your life," the Beast said. He moved forward. Rusty saw the step. But he could move no further and still be on the roof. It was seven floors to the street.

"Sure you saved—saved me," nervousness ticked in Rusty's words. "I hadn't done the job for you yet."

The Beast jumped. He grabbed for Rusty and caught him by the jacket. Rusty struggled and struck out blindly, feeling himself falling. The Beast dragged him back and held him in a crushing bear-hug. Rusty gasped, and ooophed as every rib in his body was crushed inward. He spread both hands and tried to shove the huge chest away from him, but it was no good. The

Beast gasped deeply, sucking in more air for the job, and bent Rusty backwards, till the boy felt the night breeze blowing his hair. His head was over the side of the building. He could barely feel his legs. There was no strength from his waist down. He had to get away.

He—had—to—get—away—

Rusty's legs brushed the brick of the roof ledge. It was a bare reflex, but he planted what he thought must be his heels against the brick, and shoved. The Beast stumbled a step backward, and his grip loosened just a fraction. Rusty brought both hands up from his waist, and dug the crooked fingers into the two small, evil eyes before him. He dug and felt wetness.

The Beast screamed. His voice let out across the canyon of the tenements and rattled down to the street. Rusty dug in deeper, feeling something under his left hand go soft and moist and start to run down the Beast's cheek. He gagged at the thought, but shoved harder. His fingers broke into the clear and the screams continued. The Beast retched down across Rusty's jacket and the smell was terrible. But the screams were worse. He let go, then, and Rusty fell on his back.

The Beast clutched at his streaming face, at the black pits that had been eyes, and as he stumbled he tripped across the shank of the TV antenna. His arms flailed out and he started to fall, holding tight to the antenna.

The shaft of the antenna bent and creaked and the bolts held, but the length of it swayed and gave. The Beast tumbled over the side of the apartment building, still holding tight to the antenna. He hung there, on the end of the bent aluminum, like a fish on a line. He swayed and bumped the building, and his great weight put a strain on the aluminum. It started to crack and the metal bent even more, rubbing against the brick.

The Beast's screams had not ceased for a moment and now

the street was again dotted with a crowd. People stared and
pointed up at the great hulk who was suspended on a spider-
web from nowhere.

"Aaah! Help me! Help me!" The Beast screamed and Rusty
stared down at him. A dazedness had come over the boy when
he had been released. He had risen to his feet only with the
greatest difficulty. Pain thrashed about in him, dying and pulling
his nerves along with it.

He looked down at the blind hulk that had killed his sister.
"Why'd you do it?" he asked, leaning over, hardly realizing the
Beast was on the edge of oblivion. He had to know. It was a
compulsion in there somewhere. He had to know why this
thing had started.

He knew when it had started, back when he was born, but
why.

The Beast screamed again and more windows flew up. Heads
popped out and the entire neighborhood watched—and listened. A woman yelled, "Call a cop!" But no one moved. They
watched, immobile. The Beast swayed some more. The bolts
creaked. Rusty asked him again, "Why'd you kill my sister?"

"I din't, I din't mean to do it! Help me! Help me!"

"Why, tell me why!"

"I saw'r, that was all. I saw'r and she was all alone—she left
the dance—an' I asked her for a kiss and she laughed at me, an'
I—I—ya gotta help me, ya gotta…"

A cop rounded the corner and looked up and dashed for the
building.

The bolts creaked and one snapped loose and the aluminum
straightened a little as its length was pulled over the edge.
Rusty turned away and started walking.

He passed the cop on the stairs.

The cop was too late. Rusty heard the crash in the street

below as he opened the door to the apartment. Then, when he closed the door, he heard nothing more from the street—except one high-pitched woman's wail—for Mrs. Givens had done as he had asked. Moms was asleep.

All the windows were closed.

THIRTEEN:
THE DAYS AFTER

- *rusty santoro*
- *insubstantials*

Days came, and days went. None of them paused in their relentless march to nowhere.

Everything straightened out, as straight as death could make it. Morlan was not heard from again. He was said to have left town when the police—after questioning Rusty—heard about his business ventures. Mirsky was gone, too. It was perhaps the safest thing he could do, for his life was worthless in Cherokee turf. The lot with the poppies was thoroughly excavated and the flowers destroyed. So good a job of plowing was done that the dry cleaning establishment purchased the lot for expansion purposes.

Rusty was asked a great many questions.

No one came to claim the Beast's body. It went to Potter's Field and no one took flowers for the hole. But it all straightened out, finally. With finality.

Moms got better, because she could not get worse. No one ever dies of a broken heart. Not really. At least, not on the outside. Life moves and time moves and people must move.

There were no charges that could be brought against Rusty. Over a hundred people had seen and heard what had transpired between the boy and the Beast that night, on the roof. It was clearly self-defense. And when Rusty had finished explaining how he had tracked down the Beast, the fuzz were more than happy to give him a clean turn-loose so they could spend their time breaking the dope chain that had supplied the kids.

The kids. The Cougars were another world, another time, another life. He found no hope in that direction. There was no hope at school, either. Pancoast came around, trying to find the Rusty Santoro he had taught, but like the fog that Rusty was also gone. Now there was only a quiet, dark-eyed boy who wanted peace. Too much peace.

Then one day he left.

He took a few things with him and he kissed Moms in the night, late in the night when the city was almost asleep—for the city never completely sleeps, but spins its web by night and by day—and he left. He went silently down to the street, and he stood staring at the wet-shine the water trucks had left behind when they tried vainly to clean the gutters. He looked up and saw the night of deep blue and the stars of white, and he walked away.

He walked past Tom-Tom's place, all empty and dark now, with no juke box and no stamping feet and no harsh voices. All empty, the way he was empty inside.

The street echoed back his hollowly beating footsteps, as he walked the pavement, seeing it all clearly, in retrospect. He had come from these streets, and he would someday go back to these streets, for he was umbilically joined to them and the rottenness they spawned. There was no escaping it, no getting away from it. But somehow there must be a way of fending it off for a short time.

A catalyst, some hindering factor, some buttressing force that could intercede. He had found the death and the violence and the stupidity of this life—now he had to find his way out of it. At least for a while. He had to go away and search for something insubstantial.

Decency? Was that it? Was that what he wanted? He didn't

know. Perhaps that was the word and the act and the insubstantial
he sought. But he knew one thing. There was quiet in him now.
There was no longer any anger, no hurt, no frustration. It was
all quiet, too quiet, inside him.

A quiet that these streets would not long tolerate.

Candle would end his days in some prison, it was as certain
as a token in the turnstile or no ride. But so what if one Candle
was gone, or one Beast was dead, or one Morlan had been halted?
There would be others. There had to be others. For where the
dirt and the hunger and the anger bred violence, there would
be human flies to feast on the carcasses of the weaker. As those
flies themselves were caught up in the city's suffocating web.

No, to find what it was he sought—and he had no way of
knowing what it was he sought—he must get away from here.
Not to run in fright, not to be alone, but just because there was
nothing here. These streets had held him long enough. Now
they were wasteland.

Here there was only the web and the knife and his fists.

He had sworn he would never raise his hands to anyone again.
But what good was that promise if he remained here? No good,
for the streets had their own rules, and you could not beat them.
You could only pass, and hope to escape that final jackpot. The
jackpot that bound you once more into the web. So he had to
go away.

He took the subway to Times Square and he got off and
walked past the glaring, neoned, never-asleep squares that beckoned him—and he ignored them. He walked till he came to the
movie where he had picked up the girl. How long ago was it?
Weeks? Years? Eternities? He had no way of gauging the time.
Not only had things happened, but he had become a different
person since then. He had changed so very much, and lost so
much, and found nothing to replace it.

He stood in front of the theater and waited.

He did not know if it would be a good thing or a bad thing or just another emptiness, but he knew he wanted to do it this way. She was lonely, too. She was alone and empty and tired and together they might find that insubstantial he sought. They were both alone, but at least it was better to be alone together. What had been her name? Teresa? Yes.

She would come back to that movie one night. He knew that. She would, because she had his coin and she would have to. He did not know why he knew, but he was sure.

So he left his neighborhood and he left his streets and soon he would leave his city—which held the life that had been Rusty Santoro.

All that, behind him.

But oddly, the city did not care at all.

NO WAY OUT

Originally published (as "Gutter Gang")
in the September, 1957 issue of
Guilty Detective Story Magazine

Rusty choked as the chisel bit into the leg of wood, sprayed sawdust across his face and T-shirt. He puffed air between his thin lips, continued working, and continued to ignore the stout boy who stood behind him.

The wood shop had quieted down. No one else moved, and their tools were silent. Only the constant machine-hum of lathes that had been ignored, left running, filled the shop with sound. Yet somehow the room was silent.

The boy behind Rusty took a short half-step closer, shoved his shoulder hard. Rusty was thrown off-balance, and the chisel bit too deep into the chair leg between the lathe points. The design was ruined. The chisel snapped away, and Rusty spun, anger flaming his face. He stared hard at the other boy, changed his grip on the wood chisel.

Now he held it underhand—knife-style.

The other boy didn't move.

"What's a'matter, spick? Y'don't wanna talk to your old buddy Candle no more?" His thick, square face drew up in a wild grimace.

Rusty Santoro's face tightened. His thin line of mouth jerked with the effort to keep words from spewing out. He had known the Cougars would try to get to him today, but he hadn't figured on it during school hours.

Over him, somehow—tense as he was, knowing a stand was here and he couldn't run without being chick-chick—Rusty felt the brick-and-steel bulk of Pulaski High School.

You just can't run away from them, he thought.

The boy Candle had come into the basement wood shop a minute before. He had told the shop teacher, Mr. Pancoast, that he was wanted in the Principal's office. Mr. Pancoast had left the shop untended—oh, Kammy Josephs was monitor, but hell, that didn't cut any ice with *anyone*—and Candle had moved in fast. First the little nudge. Then the dirty names. Then the shove that could not be ignored. Now they were face-to-face, Rusty with the sharp wood chisel, and Candle with a blade. Some place. Somewhere. It wasn't in sight, but Candle had a switch on him. That boy wouldn't leave home without being heeled.

Rusty looked across into Candle's eyes. His own gray ones were level and wide. "You call me spick, craphead?"

Candle's square jaw moved idly, as though he were chewing gum. "Ain't that what you are, man? Ain't you a Puerto? You look like a *spick…*"

Rusty didn't wait for the sentence to linger in the air. He lunged quickly, slashing upward with the chisel. The shank zipped close to Candle, and the boy sucked in his belly, leaped backward. Then the switchblade was in his square, short-fingered hand.

The blade was there, and it filled the room for Rusty. It was all live and flashing, everything that was, and the end to everything else. Rusty Santoro watched—as though what was about to happen was moving through heavy syrup, slow, terribly slow—and saw Candle's hairy arm come up, the knife clutched tightly between white fingers. He heard the *snick* of the opening blade, even as the other's thumb shoved the button.

Then there was a green plastic shank, and a strip of light that was honed steel.

The shop was washed by bands of lazy sunlight slanting through the barred windows; and in those bands of light, with sawdust motes rising and turning slowly, Rusty saw the blade of the switch gleam. Saw it turn in Candle's hand, saw the way his flesh cleaved to it with more than need; this was part of Candle. Part of his thoughts and part of his life. His hand had been formed to end in a knife. Anything else would have been wrong, all wrong.

He heard himself speaking. "Don't you ever call me that again, man. Just don't you call me no spick again!"

Candle dropped his shoulders slightly. He automatically assumed the stance of the street-fighter. No spick bastard was going to buck him. There was more to this than just a wood chisel. Nobody, but nobody, leaves the gang.

"Well, ain't you gettin' big these days! One minute you're too good for the Cougars, and the next you're particular who calls ya what." His green eyes narrowed, and the knife moved in aimless, circling movements, as though it were a snake, all too anxious to strike.

"I don't dig you, spick man…"

And he whaled in.

The knife came out and up and around in one movement that was all lightning and swiftness. Rusty slipped sidewise, lost his footing and went down, his shoulder striking hard against the base of the lathe. He saw Candle strut back and get ready to pounce. Then there was all that knife in his vision, and he knew he was going to get it at last. Not later, not sometime never, but here, gutted and cut, right here on the floor, and there was nothing he could do about it.

Candle rose high, and his arm drew back, and then his arm was dragged back of his head by someone else. Rusty looked up and everything was out of focus, and his head hurt; but a man with dull red hair had Candle around the throat, had the knife-hand bent back double. Candle screamed high and loud, over the whine of the machines, and the man twisted the arm an inch more.

The blade clattered to the floor.

The man kicked it out of sight under a drill press, into saw-dust debris. Then the man had Candle by the front of his dirty T-shirt, was leaning in close, and saying, "You get the hell out of here, or I'll turn you over to the Principal. I'll tell him you lied to get me out of my shop while you attacked a pupil with a switch. With your record around here, Shaster, you couldn't stand it. Now beat it!" He shoved Candle Shaster away from him, sent him spinning into the door.

Candle threw it open, and was gone in a moment.

Rusty still found himself unable to focus properly, but Mr. Pancoast was lifting him to his feet and yelling to the other boys, "Okay, let's get back to work."

The rising clatter of shop work filled his universe, and then he was out in the basement hall, in the cool depths of the school. "Sit down," Pancoast directed him, pushing him gently toward the stairs.

Rusty sat down heavily, felt the incessant throbbing in his shoulder, and for the first time realized he had struck his head also. It throbbed mercilessly.

Pancoast slid down next to the boy. He was a short man, with hair just a few shades darker than orange. His face was tired, but there was something alive in his eyes that gave the lie to his features. He had been dealing with high-school boys so long that he had difficulty with adults, so geared to the adolescent mind were his thoughts.

He pursed his lips, then asked, "What was that all about, Rusty? I thought after that last scrape you were going to stay away from the Cougars, from Candle and his bunch."

Rusty Santoro tapped gently at the bruise that ached on his head. He swung his body back and forth, as though he were caught in some tremor that would not release him. His entire body shook. The after-effects were setting in; they always did, just this way. He shook and quivered and wished he'd never heard of the Cougars.

"I told 'em I was quitting. Yesterday. They don't like that. They tell me nobody leaves the gang. I said *I* did."

Pancoast rubbed the short stubble on his small chin. He stared levelly at Rusty. "That's all, Rusty?"

"Isn't that enough?"

Pancoast replied, "Look, Rusty. When they caught you, along with those other Cougars, trying to break into that liquor store, I went out for you. Remember?" He waited for an answer. Finally, Rusty nodded his remembrance.

The teacher went on. "I had them release you into my custody, Rusty, and you've been good as your word ever since. At first I thought you were like all the rest of them—hard, no real guts, just a little killer inside—but you've shown me you're a man. You've got real woodworking talent, Rusty. You could be a sculptor, or a designer, even an architect, if you wanted to be."

Rusty was impatient. Being praised like this, in the crowd he ran with, usually meant a slap was coming. "So?"

"So, we're *both* going to have to go over there, Rusty, and let them know for sure that you're out of the gang, that you don't want any part of it."

Rusty shook his head. "It ain't that easy. You don't understand, Mr. Pancoast. It ain't like being a member of Kiwanis or the P.T.A. It ain't like nothin' else in the world. When you're in, you're in. And the only thing that gets you out is if you land in the can, or you get a shank in your gut. That's what I tried to tell ya when ya made me quit."

He stared at the teacher with mute appeal. He was boxed in, and he knew it. There was going to have to be a face-up soon, and he wasn't sure he was man enough.

Carl Pancoast leaned closer to the boy, put an arm on his

knee, tried to speak to him so the words went deeper than the ears. So they went right down to the core. He *had* to make it with this kid. There had been too many others who had come by him, like lights in the night, and he had never reached out to take that light in his hands, to stop it from rushing down that road to destruction. He had tried with Rusty Santoro—a good boy, a damned good boy—and he wasn't going to fail now.

"Look, Rusty. Let me tell you something. You can go on doing what the Cougars do, all your life, and wind up the way Tony Green did. You knew Tony. You remember what happened to him?"

Pancoast could see the memory in Rusty's eyes. He could see the vision of Tony Green, who had been top trackman at Pulaski, laid out on a slab, with a D.O.A. tag around his big toe. A zip gun .22 slug in his head. Dead in a rumble.

"Remember why he got killed, Rusty?"

Pancoast was pushing thoughts tightly, forcing them to the fore, making Rusty analyze his past. It wasn't a pleasant past.

Drenched in violence. Product of filth and slum and bigotry. Mothered by fear. Fathered by the terror of nonconformity and the fate that waited for those who did not conform. Rusty remembered. His stomach tightened, and his seventeen-year-old brain spun, but he remembered.

Tony Green, tall and slim and dead. Stretched out on a slab, because someone had danced with his steady girl at a club drag. Nothing more important. Just that.

"I'm through, Mr. Pancoast. You don't have to worry about that. I'm through, but man, it's gonna be rough all the way."

Carl Pancoast clapped the boy on the back. It would be tough all right, tough as banana skins, but that was the way it had to be. Not only for himself—and god knows he had a stake in this boy; his own redemption for the sins of failure he had committed with other boys—but for Rusty. Because Rusty had to live out there in that stinking city. He had to live and learn and sweat beside those kids.

But, Carl Pancoast swore inside himself, Rusty Santoro was going to come out of it whole. Come out of it with his guts and his mind intact. For Rusty, and for himself.

"What are you going to do?"

Rusty bit his lip, shrugged. "Don't know, man. But I got to do something. They ain't gonna give me much longer. Maybe I'll go over there tonight, club night. Maybe I'll go over and have a talk with some of the kids."

Pancoast's forehead assumed V-lines of worry. "Want me to go along? Most of the Cougars know me."

Rusty sloughed away his offer.

"No go. They know you, but you're still out of it, man. Way out. You're boss-type, and they don't dig that even a little. I come walking in with you, and I'm dead from the start…No, I can handle it."

He stood up unsteadily, clung to the banister for a minute. It rocked under his weight.

"Damned school," he mumbled, slamming the banister, "gonna fall apart under ya."

He walked back into the shop, and a minute later Pancoast heard the chisel on the ruined chair leg. Violently.

It's going to be rough, he thought. Real rough.

Rough as banana skins.

He went back to his class, worried as hell.

After school, Rusty avoided Mr. Pancoast. The teacher had done too much for him, and whatever was coming was going to have to come to him alone. Rusty slouched against the sooty brick wall of Pulaski High, and drew deeply on a cigarette. The kids avoided him; the stench of trouble was all about him.

Finally, Louise came out of the building, her books clutched tightly to her chest. She saw Rusty, and stopped. Rusty knew what was pelting around inside her head. Should she go to join her steady, walk home with him, stop to have a Coke with him? Or should she walk past and get the hell away from what might be coming?

It was a big choice. One way she would lose Rusty—he was like that, just like that—and the other, she might lose her pretty face. It was tough all right.

Rusty knew what was happening within her, and he abruptly felt so alone, so terribly, desperately alone; he had to remove the burden of decision from her, had to hold on to one person in this thing...if only for a short while. He pushed away from the wall, walked over to her.

"Wanna stop for a Coke, Weezee?"

Louise Chaplin, more "Weezee" than Louise, was a highly attractive girl, with the natural features that made up her beauty marred by imperfect application of makeup. Her eyes were a clear blue, her skin smooth, her hair a rich chestnut brown, drawn back into a full, rippling ponytail. Her young body was already making attractive bulges and curved areas within her sweater and skirt. She was aware of the growing body, and so the sweater was a size too small.

Now her eyes darkened and she blinked rapidly, pausing a moment before answering—an agonizing moment for Rusty—finally answering, "Sure. Guess so. What's new?"

It was like that all the way down the street.

Chitchat. She was scared. Really, terribly scared, and though Weezee wasn't a member of the Cougars' girl auxiliary, the Cougie Cats, she was still in Cougar turf, and if a war started, she would be one of the first to get it. Right after Rusty.

The streets were crowded. Late Friday afternoon, with fat Polish women going from butcher to butcher, trying to get the best cuts of meat for the weekend; little kids playing hopscotch and baseball on sidewalks, against walls; radios blasting from every direction with the Giants or the Dodgers beating the pants off someone. Normal day, with the sun shining, with gutters dirtied by candy wrappers and dogs that had been curbed, with the sound of the subway underfoot, with everything normal. Including the stink of death that hung not unknown above everything else.

It was funny how the territory—the turf—knew when something was burning. Even the old women in their antimacassared single rooms, waiting for their government checks, knew the gangs were about to rise. The shopkeepers knew it, and they feared for their windows. The cops knew it, and they began to straighten in harness. The cabbies knew it, and they shifted territories, hurrying back downtown to catch the Madison Avenue crowd.

Everyone knew it, yet a word was never spoken, an action never completed. It hung rank in the air, dampening everyone's mood of the weekend joviality. Rusty walked through it, dragging his feet as if he were under water.

Weezee walked along beside him, clutching her books to her firm young breasts too tightly, till her fingers whitened on the notebook. The scare was so high in her, it came out of her pores, and Rusty wished he had not approached her. No sense dragging her into this.

But at the same time, he was perversely glad she was there; he was determined to make *her* sweat, if *he* had to sweat. They turned in at Tom-Tom's Ice Cream Parlor. Rusty gave the place a quick look-over before entering, and then pushed open one of the wooden doors with the glass almost covered by soft drink advertisements. They walked past the counter, past the magazine racks, to the booths in the back.

Weezee slipped into one far back, and, even as Rusty watched, she drew in on herself, slid closer to the wall, made herself ready for what *had* to come.

Rusty sat down across from her, two-fingered a cigarette from the pack in his jacket pocket. He offered it to the girl, but she shook her head slowly. He lit it with a kitchen match and settled back, one foot up on the bench, watching her steadily.

Finally, Tom-Tom came back to get their order.

He was a stubby man, built like a beachball, with rolls of baby fat under his chin where a neck should have been but was not. He had been in the neighborhood a long time, and his hair was white, but his appearance was always the same. So was his service. Bad.

Rusty looked across at Weezee. "Coke?" She nodded. "Make it a pair," he said to Tom-Tom.

The beachball rolled away, shaking its head; these damned kids sat here for three hours over one lousy Coke, and if he tried to bounce them he'd get a staved-in candy counter for his trouble. Damned neighborhood. One of these days, he was going to move, open a high-class little shop down in the Village somewhere.

Rusty sat silently watching his girl. Weezee bit her red, red lips, and her hands moved nervously. Finally she asked, "Why are you quitting the Cougars?"

Rusty made a vague movement with his hand, uneasy that she had broken the law: she had let her feelings be known, had asked him a straight question he could not goof out of answering. "Dunno. Just tired, I guess."

Her face grew rigid. "It's that goddamned teacher, that Pancoast, isn't it?" she asked.

Rusty leaned forward an inch, said tightly, "Just forget about him. He's okay. He saved my tail from the can a month ago, that's all I know."

"But it *is* him, isn't it?"

"For Christ's sake, can't you knock it off? I just quit because I wanted to, and that's it, period."

She shook her head in bewilderment. "But you were prez of the Cougars for three years. They ain't gonna like you leeching out that way."

"That's their row to hoe."

She tried desperately to pierce the shield he had erected around himself. What he was doing was suicide, and she felt a desperate need to communicate with him, to get him to see what he was doing to himself…and to her. For as Rusty's drag, she was as marked as he.

"Are you chick-chick?"

Rusty slammed forward against the table. His hand came down flat with a smash, and his eyes burned fiercely. "Look, don't you never call me that, understand? I'm no more chickie than anybody else." His face smoothed out slowly, the anger ebbed away even more slowly.

Finally he added, "Weezee, I been runnin' the streets with the Cougars for three years. I got in lots of trouble with 'em. Look at me. I'm seventeen, an' I got a record. Nice thing to have? Like hell it is! I been usin' my fists since I could talk, and I'm just up to here with it, and that's on the square. I just want out, is all."

The girl shook her head. The brown hair swirled in its pony-tail, and she began twirling it nervously. "They're gonna make it rough on you, Rusty."

He nodded silently.

Tom-Tom brought the Cokes, collected the two dimes Rusty laid out, and went back to his fountain.

Five minutes later, they arrived.

Not the entire gang, just ten of them. With Candle in the front. Many of Rusty's old buddies were there—Fish, Clipper, Johnny Slice, even the kid they called the Beast—and they all had the same look in their eyes. All but the Beast. He was half-animal, only half-human, and what he had behind *his* eyes, no one knew. But all the rest saw Rusty as an enemy now. Two days before he had been their leader, but now the lines had changed and Rusty was on the outside.

Why did I come here with Weezee? Why didn't I go straight home? His thoughts spun and whirled and ate at him. They answered themselves immediately: there were several reasons. He had to prove he wasn't chicken, both to himself and to everyone else. That was part of it, deep inside. There were worse things than being dead, and being chicken was one of them. Then too, he knew that running and hiding were no good. Start running—do it once—and it would never stop. And the days in fear would be all the worse.

That was why he was here, and that was why he would have to face up to them.

Candle made the first move.

He stepped forward, and before either of them could say anything, he had slid into the booth beside Weezee. The boy's face was hard, and the square, flat, almost-Mongoloid look of it was frightening. Rusty made a tentative move forward, to get Candle away from his girl, but three Cougars stepped in quickly and pinned his arms.

One of them brought a fist close to Rusty's left ear, and the boy heard a click. He caught the blade's gleam from the corner of his eye.

"Whaddaya want?" Rusty snarled, straining against their hands.

Candle leaned across, folding his arms, and his face broke into a smile that was straight from hell. "I didn't get called onna carpet by Pancoast. He kept his mouth shut."

"Why don't you?" Rusty replied sharply.

Candle's hand came up off the table quickly, and landed full across Rusty's jaw. The boy's head jerked, but he stared straight at the other. His eyes were hard, even though a five-pronged mark of red lived on his cheek.

"Listen, teacher's pet. That bit this mornin' was just a start. We had us a talk in the Cougars, after I was elected prez, after you ran out on us like a—"

Rusty cut in abruptly. "What's it all about, big mouth? What's your beef? You weren't nothin' in the gang till I left, now you think you're god or somethin'."

This time it was a double-fisted crack, once, twice, and blood erupted from Rusty's mouth. His lip puffed, and his teeth felt slippery wet.

"I'll hand all that back to you real soon, big deal." But Rusty was held tightly.

"Nobody checks out on the gang, y'understand?" He nodded to one of the boys holding Rusty's left hand, and the boy drew back. Candle's fist came out like a striking snake, and the fingers opened and grasped Rusty's hand tightly. Rusty flexed his hand, trying to break the grip; but Candle was there for keeps, and the knife was still at his ear. He let the other boy squeeze… and squeeze…and squeeze…and…

Rusty suddenly lunged sidewise, cracking his shoulder into the boy with the knife. The force of his movement drew Candle partially from the booth, and he released his grip.

Then Rusty moved swiftly, and his hand, flat and fingers tight together, slashed out, caught the boy with the knife across the Adam's apple. The boy gagged, and dropped the blade. In an instant it was in Rusty's hand, and he was around the booth, had the tip of the switchblade just behind Candle's ear.

"Now," he panted, trying to hold the knife steady, having difficulty with nervous jerks of his hand, "you're all gonna listen to me.

"I left the Cougars cause I'm through. That's all, and it doesn't gotta make sense to any of you. I'm out, and I want out to stay, and the first guy that tries to give me trouble, I'll cut him, so help me god!"

The other Cougars moved forward, as if to step in, but Candle's face had whitened, and his jaw worked loosely. "No, for Christ's sake, stay away from him!"

Rusty went on: "Listen, how long you figure I gotta run with this crowd? How long you figure I gotta keep gettin' myself in bad with the school, with my old lady, with the cops? You guys wanna do it, that's *your* deal, but leave me alone. I don't bother you. Just don't you bother me."

Fish—tall, and slim, with long eyelashes that made him think he was a lady's man—spoke up. "You been fed too much of that good jazz by that Pancoast cat, Rusty. You believe that stuff, man?"

Rusty edged the knife closer, the tip indenting the soft skin behind Candle's ear, as the seated prez tried to move. "He dealt me right all along. He says I got a chance to become an industrial designer if I work hard at it. I like the idea. That's the reason and that's it.

"Now whaddaya say? Lemme alone, and I let your big-deal prez alone."

At that instant, it all summed up for Rusty. That was it; that was why he was different from these others. He *wanted* a future. He *wanted* to be something. Not to wind up in a gutter with his belly split, and not to spend the rest of his life in the army— because that was where most of these guys were going to wind up finally.

He wanted a life that had some purpose. And even as he felt the vitality of the thoughts course through him, he saw the Cougars were ready to accept it. He had been with them for three years, and they had all rumbled together, all gotten records together, all screwed around and had fun together. But now, somehow, he had outgrown them.

And he wanted free.

Fish spoke for all of them. Softly, and with the first sincerity Rusty had ever heard from the boy. "I guess it sits okay with us, Rusty. Whatever you say goes. I'm off you." He turned to the others, and his face was abruptly back in its former mold. He was the child of the gutters; hard, and looking for opposition.

"That go for the rest of you?"

Each of them nodded. Some of them smiled. The Beast waggled his head like some lowing animal, and there was only one dissenter as Rusty broke the knife and tossed it to its owner.

Candle was out of the booth, and his own weapon was out. He walked forward, and backed Rusty into the wall with it. His face was flushed, and what Rusty had always known was in the boy—the sadism, the urge to fight, the animal hunger that was there and could never really be covered by a black leather jacket or chino slacks—was there on top, boiling up like a pool of lava, waiting to engulf both him and Rusty.

"I don't buy it, man. I think as long as you're around, the Cougars won't wanna take orders from their new prez. So there's gotta be a final on this. I challenge."

Rusty felt a sliver of cold, as sharp as the sliver of steel held by Candle, slither down into his gut. He had to stand with Candle. It was the only way. As long as you lived in a neighborhood where the fist was the law, there could be no doubt. Either you were chickie or you weren't. If an unanswered challenge hung around his neck like an albatross, his days on the street were numbered.

Slowly, hesitantly, he nodded agreement. Knowing he was slipping back. Knowing all the work Pancoast had done might be wasted. Knowing his future might wind up in the gutter with him.

"When?" he asked.

"Tomorrow, after school. Out at the dump. Come heeled, man, cause I'm gonna split you to your groin."

He broke his knife, shoved it into his sleeve, walked away angrily, shoving aside the Cougars. He was gone then, and the ice cream shop was silent for a long moment.

Then Fish shrugged, said lamely, "Gee, I'm—well, hell, Rusty, there ain't—"

Rusty cut him off, running a hand through his own hair. "I know, man. Don't bother. Ain't nothin' *you* can do. I gotta stand with Candle. Gonna be rough bananas though."

Why was his past always calling? Always making grabs on him? The blood was flowing so thick, so red, and it smothered him. He felt as though he was drowning.

Wouldn't he ever be free?

It was gonna be a rough week.

The next day went like a souped-up heap. The kids stayed away from Rusty like he was down with the blue botts, and even the teachers seemed to sense something was hot on the fire, because they didn't press him about his homework, or ask him to recite.

Rusty saw Candle only once during the day, and that was in the cafeteria. It was rugged inside him. He didn't want to fight. He wanted to leave the thing alone, and reconcile it with Candle. He had to talk to the boy. The hard-faced prez of the Cougars was sitting at a table with Joy, feeling her up, and laughing loudly with his side-boys. Rusty cut wide around them, and got a tray for himself. The food was the usual steam-table garbage, and he only took a peanut-butter-and-jelly sandwich, a piece of apple pie and a container of milk. He wasn't hungry, not at all.

Finally, when he had polished off the food, he got up, took the tray to the check-in window where a colored boy was scraping them with a rubber tool, and turned around.

Everyone was watching him. He realized suddenly that they had been watching him all through lunch. But he had been thinking as he ate, and had not noticed. Now they stared at him, and from the middle of the room he heard the derisive voice of a punk.

"Here chick-chick-chick-chick-chick! Cluck, cluck, cluck, cluck, cluck. Chick-chick-chick…" It went on and on, leaving the first boy, swinging to another, then pretty soon the entire room was carrying it, like a banner. The sound was a wave that washed against the shores of Rusty's mind. It was the worst. It was a chop low like no other he'd ever heard.

He had been top man of the Cougars for so long, to have this kind of indignity pushed on him was something frightful. He clenched his fists and stood where he was.

Behind him, he heard the colored boy disappearing from behind the window. If things were going to be heaved, *he* didn't want to be in the way.

Rusty knew he had to talk to Candle now. Now was the time, because if he spent the day with that chick-chick festering in his brain, he'd fight sure as hell!

Somebody yelled, "Oooooh, *Russell*! Oh, Russell, baby, do your hen imitation fer us! Go man, go, Russell!"

He hated that name. It was the first time they'd called him that since it had been abbreviated to Rusty.

The boy stepped slowly away from the window, and walked over to Candle's table. The Cougar's prez had been talking to his broad, not even looking at Rusty while the call had been going up. Now, as Rusty approached, he paid even more attention to

Joy, but the three side-boys stood up slowly, their hands going into the tight pockets of their jeans. There were shanks in there, waiting to cut if Rusty made a snipe move.

Rusty stopped. "Candle."

The boy with the almost-Mongoloid features did not look up. He had his hand clutched to the girl's knee, and he seemed totally oblivious to what was happening behind him. But Joy's blue eyes were up and frightened. She stared straight at Rusty, and the wild excitement in her face made him sick; they all wanted their boots. They all wanted kicks. They didn't care who got nailed, so long as sparks flew and they could bathe in them. Then Candle turned carefully around. He looked up.

"Well, read this," he said arrogantly, more to his side-boys than Rusty. "Check who just dropped in for a chat. Welcome, spick."

Rusty felt the blood surging in him, and he wanted to drive a fist straight into the bastard's mouth. But that was what Candle wanted. That would be the clincher. They'd slice him up like fresh bacon, right there, and everyone would dummy up. No one wanted the Cougars mad at them.

"Candle, I wanna talk to you," Rusty said softly.

The others grinned hugely, and Candle swung one foot up on to the bench, just touching the edge of Rusty's pants, putting a bit of dirt there.

"What you got to say to me you can say out at the dump after school, spick."

"Look, don't make it rougher than now," Rusty cautioned him. "I wanna knock this off. I don't feature the idea of a stand. I got enough trouble with the cops already. No sense my getting picked up and tossed in the farm."

Candle reared back and laughed. Loud. His voice cut off all the chickie-chickie around the room, and everyone waited to find out what would happen. They knew Rusty was no chicken, they knew he had been rough as prez of the Cougars, and did not understand what had changed him.

But they also knew Candle was a rough stud, and it would be top kicks to see these two go at each other.

"You don't wanna stand, man? You don't wanna come out and show all these kids you ain't yellow?" His grin grew wider as he grabbed a cardboard carton of milk, ripped open across the top. "That sits fine with me, man, but I still got a beef with you.

"So," he said, lifting the carton, "if you wanna bow out, I'll just settle my beef like *this*!" and he threw the milk at Rusty.

They laughed. The crowd burst into sound, and Rusty stood there with milk running down over his face, soaking quickly through his shirt and running down to his pants.

Before he could restrain himself, he had lunged, and had his hands around Candle's throat. The prez of the Cougars gave a violent gasp, and brought his own hands up in an inward swinging movement, breaking Rusty's grip. Then he choked out, "Grab— grab him!" and the side-boys had Rusty's arms pinned.

Candle swung over the bench and stood up. His face was a violent blued mask of hate. "Now you read this, man. I'm not gonna work you over like I should now. Mostly cause I want to have more time at you, without nobody holding you back, yellow-belly. So you be out at the dump after school, and we'll settle this down once and for all."

Then he shoved Rusty in the stomach, not hard enough to knock the boy out, but hard enough to suck the energy from him. Then he and his side-men walked away quickly.

Rusty stood there for a full five minutes, listening to the cackles and catcalls ringing around him.

He could not move.

There was no way free. He would fight and he would win. He would carve that sluggy sonofabitch from gut to kisser and leave him for the dump rats to chew on.

The ringing of the sixth-period bell brought him around abruptly, and he moved to his locker to get his books.

It was gonna be tough as banana peels.

Pancoast got to him just before school let out.

"Rusty, I heard what happened yesterday. You going out there?"

Rusty shifted from foot to foot. What could he say to him? He knew if he went out there and fought, he was throwing it all away. But he couldn't yank loose now if he wanted to, even though he knew it was the worst thing he could do.

"I—I *gotta*, Mr. Pancoast. I got into this, and if I don't finish it once and for all, they won't ever let me alone. One way or the other, I got to put a tail to this thing."

Pancoast shook his head, grabbed the boy by the biceps. "Listen to me, Rusty. Listen to me now.

"You've been doing real well. You've been growing with every day. You go out there and come down to their level, and you'll be right back where you started three months ago when I fished you out of jail. Do you understand?"

"I understand," Rusty said, not looking at him, "but it's gotta be this way. Final."

Pancoast dropped his grip. His voice got steely hard. "I'll call the police, Rusty. I'll come out there with them and stop it."

Rusty looked up at the man, and a warm bond of friendship —and more—existed between them. He knew he might sever that bond with what he was about to say, but he had to say it nonetheless.

"You come out there, or you call the fuzz, and I'll cut you off even myself."

Pancoast had been around the kids long enough. He knew that "cutting off even" was tantamount to a threat of revenge.

He said nothing, but his eyes were filled with a nameless

hurt. His hands moved aimlessly at his sides. Then he turned and walked away.

Rusty was alone.

So damned, finally, horribly alone.

He walked out of the school, knowing two Cougars followed him. He moved down the street, and when Fish pulled alongside in his heap, Rusty was not surprised.

"Hey, man. They give me the word to bring you out. You know, like they told me." He was always alibiing, Rusty thought ruefully.

"Yeah. Yeah, I know. Just a job like."

"So like get in, huh, man?"

Rusty got into the car, and Fish waited while Tiger and the Greek got in the back seat. No one said a word; the car pulled away from the curb, swung out into traffic heading uptown toward the dump.

Rusty was scared, and his mouth was dry.

At least the knife in his shoe felt reassuring.

But not much.

As they passed the burning piles of garbage and refuse, the sky darkened appreciably. It was still early, not quite four yet, but the day seemed blacker than any Rusty could remember.

Fish tooled the beat-up Plymouth along the bumpy road, avoiding chuck holes and pits in the packed dirt. "One of these days, dammit, I'm gonna crack a parts shop and get me enough cams and crap to juice up this buggy."

Rusty didn't answer. He had more important things to worry about.

If he chickened here, he would not only have to ward off the antagonism of the neighborhood for the rest of his days—that was minor compared to what else would happen. Dolo would have to live him down, and that could mean any number of

things in the streets. She might have to get more deeply involved with the Cougie Cats and their illegal activities. He had
gotten Dolores into the Cougie Cats at her own request, and
even though she was his sister, or perhaps *because* of it, he
would have to watch out for her as much as himself. She was in
the gang for keeps; she liked it, liked the excitement of it. So he
had to make sure her row wasn't as hard as his own to hoe. If *he*
had trouble, he had to make certain she didn't get the stick side
of it.

It surprised him, suddenly, that he should think of his sister.
She meant a great deal to him, and yet he hardly gave her a
thought; the gang had taken up too much of his time. But she
figured in this big. He had to watch himself. And then his ma.
She would be bugged in the street. His old man…

That crumbum wouldn't have to worry, but if he was here,
maybe he could have done something, maybe he could have
helped. Rusty set those bitter thoughts aside. Pa Santoro was a
wine-gut, and there was no help coming from *that* angle.

The heap pulled around a bend, and Rusty saw a dozen or so
cars all drawn into a circle, their noses pointed into the center.
The place was crawling with kids, and a great cheer went up as
they saw him in the front seat.

Rusty's belly constricted. He didn't want to fight Candle; he
didn't want to fight anybody. He wanted to go home and lie down,
put on some records and lay very very still. His belly ached.

Fish took off at top speed around the ring of cars, spraying
dirt in a wide wedge as he rounded the circle on two wheels. It
was all Rusty needed to finish the nerve-job on him. He leaned
against the right side of the car, and puked so hard he thought
the tendons in his neck would split.

Fish was spinning the wheel as Rusty came up with it, and
his eyes bugged. "Hey, man! What the hell ya doin'?"

He slammed his foot on to the brake pedal and the Plymouth

ground to a skittering halt, the tires biting deep into the dirt of the dump grounds and spinning wildly.

The car stalled, and Fish was out, around the other side and opening the door in an instant. He grabbed Rusty by the collar of the boy's jacket, and hauled him bodily from the car.

The kids were running over from the circle, violence lighting up their faces. What was happening there? This was a real kick!

Fish pulled Rusty down and the Puerto Rican boy fell to his knees in the dirt, Fish still clinging to his jacket. He began dry-vomiting, hacking in choking spasms.

Finally he slapped Fish's hand away, and laid his palms flat on the ground, tried to push himself up; it took three cockeyed pushes till he was standing unsteadily. Everything was fuzzy around the edges and he could only vaguely hear the jeers coming from the crowd.

"Man, what a punk *he* turned into!"

"Chicken all the way. No guts."

"Candle's gonna slice you up good, wait an' see."

Every face was one face; every body was a gigantic many-legged body. He was swaying, and he felt a hand shoved into his back, and, "Stand up, fer chrissakes!"

His throat chugged and he thought for an instant he was going to bring up what little of his lunch was left lying uneasily in his stomach. But it passed as he gulped deeply, and he began to get a clear picture of what was around him.

He saw all the faces. Poop and Boy-O, Margie, Connie, Cherry, Fish beside him looking angry and worried at the same time, Shamey, the Beast, Greek, Candle with his eyes bright and daring, and—he stopped thinking for a moment, when he saw her.

Weezee. She was here too. Who had brought her?

He started forward in her direction, but Candle moved in and stopped him. "She came with me. I brought her. Any complaints?"

Before he could answer, Weezee started to say something. "I couldn't help it, Rusty. He saw me—"

"Shaddup!" Candle snapped over his shoulder. He turned back to Rusty. "You got any beefs, you can settle 'em the knife way."

The sickness and the fear had passed abruptly. Rusty was quite cold and detached now. If it was a stand Candle wanted, all the rest of these sluggy bastards wanted, then that was what they'd get. Right now.

"Who's got the hankie?" he yelled.

Magically, a handkerchief fluttered down on to the ground between the two boys. Neither touched it. Candle's arm moved idly in his sleeve, and the switchblade dropped into his hand. Even as he pressed the stud and the bright blade flicked up, Rusty was bending sharply, and he came erect with his own weapon in his fist, already open.

They faced each other across the white handkerchief, and then Candle watched stonily as Rusty bent down and picked it up. From the crowd cries of "Get him! Sling him!" and, once in a while, "Go, go, go, chickie-man!" rang out.

Rusty shook out the hankie and put one corner in his mouth, wadding it slightly behind his clenched teeth. He extended the opposite corner to Candle delicately, and when Candle took it, his eyes were sharp on Rusty's own.

Caution: when you knife fight, don't bother watching the knife as much as the other guy's eyes. *They* tell when he's gonna strike.

Candle knew it, and took the hankie in his mouth with care. He maneuvered his tongue and teeth a bit till the cloth was settled properly. They were separated across a two foot restraining line of taut cloth, their backs arched, their bodies curved to put them as far away at swinging level as possible.

Then they circled.

Keeping the knife tight in the fist, keeping the hankie tight in their mouths, they stirred the dust with their heavy stomping shoes as they walked around each other.

Then Rusty swung.

He came out with the blade from the right, swinging hard and flat-stepping in. Candle jumped back, sucking in his belly just as the knife zipped past. Rusty sliced nothing but air. Then *he* was off-balance, and Candle jumped, bringing the blade up from underneath in a splitting swing. Rusty careened sidewise, dragging Candle with him, and the knife lanced past the Puerto Rican's right shoulder.

Circling again, circling carefully as Candle bit down harder on the hankie, and Rusty made a fist with his free hand. They moved around each other slowly, like two tigers smelling each other's spoor.

Every few seconds one would make a sharp, starting movement, and the other would leap back, dragging the other with him. They were feeling each other out.

Suddenly Candle cut sidewise, let the hankie loosen and sag in the middle, and he was in close. One arm snaked around Rusty's shoulder, and his knife arm came back for the kill.

Rusty screamed loudly through the hankie, and twisted hard, throwing his hip into Candle. The stout boy was rocked by the blow, and fell back. Then Rusty was on him.

The knife came up once…

…and down once.

And Candle was through fighting.

Rusty stood looking down at the boy. The blood had begun to stain the ground around him, and a fine trickle emerged from the Mongoloid mouth. Candle died as he watched, with a sucking gasp and open, staring eyes.

There it was. All laid out cold and empty. There it was, and Rusty knew he was trapped again. Knew he was boxed in and nailed shut again. He had almost been free, but now the truth of it all came to him.

There was *no* freedom in these deadly streets. The kids of the gutter gang were never *really* free. There was always a claim, a tag, a rescinding order that canceled their freedom.

From close by he heard the wail of police sirens. Had Pancoast called them, or had a passer-by seen the kids and phoned in? Maybe a million answers, but none of them mattered. He was caught, and there was only one way out.

With a leaden heart he said, "Listen, listen to me." The Cougars and the Cougie Cats looked at him with renewed respect as he buried the knife in a pile of garbage where it could not be found.

"I'm prez of the Cougars again, see. An' nobody, but *nobody*, talks about this. We just found him out here. The gang that did it ran away. Got that?

"Listen to me and we'll be okay. We'll get away free."

They nodded. It would be all right; but *was* it all right? They would not go to jail—at least not now—but the deadly streets had called them back once more.

They knew inside them what it meant.

The gutters had claimed their own.

NO GAME FOR CHILDREN

*Originally published in the
May, 1959 issue of* Rogue

Herbert Mestman was forty-one years old. He was six feet two inches tall and had suffered from one of the innumerable children's diseases at the age of seven, leaving him with a build that was decidedly sink-chested and just barely slim to the point of emaciation. He had steel-gray hair and wore bifocals. It was his avocation, however, that most distinguished him from all other men: Herbert Mestman knew more about Elizabethan drama than anyone else in the country. Perhaps even in the world.

He knew the prototypes and finest examples of that genre of drama known as the "chronicle history." He knew Marlowe and Shakespeare (and believed firmly the original spelling had been Shexpeer), he was on recitation terms with Dekker and Massinger. His familiarity with *Philaster* and Jonson's *The Alchemist* bordered on mania. He was, in essence, the perfect scholar of the drama of Elizabeth's period. No slightest scrap of vague biographical or bibliographical data escaped him; he had written the most complete biography—of what little was known —on the life of John Webster, with a lucid and fantastically brilliant errata handling all early versions of *The Duchess of Malfi*.

Herbert Mestman lived in a handsome residential section in an inexpensive but functional split-level he owned without mortgage. There are cases where erudition pays handsomely. His position with the University was such a case, coupled with his tie-up on the Britannica's staff.

He was married, and Margaret was his absolute soulmate. She was slim, with small breasts, naturally curly brown hair, and an accent only vaguely reminiscent of her native Kent. Her legs were long and her wit warmly dry. Her eyes were a moist brown and her mouth small. She was in every way a handsome and desirable woman.

Herbert Mestman led a sedentary life, a placid life, a life filled with the good things: Marlowe, Scarlatti, aquavit, Paul McCobb, Peter Van Bleeck, and Margaret.

He was a peaceful man. He had served as a desk adjutant to the Staff Judge Advocate of a small southern Army post during the Second World War, and had barely managed to put the Korean Conflict from his notice by burying himself in historical tomes. He abhorred violence in any form, despised the lurid moments of television and Walt Disney, and saved his money scrupulously, but he was not a miser.

He was well-liked in the neighborhood.

And—

Frenchie Murrow was seventeen years old. He was five feet eight inches tall and liked premium beer. He didn't know the diff, but he dug premium. He was broad in the shoulders and wasped at the waist. The broads dug him neat. He had brown hair that he wore duck-ass, with a little spit erupting from the front pompadour to fall Tony Curtis-lackadaisical over his forehead. He hit school when there wasn't any scene better to make, and his '51 Stude had a full-race cam coupled to a '55 Caddy engine. He had had to move back the fire wall to do the soup job, and every chromed part was kept free of dust and grease with fanatical care. The dual muffs sounded like a pair of mastiffs clearing their throats when he burned rubber scudding away from the Dairy Mart.

Frenchie dug Paul Anka and Ricky Nelson, Frankie Avalon and Bill Haley. His idols were Mickey Mantle, Burt Lancaster (and he firmly believed that was the way to treat women), Tom McCahill, and his big brother Ernie who was a specialist third class in Germany with the Third Infantry Division.

Frenchie Murrow lived in a handsome residential section in an inexpensive but functional split-level his old man had a double mortgage on. His old man had been a fullback for Duke many years before, and more green had been shelled out on the glass case in the den—to hold the trophies—than had been put into securities and the bank account.

Frenchie played it cool. He occasionally ran with a clique of rodders known as the Throttle-Boppers, and his slacks were pegged at a fantastic six inches, so that he had difficulty removing them at night.

He handled a switch with ease, because, like, man, he *knew* what he could do with it.

He was despised and feared in the neighborhood.

Herbert Mestman lived next door to Frenchie Murrow.

HERBERT MESTMAN

He caught the boy peering between the slats of the venetian blind late one Saturday night, and it was only the start of it.

"You, there! What are you doing there?"

The boy had bolted at the sound of his voice, and as his head had come up, Mestman had shone the big flashlight directly into the face. It was that Bruce Murrow, the kid from next door, with his roaring hot rod all the time.

Then Murrow had disappeared around the corner of the house, and Herb Mestman stood on the damp grass peculiarly puzzled and angry.

"Why, the shitty little Peeping Tom," he heard himself exclaim. And, brandishing the big eight-cell battery, he strode around the hedge, into Arthur Murrow's front yard.

Margaret had been right there in the bedroom. She had been undressing slowly, after a wonderful evening at the University's organ recital, and had paused nervously, calling to him softly: "Oh there, Herb."

He had come in from the bathroom, where the water still ran into the sink; he carried a toothbrush spread with paste. "Yes, dear?"

"Herb, you're going to think I'm barmy, but I could swear someone is looking through the window." She stood in the center of the bedroom, her slip in her hand, and made an infinitesimal head movement toward the venetian blind. She made no move to cover herself.

"Out there, Margaret? Someone out there?" A ring of fascinated annoyance sounded in his voice. It was a new conception; who would be peering through his bedroom window? Correction: his and his *wife's* bedroom window. "Stay here a moment, dear. Put on your robe, but don't leave the room."

He went back into the hall, slipped into the guest room and found an old pair of paint-spattered pants in the spare closet. He slipped them on, and made his way through the house to the basement steps. He descended and quickly found the long flashlight.

Upstairs once more, he opened the front door gingerly, and stepped into the darkness. He had made his way through the dew-lipped grass around the house till he had seen the dark, dim form crouched there, face close to the pane of glass, peeking between the blind's slats.

Then he had called, flashed the light, and seen it was Arthur Murrow's boy, the one they called Frenchie.

Now he stood rapping conservatively but brusquely on the front door that was identical to his own. From within he could hear the sounds of someone moving about. Murrow's house showed black, dead windows. *They've either got that television going in the den, or they're in bed*, he thought ruefully. *Which is where I should be.* Then he added mentally, *That disgusting adolescent!*

A light went on in the living room, and Mestman saw a shape glide behind the draperies drawn across the picture window. Then there was a fumbling at the latch, and Arthur Murrow threw open the door.

He was a big man; big in the shoulders, and big in the hips, with the telltale potbelly of the ex-football star who has not done his seventy sit-ups every day since he graduated.

Murrow looked out blearily, and focused with some difficulty in the dark. Finally, "Uh? Yeah, what's up, Mestman?"

"I caught your son looking into my bedroom window a few minutes ago, Murrow. I'd like to talk to him if he's around."

"What's that? What are you talking about, your bedroom window? Bruce has been in bed for over an hour."

"I'd like to speak to him, Murrow."

"Well, goddammit, you're not going to speak to him! You know what time it is, Mestman? We don't *all* keep crazy hours like you professors. Some of us hold down nine-to-five jobs that make us beat! This whole thing is stupid. I saw Bruce go up to bed."

"Now listen to me, Mr. Murrow, I *saw*—"

Murrow's face grew beefy red. "Get the hell out of here, Mestman. I'm sick up to here," he slashed at his throat with a finger, "with you lousy intellectuals bothering us. I don't know what you're after, but we don't want any part of it. Now scram, before I deck you!"

The door slammed anticlimactically in Herbert Mestman's face. He stood there just long enough to see the shape retreat past the window, and the living-room light go off. As he made his way back to his own house, he saw another light go on in Murrow's house.

In the room occupied by Bruce.

The window, at jumping-height, was wide open.

FRENCHIE MURROW

Bruce Murrow tooled the Studelac into the curb, revved the engine twice to announce his arrival, and cut the ignition. He slid out of the car, pulling down at the too-tight crotch of his chinos, and walked across the sidewalk into the malt shop. The place was a bedlam of noise and moving bodies.

"Hey, Monkey!" he called to a slack-jawed boy in a stud-encrusted black leather jacket. The boy looked up from the comic book. "Like cool it, man. My ears, y'know? Sit." Frenchie slid into the booth opposite Monkey, and reached for the deck of butts lying beside the empty milk shake glass.

Without looking up from the comic book Monkey reached out and slapped the other's hand from the cigarettes. "You're old enough to smoke, you're old enough to buy yer own," he commented, thrusting the pack into his shirt pocket.

He went back to the comic.

Frenchie's face clouded, then cleared. This wasn't some stud punky from uptown. This was Monkey, and he was prez of the Laughing Princes. He had to play it cool with Monkey.

Besides, there was a reason to be nice to this creep. He needed him.

To get that Mestman cat next door.

Frenchie's thoughts returned to this morning, when the old man had accosted him on the way to the breakfast table:

"Were you outside last night?"

"Like when last night, Pop?"

"Don't play cute with me, Bruce. Were you over to Mestman's house, looking in his windows?"

"Man, I don't know what you're talkin' about."

"Don't call me 'man'! I'm your father!"

"Okay, so okay. Don't panic. I don't know nothin' about Mr. Mestman."

"You were in bed?"

"Like I was in bed. Right."

And that had been that. But can you imagine! That bastard Mestman, coming over and squeaking on him. Making trouble in the brood, just when the old man was forgetting the dough he'd had to lay out for that crack-up and the Dodge's busted grille. Well, nobody played the game with Frenchie Murrow and got away with it. He'd show that creep Mestman. So here he was, and there Monkey was, and—

"Hey, man, you wanna fall down on some laughs?"

Monkey did not look up. He turned the page slowly, and his brow furrowed at the challenge of the new set of pictures. "Like what kinda laughs?"

"How'd you like to heist a short?"

"Whose?"

"Does it matter? I mean, like a car's a car, man."

Monkey dropped the comic book. His Mongoloid face came up, and his intense little black eyes dug into Frenchie's blue ones. "What's with you, kid? You tryin' ta bust the scene? You want in the Princes, that it?"

"Hell, I—"

"Well, blow, Jack. We told ya couple times; you don't fit, man. We got our own bunch, we don't dig no cats from the other end of town. Blow, will ya? Ya bother me."

Frenchie got up and stared down at Monkey. This was part of it; these slobs. They ran the damned town, and they wouldn't take him in. He was as good as any of them. In fact, he was better.

Didn't he live in a bigger house? Didn't he have his own

souped short? Didn't he always have bread to spread around on the chicks? He felt like slipping his switch out of his high boot-top and sliding it into Monkey.

But the Laughing Princes were around, and they'd cream him good if he tried.

He left the malt shop. He'd show those slobs. He'd get old busybody Mestman himself. He wouldn't bother with just swiping Mestman's crate either. He'd really give him trouble.

Frenchie coasted around town for an hour, letting the fury build in him.

It was four thirty by the car's clock, and he knew he couldn't do anything in broad daylight. So he drove across town to Joannie's house. Her old lady was working the late shift at the pants factory, and she was minding the kid brother. He made sure the blinds were drawn.

Joannie thought it was the greatest thing ever came down the Pike. And only sixteen, too.

HERBERT MESTMAN

There was something about orange sherbet that made an evening festive. Despite the fact that no one these days ate real ice cream, that everyone was willing to settle for the imitation Dairy Squish stuff that was too sweet and had no real body, Herbert and his wife had found one small grocery that stocked orange sherbet—in plastic containers—especially for them. They devoured a pint of it every other night. It had become a very important thing to them.

Every other night at seven thirty, Herbert Mestman left his house and drove the sixteen blocks to the little grocery, just before it closed. There he bought his orange sherbet, and returned in time to catch the evening modern classics program pulled in on their FM, from New York City.

It was a constant pleasure to them.

This night was no different. He pulled the door closed behind him, walked to the carport, and climbed into the dusty Plymouth. He was not one for washing the car too often. It was to be driven, not to make an impression. He backed out of the drive and headed down the street.

Behind him, at the curb, two powerful headlamps cut on, and a car moved out of the darkness, following him.

It was not till he had started up the hill leading to that section of town called "The Bluffs" that Herbert realized he was being tailed. Even then he would have disbelieved any such possibility had he not glanced down at his speedometer and realized he was going ten miles over the legal limit on the narrow road. Was the car behind a police vehicle, pacing him? He slowed.

The other car slowed.

He grew worried. A twenty-dollar fine was nothing to look forward to. He pulled over, to allow the other car to pass. The other car stopped also. Then it was that he knew he was being followed.

The other car started up first however. And as he ground away from the shoulder, the town spreading out beneath the road on the right-hand slope, he sensed something terribly wrong.

The other car was gaining.

He speeded up himself, but it seemed as though he was standing still. The other car came up fast in his mirror, and, the next thing he knew, the left-hand lane was blocked by a dark shape. He threw a fast glance across, and in the dim lights of the other car's dash, he could see the adolescently devilish face of Frenchie Murrow.

So that was it! He could not fathom why the boy was doing this, but for whatever reason, he was endangering both their lives. As they sped up the road, around the blind curves, their headlight shafts shooting out into emptiness as they rounded each turn, Mestman felt the worm of terror begin its journey. They would crash. They would lock fenders and plummet over the side, through the flimsy guard railing…and it was hundreds of feet into the bowl below.

The town's lights winked dimly from black depths.

Or, and he knew it was going to be that, finally, a car would come *down* the—

Two spots of brightness merged with their own lights. A car was on its way down. He tried to speed up. The boy kept alongside.

And then the Studebaker was edging nearer. Coming closer, till he was sure they would scrape. But they did not touch. Mestman threw a glance across and it was as though hell shone out of Frenchie Murrow's young eyes. Then the road was illuminated by the car coming down, and Frenchie Murrow cut his car hard into Mestman's lane.

Herb Mestman slammed at the brake pedal. The Plymouth heaved and bucked like a live thing, screeched in the lane, and slowed.

Frenchie Murrow cut into the lane, and sped out of sight around the curve.

The bakery truck came down the hill and passed Mestman where he was stalled, with a gigantic whoosh!

FRENCHIE MURROW

This wasn't no game for kids, and at least old man Mestman realized that. He hadn't spilled the beans to Pop about that drag on the Bluffs Road. He had kept it under his lid, and if Frenchie had not hated Mestman so much—already identifying him as a symbol of authority and adult obnoxiousness—he would have respected him.

Frenchie held the cat aloft, and withdrew the switchblade from his boot-top.

The cat shrieked at the first slash, and writhed maniacally in the boy's grasp. But the third stroke did it, severing the head almost completely from the body.

Frenchie threw the dead cat onto Mestman's breezeway, where he had found it sleeping.

Let the old sonofabitch play with *that* for a while.

He cut out, and wound up downtown.

For a long moment he thought he was being watched, thought he recognized the old green Plymouth that had turned the corner as he paused before the entrance to the malt shop. But he put it from his mind, and went inside. The place was quite empty, except for the jerk. He climbed on to a stool and ordered a chocolate coke. Just enough to establish an alibi for the time; time enough to let Mestman find his scuddy cat.

He downed the chocoke and realized he wanted a beer real bad. So he walked out without paying, throwing at the jerk a particularly vicious string of curse words.

Who was that in the doorway across the street?

Frenchie saw a group of the Laughing Princes coming down the sidewalk, a block away. They were ranged in their usual belligerent formation, strung out across the cement so that anyone wanting past had to walk in the gutter. They looked too mean to play with today. He'd cut, and see 'em when they were mellower.

He broke into a hump, and rounded the corner. At Rooney's he turned in. Nine beers later he was ready for Mr. Wiseguy Mestman. Darkness lapped at the edge of the town.

He parked the Studebaker in his own folks' garage, and cut through the hedge to Mestman's house.

The French doors at the back of the house were open, and he slipped in without realizing he was doing it. A fog had descended across his thinking. There was a big beat down around his neck some place, and a snare drummer kept ti-ba-ba-ba-powing it till Frenchie wanted to snap his fingers, or get out the tire jack and belt someone or get that fraykin' cat and slice it again.

There was a woman in the living room.

He stood there, just inside the French doors, and watched her, the way her skirt was tight around her legs while she sat watching the TV. The way the dark line of her eyebrows rose at something funny there. He watched her and the fog swirled higher; he felt a great and uncontrollable wrenching in his gut.

He stepped out of the shadows of the dining room, into the half-light of the TV-illuminated living room.

She saw him all at once, and her hand flew to her mouth in reflex. "What do you—what…"

Her eyes were large and terrified, and her breasts rose and fell in spastic rhythm. He came toward her, only knowing this was a good-lookin' broad, only knowing that he hated that bastard Mestman with all his heart, only knowing what he knew he had to do to make the Princes think he was a rough stud.

He stumbled toward her, and his hand came out and clenched in the fabric of her blouse, and ripped down…

She was standing before him, her hands like claws, raking at him, while shriek after shriek after shriek cascaded down the walls.

He was going to rape her, damn her, damn her louse of a big-dome husband, he was going to…

Someone was banging at the door, and then he heard, ever so faintly, a key turning in the lock, and it was Mestman, and he bolted away, out the French doors, over the hedge, and into the garage, where he crouched down behind his Stude for a long time, shivering.

HERBERT MESTMAN

He tried to comfort her, though her hysteria was beginning to catch. He had followed the boy after he had come home and found the cat. Sir Epicure had been a fine animal; quick to take dislike, even quicker to be a friend. They had struck it off well, and the cat had been a warmth to Herbert Mestman.

First the peeping, then the trouble on the Bluffs Road, and so terribly this evening, Sir Epicure, and now—now—

This!

He felt his hands clenching into fists.

Herbert Mestman was a calm man, a decent man; but the game had been declared, and it was no game for children. He realized, despite his pacifist ways, there were lice that had to be condemned.

He huddled Margaret in her torn blouse closer to him, soothing her senselessly with senseless mouthings, while in his mind he made his decision.

FRENCHIE MURROW

Mornings had come and gone in a steady, heady stream of white-hot thoughtlessness. After that night, Frenchie had stayed away from Mestman and his house, from even the casual sight of Mestman's house. Somehow, and he was thankfully frightened about it, Mestman had not reported him.

Not that it would have done any good—there was no proof and no way of backing up the story, not really. A stray finger-print here or there didn't count too much when they lived next door and it might easily be thought that Bruce Murrow had come over at any time, and left them.

So Frenchie settled back into his routine.

Stealing hubcaps for pocket money.

Visiting Joannie when her old lady was swing-shifting it.

And then there were the Laughing Princes:

"Hey, man, you wanna get in the group?"

Frenchie was amazed. Out of a clear field of vision, this afternoon when he come into the malt shop, Monkey had broached the subject.

"Well, hell, I mean yeah, *sure!*"

"Okay, daddy, tell you what. You come on out to the chickie-run tonight, and we'll see you got gut enough to be a Prince. You dig?"

"I dig."

And here he was, close to midnight, with the great empty field stretching off before him, rippled with shadows where the lights of the cars did not penetrate.

It had been good bottom land, this field, in the days when the old city reservoir had used water deflected from the now-dry creek. Water deflected through the huge steel culvert pipe that rose up in the center of the field. The culvert was in a ditch ten feet deep, and the pipe still rose up several feet above the flat of the field. The ditch just before the pipe was still a good ten feet deep.

The cars were revving, readying for the chickie-run.

"Hey, you, Frenchie! Hey, c'mon over here!"

It was Monkey, and Frenchie climbed from his Stude, pulling at his chinos, wanting to look cool for the debs clustered around the many cars in the field. This was a big chickie-run, and his chance to become one of the Princes.

He walked into the group of young hot-rodders clustered off to one side, near a stunted grove of trees. He could feel everyone's eyes on him. There were perhaps fifteen of them.

"Now here's the rules," Monkey said. "Frenchie and Pooch and Jimmy get out there on either side of the road that runs over the cul. On the road is where I'll be, pacin' ya. And when Gloria"—he indicated a full-chested girl with a blonde pony-tail—"gives the signal, you race out, and head for that ditch, an' the cul. The last one who turns is the winner, the others are chickie. You dig?"

They all nodded, and Frenchie started to turn, to leave. To get back in his Stude and win this drag.

But the blonde girl stopped him, and with a hand on his arm, came over close, saying, "They promised me to the man who wins this run, Frenchie. I'd like to see you bug them other two. Win for me, will ya, baby?"

It sounded oddly brassy coming from such a young girl, but she was very close, and obviously wanted to be kissed, so Frenchie pulled her in close, and put his mouth to hers. Her lips opened and she kissed him with the hunger and ferocity of adolescent carnality.

Then he broke away, winking at her, and throwing over his shoulder, "Watch my dust, sweetheart," as he headed for the Stude.

A bunch of boys were milling about the car as he ran up.

"Good luck," one of them said, and a queer grin was stuck to his face. Frenchie shrugged. There were some oddballs in this batch, but he could avoid them when he was a full member.

He got in and revved the engine. It sounded good. He knew he could take them. His brakes were fine. He had them checked and tightened that afternoon.

Then Monkey was driving out on to the road that ran down the center of the old field, over the grade atop the culvert pipe. His Ford stopped, and he leaned out the window to yell at Gloria. "Okay, baby. Any time!"

The girl ran into the middle of the road as the three racers gunned their motors, inching at the start mark. They were like hungry beasts waiting to be unleashed.

Then she leaped in the air, came down waving a yellow bandana, and they were away, with great gusts of dirt and grass showing behind.

Frenchie slapped gears as though they were all one, and the Studelac jumped ahead. He decked the gas pedal and fed all the power he had to the engine.

On either side of him, the wind gibbering past their ears, the other two hunched over their wheels and plunged straight down the field toward the huge steel pipe and the deep trench before it.

Whoever turned was a chicken, that was the rule, and Frenchie was no coward. He knew that. Yet—

A guy could get killed. If he didn't stop in time, he'd rip right into that pipe, smash up completely at the speed they were doing.

The speedometer said eighty-five, and still he held it to the floor. They weren't going to turn. They weren't going...to... turn...damn...you...*turn!*

Then, abruptly, as the pipe grew huge in the windshield, on either side of him the other cars swerved, as though on a signal.

Frenchie knew he had won.

He slapped his foot on to the brake.

Nothing happened.

The speedometer read past ninety, and he wasn't stopping. He beat at it frantically, and then, when he saw there was no time to jump, no place to go, as the Studelac leaped the ditch and plunged out into nothingness, he threw one hand out the window, and his scream followed it.

The car hit with a gigantic whump and smash, and struck the pipe with such drive the entire front end was rammed through the driver's seat. Then it exploded.

It had been most disconcerting. That hand coming out the window. And the noise.

A man stepped out of the banked shadows at the base of the grove of trees. The fire from the culvert, licking toward the sky, lit his face in a mask of serene but satisfied crimson.

Monkey drove to the edge of the shadows, and walked up to the man standing there half-concealed.

"That was fine, son," said the tall man, reaching into his jacket for something. "That was fine.

"Here you are," he said, handing a sheaf of bills to the boy. "I think you will find that according to our agreement. And," he added, withdrawing another bill from the leather billfold, "here is an extra five dollars for that boy who took care of the brakes. You'll see that he gets it, won't you?"

Monkey took the money, saluted sloppily, and went back to his Ford. A roar and he was gone, back into the horde of hot-rods tearing away from the field, and the blazing furnace thrust down in the culvert ditch.

But for a long time, till he heard the wail of sirens far off but getting nearer, the most brilliant student of Elizabethan drama in the country, perhaps the world, stood in the shadows and watched fire eat at the sky.

It certainly was not—not at all—a game for children.

STAND STILL AND DIE!

Originally published in the September, 1956 issue of Guilty Detective Story Magazine

It wasn't pretty, the way they were beating him to death. They were using bricks.

I've been driving a hack in New York ever since I picked up a hunk of shrapnel in my elbow, on the backwash of the Yalu. I'd seen some pretty rough things in Korea, and I've seen some even rougher behind the wheel of that cab, but the way they were working that guy over—cool, smooth and without a wasted movement—made my throat dry out.

I turned my cab into 25th Street, off Second Avenue, a few blocks from the East River—I'd just taken an old-maid school-teacher home and was cutting back to the main drag—when my headlights caught the six of them.

There were five kids, all in black leather jackets, and a guy with a briefcase handcuffed to his wrist. The kids had him up against the wall of a clothing factory, and they were clipping him in the head and belly with those bricks. I roared down the street at them, going over the sidewalk to keep them in the beams, and honking my horn like mad.

When they heard me, they backed off, and the guy fell on his face. They thought that was a good deal, thought they could finish him quicker that way, and went back at him.

The kids started stomping him in the groin when he tried to struggle to his knees, then they kicked his head. They were wearing heavy army boots, and the guy on the sidewalk started bleeding. I could see it all as clearly as if it were daylight.

They must have figured they'd done all they could to the guy, because they bent down trying to get the briefcase off him. I saw one of the kids bring his foot down full on the guy's wrist.

I screeched the cab to a stop right beside them and hauled my Stillson wrench off the floor.

Then I was out the door and around the cab. "Hey!" I yelled, not actually thinking it would do any good, but what the hell, at least it would keep them off that bleeding slob on the sidewalk.

Two of them came at me, both with bricks in their hands. Those kids weren't sloppy street-fighters. They knew what they were doing. I'm a big boy, almost six-two, and they could see that; one came in high, the other low. The other three were busy breaking the guy's wrist, trying to get that briefcase off him.

The first kid was a puffy-nosed character, with long brown hair combed back into a duck's-fanny hairdo, and he swung his brick the long way, aiming it at my chops. I swiveled a hip, and tossed a foot out. He stumbled over it, and I only hesitated a moment before chopping him with the wrench. I didn't much care for the idea of clobbering a kid, but I saw the size of that brick, and my mind changed itself *so* fast!

The wrench caught him alongside the head and he yowled good and loud. Then he went down, spilling into the gutter just as his buddy smashed me in the middle with *his* brick!

It felt like someone'd overturned a cement wagon on me. The pain shot up my body, ran through my nerves, tingled in my fingertips, and numbed my legs, all at the same time. What a shot *that* kid was!

I spun aside, before he could get leverage for a second pot at me, and kicked out almost wildly. It was my numbed leg, and I wasn't quite sure what the damned thing would do. But it caught him on the knee, and his almost handsome face screwed up till he looked like I'd ripped out his liver. I took a short step and chopped him fast with the flat of my hand behind his ear. The kid moaned once and went down on one knee. I used my good leg and brought a knee up under the chin. A K.O. real fast; he went the way of his buddy.

I started to spin halfway around to get the other three. All I saw was the guy lying there, bleeding like a downed heifer, and two of the kids tearing that briefcase off him, swearing like Civil War veterans. I had about a half-second to wonder where the third punk was; then I found out real fast.

He was right beside me, with a sockful of quarters. They must have been quarters. Pennies wouldn't have put me to sleep that quickly. One full-bodied swipe.

I went down, and everything was ever so black.

Coming out of it was sicker than going down. I remembered when I had come to in the field hospital five miles from the front in Korea. I'd thought I was in a long white corridor, and somebody was calling my name, over and over, echoing down that long corridor of my mind for ever and ever.

That's what it was like. Someone was standing over me saying, "Campus, Campus, Campus," over and over again, and it was echoing in my head *so* loud.

I screwed my eyes shut as tight as I could, and right about then the little man turned on his trip hammer inside my skull. He was mining for gray matter, and I thought sure my brains would tumble out of my ears. "W-water," I managed to gasp.

A shadowy thing extended a tentacle, and there was a glass of water on the end of it. When another shadow propped me up, I let a little of the water slop into my mouth, and slowly my eyes sank back into my head. They cleared and I looked up into a four-day growth of beard.

The growth was on a cop. I shut my eyes carefully; the last thing on this Earth I wanted to see was a cop. "Go away," I muttered, getting a nauseating taste of my own raw-blood lips.

"You're Neal Campus, right?" he asked. His voice matched

his face. His face had been hard, rough, and grizzled. I looked up at him again.

"I wasn't doing more than fifty, so help me god!" That was when I realized I was in the hospital. "What the hell am I doing here?" I almost shouted. I tried to sit up, but someone on the other side of the bed that I hadn't seen before pushed me back.

I tossed a look at the guy—it was an interne—and it must have been a pretty vicious look, because he let go quick. I sat up again. "I said what the hell am I doing here?" I was so confused, I didn't realize I was fainting again till they all slid off my vision, and black gushed into my head.

The next time I came up the cops were gone and it was semi-dark in the room. The sterilized odor almost made me puke, and I came upright on the bed, clawing out.

They pushed me back—or I should say *she* pushed me back. It was a nurse. As sweet and virginal-looking a thing as Johns Hopkins ever issued.

Her voice floated to me, almost detached from her body. "You've had a nasty spill, Mr. Campus. Take it easy now." I let her push me back without any trouble.

"How—how long have I been here?" I asked. My throat was dry as an empty gas tank.

"Three days, Mr. Campus. Now just lie back and take it easy. Doctor Eshbach said you were coming along nicely."

Three days. I'd been in the hospital three full days. Suddenly, faces came back to me. Three. Three days. Three faces on three hoods. A puffy-nosed kid with brown hair, slightly pudgy. An almost handsome kid with a Barrymore profile and sleepy eyes. A kid with buck teeth and a crew-cut—bringing an argyle sock full of coins down on my head.

They were so clear in my mind, I felt I could reach out and touch them. I tried it. She took my hand. Then I peeled off again.

This time the cop was clean-shaven, but it didn't help his general appearance much. He said he had been to see me two days before—which made it five I'd been in the hospital—and that his name was Harrison, operating out of Homicide. I don't quite know how I knew he was a cop, because he wasn't in uniform. But I knew. He was stockily built, square and almost immovable looking. His face was a pasty white, broken by dark shadows and black, bushy eyebrows. He looked like a short stack of newspapers.

Harrison wore glasses—the old thin-rimmed wire kind—but it didn't distract from his ferocious appearance. There was something in the rock-ribbed squareness of his jaw, the snapping expression in his flinty eyes, that instantly made me aware this cookie wasn't playing games.

They must have told him I was ready for visitors; he hurricaned into the room, slung a chair away from the wall and banged it down next to the bed.

"You've been able to conk out of answering a few questions for five days now, Campus, but they tell me you're okay today. I suggest you answer fast and straight. There's an electric chair waiting if you don't!"

He spat it out fast, without any room for niceties or subtleties. He meant it. I didn't know what he was talking about, though.

"Why the chair?" I was surprised at my voice; it was a duckrasp. It rattled out like hailstones and fell onto the floor.

He worked his jaw muscles. The guy looked like he was trying to hold back from belting me. I didn't know why he was so damned angry—*I* hadn't done anything but get clobbered! Then he told me why they had the chair greased and waiting.

"Pessler was dead when we got to him. His head stomped into raspberry jelly and three hundred thousand dollars' worth of uncut diamonds missing. I was sent down there, Campus, and I saw that guy. He looked real bad."

I've seen and dealt with a lot of cops. The ones that gave me tickets, and the ones that took my statement at accidents; the ones that broke up tavern brawls and the ones that hauled me in with MP bands on their uniforms. I've seen them mad and indifferent, annoyed and savage. But I never saw one like this Harrison.

"Look, fella," I said, "maybe you better back off some and let me in on what this is all about. All I know is that five kids were clubbing a guy, and when I tried to help him out, I got smacked for my trouble."

"Maybe that's what you *wanted* it to look like," he shot back at me.

I could feel my face getting red, like it does when I'm boiling, and my duck-rasp had a real waspish tone. "Now you come patty-caking in here trying to whipsaw me and scare me with tales of the fry-seat. I don't much care for it! So unless you got something logical to say, or a charge to make, or a warrant to back you, or you want to talk more civilly, beat it. I don't feel so hot right now." I turned toward the wall.

Instead of cowing him, it got him all the madder. He grabbed me by the shoulder, yanked me back facing him. He was all the harder looking.

"Listen, Campus, this isn't any catered affair! We've been having trouble with this bunch of juvie hoods for six months now, and we've got a hunch they aren't figuring out three hundred thousand dollar muggings on their own. We've got a hunch someone is ringing these jobs for them—and we've got a hunch the guy that's been spotting for them is you."

His finger was in my face. I felt like biting it, but I didn't. His arm looked too big behind it.

"Nurse!" I hollered, and the sweet young thing appeared as though by magic. "Haul this character off me, or call my company to send me a lawyer. I'm supposed to be an invalid, aren't I?"

She shrugged her neat shoulders, made a futile motion with her hands and said, "Doctor Eshbach said it was all right for Lieutenant Harrison to speak to you. Nothing I can do." She shrugged again and promptly disappeared at a wave from Harrison.

"She on strings?" I asked sarcastically.

"Okay, Campus," Harrison chimed me off. "Now you got the word, let's have a few answers." I pursed my lips. My head was splitting, and I rather thought I'd gotten a concussion, though they hadn't mentioned it. But it was better to get this cop off my back early, and just lie back—till I could catch up with those punks.

Oh, I'd decided to get them. *That* was settled in my mind by the time I started talking to Harrison.

"Shoot," I said.

"Yeah," he answered nastily, "that too." He reached into his topcoat pocket and brought out a little black notebook. "I've got to warn you, it says here, that anything you say may be used against you, and…" He went on like that, the usual patter, all in a bored tone of voice. I told him to can it and get his questions over with.

"What do you know about the mugging of a guy named Tanenbaum? A rug importer. About two months ago?"

I looked at him blankly. Then a memory stirred. "That was in the papers. Got robbed of close to fifteen thousand dollars, didn't he? On the way to pay someone for a big shipment of goods, wasn't that it?"

"Unusual you'd remember the exact amount, that long ago," Harrison shot at me.

"I've got a good memory—any law against *that*?" I drove back at him. He lowered his bushy brows in anger, and his glasses slid an inch down his nose.

Then the grilling started for real. About halfway through, another cop came in—a detective—and *he* went at me when Harrison was taking five.

I managed to piece the story together. It was interesting and made me all the more anxious to get the hoods that had plastered me. The story ran something like this:

About six months before, big robberies and muggings had started cropping up, all of them pulled off by trained teenage punks in black leather jackets—the juvie set. One guy had been shot through the head with a zip-gun .32, another had been knifed in the chest a couple of times, this Tanenbaum had lost an eye when they'd stomped him—and now Pessler, a diamond merchant, was dead.

It appeared to the police—and I could easily see why they were casting out for such unlikely suspects as me—that someone was ringing for the pack. And a cabbie was as neat a sentry as they could hope for.

Particularly since they'd found a couple of diamonds, raw, uncut, and pretty, nestling in my pants cuff.

"A plant!" I yelled when they popped *that* to me.

"Maybe," Harrison answered.

"Maybe, hell," I jumped back. "Look, I got a good record. I've never had any trouble more serious than a locked bumper. Now why the hell are you trying to pin this thing on me?"

He didn't have to say it. I could read it in his eyes. He was being crucified like a voodoo doll, from Downtown. All the way up the line, they were getting hot pants. From detective to lieutenant, to inspector, to chief, to D.A., even up to the mayor—all of them were roasting. To pull the pan off the flame, they'd decided to temporarily fry a guy named Neal

Campus. Because I'd been there, I looked good, and I had a couple of blue-whites in my pants cuff.

"Look, Harrison," I said, a little more quietly, "I know you've got it rough, but don't try to hang any of this wash on *my* line. I'm clean and you know it. Now if it's just that you've got to make a pinch to shut the papers off, then find someone else. Because you know damned well you haven't got a shred of a case to take before a jury. You'll look like a sap, and I'll sue you for ten years' pay.

"Those diamonds were planted on me just to throw you off, as they have. Now if you want a line on what happened—as much of it as I saw—maybe I can fish that out for you. But otherwise, I'm not your boy."

We went around and around for a while longer, and then they asked me, "What did these kids look like?"

"I didn't see their faces," I answered, smoothing the sheet across my lap. "Too dark."

Harrison leaped up, the chair fell over, he was bellowing at me, "You were up over the curb, Campus. You must have had them dead in your spots. If you're telling the truth, and haven't got anything to hide, why are you holding out on us?"

They were damned mad, and I didn't want to rub them any more. I clammed, and put on the honest-to-god-I'm-not-holding-back attitude. After a while, they took it for straight talk.

I didn't want to turn them loose on those kids just yet. If those kids had planted the diamonds on me, they must have wanted me for a patsy. They probably didn't realize I'd gotten a good look at them. I'd had enough guys shoving me around in Korea, and I'd learned to dislike it real intense. Now, to have anybody start shoving me in my own city—that was too much.

I wanted a crack at them before Harrison and his squad got to them.

It took them an hour and a half to pump me dry. Or at least to pump me what they *thought* was dry.

They got up to leave. Harrison clapped a battered porkpie down on his head and stood up. "That's it for now, Campus. We don't have anything really solid on you yet, but it's still smelly, some of the dodges you've handed us. So take it true when I tell you not to leave town, or the fare you run up on that hack of yours may pay off in a trip to the fry-seat."

He wasn't kidding, and it was easier just to shut my eyes than to try reassuring him. I wasn't leaving town.

They left, and all I could see, with my eyes shut, were three young hoods. I was going to get out of this hospital in another week, and I wanted them. Bad.

Liggett, the dispatcher, caught me on the way out one morning about a week after I'd been released. I'd been out for a week, and asking plenty of questions around town—if anybody knew the kids I'd described. Nobody had, of course, but I hadn't given up.

I'd had a bit of a time getting my cab back, but I threatened to get the union on their tailpipes, and they slapped me back on schedule fast. They didn't like the idea of a cabbie suspected of murder tooling one of their crates around, but they liked the idea of the union beating around their ears even less.

That's why it bothered me when Liggett stopped me at the garage check-out.

"Neal!" he flagged me, and I pulled over, outside the garage.

Liggett was a short man, with washed-out eyes, and a look that said, "Three years from now I can ditch all this crap and settle back on my rosy-red pension."

I lit a cigarette, waiting for him to check off the last two boats out of the pool, and come over. He walked with a slight limp from the days of the hack wars. "Neal, there was somebody asking after you last night—phone call."

My ears perked up. "Who?"

"Didn't offer any references. Just wanted to know what route you were working—obviously knew but nothing from cab policy in this town—and when you were finished. Said he was a friend and wanted to toss you a juicy out-of-limits fare. Also wanted to know where you lived."

"Tell him?"

Liggett rubbed the back of his neck reflectively. "Where you live? No. When you were off? Yes. The former because I didn't think it was any of his biz, the latter because he said he wanted to hire you to ferry him out to Newark Airport. Thought he might be on the level. After I'd told him, though, I wondered why he didn't know your address and what time you're off, if he was such a big buddy."

I pursed my lips, then stuck the butt back in my mouth. "Thanks, Lig," I said. "If anybody starts checking me out in the future, play it close. There may be a couple people don't want me to go on breathing. I've maybe been asking the right questions in the wrong places."

"That mugging business still?" he asked.

I nodded and tossed the hack into first, punched the starter. Then I thought of something. "Hey, Lig." He walked back, leaned against the window. "Any other way they can get my address uptown?"

He stopped to think a minute, nodded his head. "If you mean through our records—no. But there is just one."

"What's that?" I asked.

"Any phone book," he answered, shaking his head.

I drove a double shift that day, trying to catch up on all the time I'd lost in the hospital. I was sort of slow in wanting to quit. Finally I felt my eyes bugging, and decided it was time to sack off. I reported in and told Lig I was taking the hack home for the night.

He okayed it, and motioned me off.

I drove uptown fast, wanting to pound my ear. I found my-self getting tired fast these days. The hospital hadn't worn off completely yet.

It was after nine when I pulled into 82nd Street, and stopped in front of the brownstone where I live. It was a dusty black night, and the streets were quiet as the catacombs. Odd for May, when the kids usually stay out late in the streets. There was one parking space, just big enough for the hack, and I jim-mied it into the spot between a big Caddy and a Pontiac without too much shifting.

I was just starting across the street when the three kids jumped me.

They popped out of a dark-blue Merc parked on the wrong side of the street, in front of my brownstone, and they didn't bother slugging me. One had a .45 and the other two were han-dling vicious switchblades. They didn't say a word, just waggled their weapons in the direction of the Merc.

I got in. I didn't really have a helluva lot of choice.

They pulled out with a squeal of burning tires, and started toward the East Side.

They turned left at Amsterdam Avenue, then left again at 83rd Street. When they got down to the Hudson River Drive, they turned onto it and shot hell-for-leather uptown.

"How far you kiddies think you can carry this game?" I asked. I was so goddam mad I was ready to yank their large colons out and tie them together.

"Far enough," said the kid with the .45, leaning over the front seat.

"The hell you—" I started, and he tapped me with the barrel. He tapped me goddam good and hard. I went under, plenty annoyed. I was beginning to feel like a door knocker.

✿

I came out of it, for a change, without a headache. *I must be getting used to this stuff*, I thought. Then I realized why I'd come to. The car had stopped.

We were on a cliff, overlooking what looked suspiciously like an ocean. "Out," the lad with the pistol said.

I got out.

They marched me, at knife-point, toward the edge of the cliff. They must have driven way out, because this strip of coast didn't look familiar. It was all too painfully obvious what was coming next.

"Do you jump, wise-mouth, or do we push?" one of the punk kids said. He was a ratty-looking little thing. The kind of kid you instinctively know gets pushed around, and plays it hard so no one will notice he's scared of his shoelaces.

"I guess you're going to have to push, runny-nose," I tossed over my shoulder, looking down at the razored rocks and lacy froth of the waves crashing on them. That was gonna be a real nasty fall. I added, "But whether you push or I jump, I'm going to remember that mousy kisser of yours, and when I get to it I'm going to—"

Then the little bastard shoved me.

He planted a foot in the small of my back, gave a strangled yell of hatred, and I went can-over-tea-kettle into open air.

My arms went out in all directions. I felt the cold wind whistling past my cheeks, and I screamed so loud I'm sure my lungs wanted to take up residency elsewhere.

I didn't see my life flash in front of my eyes. All I saw was a guy named Neal Campus, mad as hell because he was being pushed around like a floor mop, looking for a way out of this.

It seemed like I'd never stop falling. Then my flailing hands grabbed something. It was a bush. It ripped loose and dirt sprayed my face. I grabbed again, another bush. It ripped loose. But I was slowing a little. The third try made it. I hooked my hand around a scrub growth and slammed up against the chinky rock wall. It shook the breath out of me, and my arms felt as though they were leaving their sockets. But I wasn't falling anymore. The rocks and debris cascaded past me, and made a helluva bang when they landed below.

I heard a thin laugh from the darkness above me, and a voice that carried down the cliff to me. "Let him spot us from down *there*, if he can, goddam big-mouthed sonofabitch!"

Two minutes later the Merc started up, and they drove away fast. I started back up. It wasn't easy. It took me half an hour to climb what I'd fallen in a few seconds. My hands were raw by the time I made it, my head ached miserably, and I fell onto the dirt, gasping.

After a while I stood up. I faced into the wind to get cooled. I faced back toward the city. "I'll get you—every one of you!" Not loud, just firm. That's the way I felt. Not loud. Just firm. *Real* firm.

I started walking.

By the time I'd hopped enough lifts, and used what little change had stayed in my pockets during the fall—the punks had lifted my wallet—to get bus rides, I had a few other things straightened out in my mind.

Number one: these weren't just kids jumping salty. There was something more here than just a particularly ugly form of organized gang crime. There was an older, smarter boy behind these leather-jacketed jockeys.

Number two: they'd know in a day or so that I wasn't dead, that I hadn't spattered into the Atlantic. Then they'd come jiving after me, and this time they'd probably make it stick. In short, if I stood still long enough for them to find me, I was dead.

Number three: I was caught between the devil and the deep blue. If the kids didn't polish me off—and I wasn't worried about being convinced on *that* score any more—the cops were going to do their damnedest.

And, most important, number four: I wanted those kids so bad I could taste it. I had to get to them and turn them in to Harrison and his stooges, just to get them off my back. Because if I didn't do it ever so fast, they were going to make sure I didn't *have* any back to get off.

But how the hell do you locate a bunch of teenage punks in a city of over eight million people? How do you get to them before they get to you?

I knew I had to take care of a few things.

I went to see Jerry Saha over in the Bronx.

Jerry had been through the freeze-mud with me, near Wonson, and we'd kept in touch once we'd gotten back. I knew he still had his army service revolver—a spanking handy .45 that shot a real straight round. Jerry was an incurable souvenir hunter. His apartment looked like an antique shop.

I called him from a drugstore on his corner, and he told me to come on up. About ten minutes later he let me in, giving me the shush-finger. The wife and kids were asleep in the next room. It was six in the A.M.

"What's up, Neal?" he said, belting his robe about him tighter. I told him he didn't really want to know, but he said, "Hell, yes. Sure I do. You don't come bursting in here at six in the morning unless something's under your fingernails. Now give!"

So I gave him the bit from the top—all the way from the mugging, and this Pessler character's being cooled to the tune of three hundred thousand bucks' worth of uncuts, through Harrison's visit in the sick ward, right up to and including the little ride I'd just come back from, and particularly about how they were going to try and cool me proper in the near future.

"I'd like to borrow your heater, Jerry," I told him.

He looked worried for a minute, then nodded slowly. "Sure, Neal. Just a second." He trotted into the next room, his bedroom slippers slap-slapping against the soles of his feet, and closed the door behind him. I heard a drawer open and close. Then the closet door opening. I heard him fishing around the closet for a few minutes, then he reappeared. He had a chamois bag and a small box in his hand.

"Here's a box of bullets for the thing," he said, handing me the box. I took out eight rounds and shoved the box in my jacket pocket. I reached into the bag, came up with the blocky thing in my hand. Jerry had taken good care of that gun. It shone.

I loaded the clip, flat-palmed it back into the butt. I shoved the .45 into my waistband. "Thanks, Jerry," I said. "Thanks a lot. You'll get it back in good shape."

He looked concerned, his collegiate, crew-cut appearance cut by a frown. "Look, take care of yourself, Neal. If there's anything else you need…"

"Not right now, Jerry. I'll keep you posted." I patted the spot under my dirty, mud-caked jacket where the .45 nestled against my tummy. "Thanks for this. It'll probably be the only thing between me and Potter's Field if it comes to a showdown with these characters."

"What kind of a showdown?" he asked, the frown deepening.

I shrugged, my hand on the doorknob. "Don't know, but there's got to be one. They want *me* real bad—or they will when they find out that cliff didn't finish me—and I want *them* real bad. I can't stop moving, because if I do, they cool me. And they can't show themselves, because when they do I'll get to them."

I closed the door quietly behind me.

I went home and sacked in with my clothes on. I didn't sleep too well. The .45 was a hard nubbin under the pillow, and I had a lousy nightmare about a switchblade cab that was trying to push me off a cliff into a sea of diamonds.

I woke up about four in the afternoon, reeking of my own sweat. The world was shattering inside my skull, there was a painful lump where the kid had tapped me the night before, and I had a horrible itch to find those kids one by one and hammer their molars back down their throats.

I showered, dressed, and phoned in to Liggett, told him I'd be right down. He told me I could work the six-to-four shift. I told him to let word seep through the vine that Campus had been jumped and dumped—but had come back.

He asked me what I meant, so I fired the story over the line real quick. I heard a gasp, and he said he'd let the word out. "But why the hell don't you just cut out and forget the whole thing?" he asked.

"Reasons," I answered, thinking about Korea and being pushed too far.

Then I hung up and went downstairs, to take up where I'd left off the day before.

Things went cozy that day. I got finished with my tour of duty about four-oh-five and went home. This time I made sure I was alone when I got out of the cab.

I sacked in, and this time the sleep was better. Not perfect, but a whole lot better.

Next morning I shoved the .45 into my belt and put my jump-jacket over it. Then I went down to the cab. I got in, took out my route book, and scribbled my tie-in time. I stuck the key in the ignition.

Then I pushed the starter.

And the bomb went off. The whole goddam universe exploded. I felt myself being shoved in the chest. It was the steering wheel. The car exploded, erupted, whanged away with a boom, and the doors flew off their hinges, thank god! I was parked next to a church. The explosion tossed me up against the holy walls.

I lay there on my face on the sidewalk, blood all over me from abrasions, while screaming metal and broken glass fell on top of me. I heard people screaming and windows flying up, and knew it must have been one hell of an explosion. I reprimanded myself mentally for swearing mentally in front of a church. Even if I *was* lying on my kisser.

It was obvious, of course. They'd planted a souper in the engine of the cab.

If the hack hadn't been so strong—mainly due to my reinforcing sections of it on my days off—I'd have been spattered across the wall of that church permanently.

I rather supposed they hadn't rigged it properly. If they had, no matter *how* strong that cab was, I would have been decapitated. These kids were novices when it came to installing a juice-box in a crate. I started to faint.

I heard people running up to me, and I tried to sit up. I managed to get my feet under me and pull myself up on the church stair railing. Someone produced a glass of something that tasted like bad sherry, and I sipped a bit, listening to the mingled bird-sounds of the people's horror-cooing.

I staggered erect, and bumbled into the house to call Lig. He could handle Harrison, if that crumb was assigned to this deal.

I wanted to call Lig to thank him for spreading the word. He'd done it real fine—the bastards knew I was still kicking.

Now it was a case of hide-and-seek.

If I was "it," I'd be "it" with a slug in my tummy or a switch shaft sticking out of my throat. If *they* were "it," I'd be rapping a few skulls good and hard, real soon.

❖

I moved later that day. Across town to a furnished flea trap. But it would do till I came up with something other than a cracked skull and empty hands.

Then started a week of real nightmare. I borrowed Jerry's car and went looking. New York's a big town. You can go for years without running into anyone you know; on the other hand, you might walk into the street and meet a guy you haven't seen in ten years. Funny, like that. But a full week without more than three hours sleep a night—running on No-Doz and black coffee—I patrolled the streets in Jerry Saha's car. All the way from Astoria to Brooklyn.

It wasn't hard to get the other hackies I knew to keep half an eye open for the kids I'd described, also.

Along about Thursday, I got word from Lig that Harrison had been around looking for me. I told Lig to stall the bull, tell him I was on routes with a new cab, tell him *anything*, but to stall the slob. He did, and I kept looking, cutting my sleep down to nothing.

Nothing. That's what I got on Friday.

Saturday was more of the same. A righteous, empty nothing; a stone loss.

But Sunday night the break came.

I was cruising on Central Park South, in the Fifties, when I saw one of them. I suddenly knew how these kids had escaped being picked up till now. He wasn't in a black leather jacket. That was cornball stuff for these punks. It was a uniform, a disguise. He had on a charcoal-gray flannel suit and he looked like the spoiled brat of a wealthy advertising executive. He was walking crosstown.

I spotted him dead at once. It was the kid with the Barrymore profile and the sleepy eyes.

I fell behind him a half block, and tagged him all the way. He turned in at a flashy apartment house in the plush section of the Park South. When he'd gone in, I parked the car around the corner and flat-footed it over to the building. The kid was gone.

But there was a doorman.

"Hello," I said, smiling, tipping my cabbie cap back on my head so the license button showed real plain. "Say, did a young boy in a charcoal suit just come in here?"

He looked at me leery. "Why?"

I yanked out my hack license, flipped it at him. "I just brought that fare up here from downtown, with a two-buck placket on the meter. He said he was broke and would run upstairs to get me my fare. I'd like to make sure he comes back. Can you tell me where he went?"

The doorman looked at me hard for a minute, then nodded his head. "Yes, I suppose so. He went up to Mr. Steckman's penthouse. That's Mr. Fritz Steckman, the broker. I'm sure the boy's all right if he's a friend of Mr. Steckman's. Probably a nephew or something. Mr. Steckman has a good many young people visiting him—mostly relatives, I guess."

"Yeah. Sure." I smiled at him. "Thanks. I'll wait in the cab. Hope he shows soon; I'd like to catch another fare."

I went out and got in the car, drove around the block, parked down and across the street. Then I waited.

About a half-hour later, the kid came out and started walking crosstown. I didn't follow him—I knew where his home roost was.

I was about to make as big a play as I could. Pray? You bet your life I did!

I called Richie Ellington on the *Daily News* and got some poop from him on this Steckman.

Big operator. Wealthy. In the social register, and a large investor in the stock market. Summer home, winter home, two yachts and a hunting lodge in the Canadian Rockies. Impeccable taste—one of the Best Dressed Somethings-or-other—and un-married. Nominated Very Eligible Hunka Meat by some group of young debs coming out, recently.

I thanked Ellington, inquired about his cats and his booze, and then started to get ready.

I changed into *my* charcoal-gray suit, and made sure the slide on the .45 was working smoothly. Then I piled into Jerry's car and headed crosstown to Central Park South. I parked up the street from Steckman's building, and waited till the doorman went off duty. When he'd been gone ten minutes, I climbed out and went into the building.

The alternate doorman opened the door for me. I brushed past him without a glance, as though I knew where I was going and as if I had every right to be there.

I climbed into the elevator, and pushed the button for the top floor.

The top floor wasn't the penthouse. There was a separate elevator for that. But I didn't take it. I took the fire stairs. When I got to the top, the door was locked; but another flight went up, and I figured it must go to a service shed atop the penthouse.

I kept climbing, and a minute later opened the fire door to the outside. I was standing next to a metal ladder that went up into a water tank.

I slammed the door, and walked around the platform. Turned out the penthouse was a duplex, with an entrance up here at roof level. It was parked far back at the rear of the area, with a glass front and a large patch of neatly tended greenery sur-rounding it, grass and shrubs and whatnot. I didn't see anyone outside the house, so I jumped into the grass.

I rolled under a bush, all in the same movement, and came up with wet grass on my back and the pistol in my hand.

The glass-doored greenhouse-looking penthouse was right across from me. I figured to lay there till it got dark enough inside and outside so that no one would see me. I wasn't sure just how many were in there.

It took a long time getting dark, and I had a long chance to get some thinking done.

I knew why they wanted to get me so bad. I was the only boy who could identify them. There was a sweet setup here, but I wasn't sure just what it was. Who was Steckman, and how did he figure into this? What were those punks doing, coming to visit him?

I wanted some answers, but more, I wanted all those kids—and the guy that was operating them. Him, most of all. I knew I couldn't call the cops till I had all of them, the whole batch of them. Let one lone juvie get away, and my days were even more numbered than right now. Those kids hold grudges longer and harder than any adult. I had to get them all together, or my life wouldn't be worth starting fare on my meter.

It pitched-out around 9:30, and I started my creep toward the penthouse.

The grass was dry now, and the sounds of traffic filtered up the face of the building. The .45 was warm in my mitt. I suddenly realized I'd been hanging onto it for over three hours, while I'd been waiting.

I crawled over to the big windows and looked inside. At first I didn't see anyone. The living room was empty. Just an overplush apartment, decorated ultramodern with hanging lamps, screwy-looking wire clocks on the walls—the works.

In a few minutes a man came into the room with a drink in his hand; he was wearing a wine-colored satin smoking jacket, with a silk scarf knotted about his throat. The guy was about forty, or forty-five, hair graying at the temples, a smooth, unlined face, almost like a baby's. He looked hard, but the mark of dissipation was on him. As though he'd just gotten rich and was letting himself go to fat enjoying it.

It was Steckman all right. Richie Ellington had described him almost perfectly. I waited a few minutes to make sure he was alone; then I shoved in.

The French doors were unlocked. He must have felt pretty secure up there in the clouds. When I stepped through into his living room, the .45 aimed at the spot behind his brandy snifter, he turned a fish-belly white.

"Who—who are you?" he asked. Real hacky phrase—no inventiveness, this guy. I disliked him more and more. But I told him anyhow.

"The name's Campus, Mr. Steckman. Neal Campus. I'm the boy you don't like."

He started sputtering something about getting out, and who the hell did I think I was, but I cut him off sharply.

"I *know* you don't like me, Mr. Steckman, because you had a few of your kindergarten associates clobber me, then toss me over a cliff, then plant a bomb in my hack. They really tried everything but staking me out and letting the ants eat me alive. Now unless that's the way you recruit new members for the Social Register, I'm certain you don't care for little old Neal Campus."

"You're out of your mind. Get out of here before I call the police!"

"Oh, you'll do some calling, all right, Mr. Steckman, but not right now. First I want to thank you in my own charming way for all the attention you've paid me."

I laid the gun down on top of the spinet piano, and chucked off my jacket.

Steckman was almost as tall as me, but he was heavier by a good twenty pounds. And he wasn't *that* soft.

I came at him, and he did something *really* old hat: he tossed the brandy in my face. Glass and all. The damned stuff burned like lye, and I fell back. The next thing I knew he had a foot in my groin, and I was getting pitchforks of pain in my abdomen.

I staggered back against the spinet and grabbed out blindly for him, while I prayed my eyes would stop tearing.

All I could see was a vague blur, but I threw a left hook at it, and it connected. He tumbled backwards over a modern chair, and brought up short against the opposite wall, next to the fireplace.

I shook my head a couple of times, and my eyes cleared just nicely so that I could see him coming whole-hog at me with an andiron in his big mitt.

He swung the thing like a golf pro, and it sizzled past my temple, parting my hair. The thing smashed into the wall, shattering a shadow box and a couple of little Chinese figurines.

I dove for him, low, and caught him around the legs. Then I was on top of him, and all the anger and frustration of the past weeks let loose. I clobbered that guy real good. I don't think I'd have stopped, except his kisser started looking like a pound of prime ground round. I figured it was time to back off him.

I hauled him to his feet, shoved him into a chair, and emptied the water from the bottom of an ice bucket in his face. He jerked like I'd harpooned him when the ice water hit, and I jerked him erect by his satin lapels.

"All right, Mr. Steckman, how's about you letting Uncle Neal in on what the pitch is here. Why the juvies? Why all the muggings?"

He seemed reluctant to talk, so I tossed him a couple of open-hand cracks across his bleeding mouth, and he came around real fast.

"I've had some serious losses in the stock market of late," he explained, "and I had to recoup the money somehow."

"Pretty high living you're doing here. Ever think if you moved back to Earth with us poverty-struck commoners you might be able to get along on less?"

He glared at me, and continued: "I got in touch with a boy named Boots, and told him to get a few of his friends in the gang, and bring them over; that I'd like to talk to them. So I brought them over and showed them how to avoid being caught—"

I interrupted, "Like changing to charcoal suits and hiding the leather jackets when they were off duty, right?"

He nodded. "Then I planned a few jobs for them, with myself handling the disposal of non-cash merchandise—"

"Like Pessler's diamonds," I put in.

"Like Pessler's diamonds," he agreed, dabbing at the trickle of blood running out of his mouth. "But I never told them to frame you, or to kill anyone. They did that on their own. I swear to god! I never told them—"

"You're lying like a rug, Steckman!" I accused him. "No matter *how* sharp those kids are, it would take a lousy fagin like you to think up that cliff deal, or the bomb."

"No, I—"

"Shut up, Steckman. You make me sick to my belly. How many are there in the gang, fagin?"

He gritted his teeth—those he had left—and told me there were eight of them, all members of a gang called the Falcons.

"Get them over here," I told him.

He looked at me sharply. "Get them!" I snapped.

He went to the phone, lifted it and dialed. He spoke to someone on the other end, and asked them if he could speak to Boots. They must have told him Boots wasn't there, because he asked who *was* there in the Falcs.

Then he said, "All right, let me talk to Stick." He waited about a minute, then he said, "Hello, Stick?" He paused and licked his lips, started to say something, but I stepped over quickly and prodded him with the .45 in the back of the head.

"This is Steckman. Yes, that's right. Come on up immediately. I've got—what's that? Yes, that's right, a big job for you. Bring the rest of the boys." He waited, listening, then said, "Yes, *all* of them. Even Carpy and Second." I stepped in front of him and mouthed that Stick should get Boots, too, in particular. "Oh, and Stick—be sure Boots is with you." He muttered a few more things, then hung up, sweating like a pig. I'd had the muzzle of that .45 behind his ear all the time he'd been talking.

Steckman looked scared.

"Sit down again," I told him. He walked over and folded up into his contour chair. I wondered about one thing more, so I asked him, "How did you know guys like Pessler would be carrying that much with them, or where they'd be?"

He shrugged sullenly, answered, "Friends of mine, or acquaintances I've met at parties. It was easy to get them to drop word of where they were going, or where they'd be at certain times, and if they were carrying much money. Then all I had to do was make sure the kids were there." He seemed proud of his little fling into crime.

A real nice guy this Steckman. "Where are those kids coming from now?" I asked.

He hesitated a second, then said, "Way over from Brooklyn. Why?"

I knew I couldn't handle all of them alone, that I'd need the help of Harrison and his Homicide boys, but I wanted those kids here first. I didn't want any of them walking up as the cops showed, and then blowing.

So I waited. After half an hour, I dialed the operator. "Get me the police! This is an emergency!"

Then a short wait, and finally a voice said, "Police Headquarters. Can I help you?"

"Homicide!" I bellowed. There wasn't any reason to yell, but I thought it might get me faster service.

In a minute I heard Harrison's dulcet tones. I briefed him in fast, and gave him the address, told him to blast over.

"Is this a gag, Campus? I know Fritz Steckman, and he doesn't front any bunch of juvie hoods!"

"Look, Harrison," I shouted at him, "either you get over here within the next ten minutes, or you're going to find a cache of corpses. And I can bet you either Mr. Steckman or I will be among them. Now for Christ's sake, back me up on this, at least till you find out whether I've got hold of something or—"

Right then, the kids blew in. Without knocking. Eight of them. With switchblades uncurled.

"*Fast, Harrison!*" I yelled into the phone. "Eight of them just showed on the scene, and they don't look as though they're here to trade bubble-gum pictures!"

I had to drop the phone then, because Steckman was grinning and clapping his hands at them. "You understood the 'Boots' warning! Good, good! Now get Campus! I can cover with the police. Get him!"

Then, maybe because the kids were too slow for him, Steckman came out of his chair at me, with a fist as big as a muskmelon aimed at my head. I ducked under it, and it swished past my ear. Beyond him I saw three of the eight kids coming at me.

Steckman had spun halfway around me with that swing, so I leaned away from him and smacked him good and hard behind the ear as he swung past. The blow didn't catch him full, but he fell across me, and threw me against the spinet again.

He tumbled to the floor, on his back. Then the kids were on me.

I felt one of their knives go into my shoulder, ripping up and out, and tearing away my shirt—some skin with it. It wasn't really a deep slash, but it hurt like hell, and I could feel warm stickiness running down my arm. I wished I'd kept my jacket on.

They were all over me, but it was as rough for them as it was for me. They couldn't get a clear shot at me and I couldn't pot any of them.

Even so, I felt another shank go into my thigh. It was close again, hit nothing vital, but much more of this and I'd bleed out!

Finally I kicked up with both knees, lying on my back as I was, and they went in all directions. The pain was blinding me, and blood was all over the place. But I staggered to my feet, holding on to the edge of the piano, and barked, "Get the hell back, you little bastards, or I'll make you look like Life Savers!"

They laughed, almost at the same time, and came at me.

I fired and caught the first one in the left leg. He slipped over and crumpled onto his side, moaning and clutching the shattered shinbone. The second one was too close to stop, and had his arm back for an overhand swipe with the knife. It was the ratty-faced kid that had pushed me off the cliff.

I couldn't help it—all I could see was that knife, so I fired at it as it slipped toward me. The shot went past his arm and caught him just under the nose. The bullet plowed upward and the back of his head flew off. He fell forward, just a lousy bloody wreck, and I shoved the knife hand aside as he fell. He tumbled on top of Steckman, who wasn't completely out and who was just rising. When Steckman saw what was on his back, he screamed like a woman, high and thin, and fainted.

The other six stopped cold. They didn't want any more of that jazz. I felt sick for a moment, thinking how I'd killed a kid, but then I remembered what Harrison had said about how Pessler's face had been stomped to goo. Then it didn't bother me so much.

I staggered back till I had them all in sight, and suddenly I felt the ceiling lowered down on me. "Back up, and drop those shanks," I mumbled. Things were starting to ooze off into grayness. I had to keep my eyes wide open and focused on them or I'd lose *them*, too.

I heard the switchblades drop dully to the rug, and they backed against the wall.

"You didn't come from Brooklyn, did you?" I rattled. They shook their heads.

One of them gave a belligerent half-laugh, said, "We live eight blocks away from here, off Broadway. You thought we'd be a whole lot longer comin'. But Steckman gave us the word."

"Now we're going to wait for Harrison and his squad boys," I said. I choked the words out, and the kids didn't look too worried about matters.

They didn't say a word. I leaned against the piano and waited.

It seemed like forever. I could feel the blood oozing off down my arm and leg, and all the clubbings I'd taken in the past few weeks were finally adding up. How I'd kept going till now suddenly shocked me. It seemed fantastic, but nervous energy accounted for most of it, and good condition answered the rest.

I glanced down at my wristwatch. It had been a good twenty minutes since I'd spoken to Harrison. Maybe the sonofabitch didn't believe me!

I didn't have a very long while to think about it though. Abruptly, somebody drained all the juice out of me, and I felt myself tilting over. The gun dropped out of my hand, and as the grayness closed in I saw the kids dipping for their shanks, with hell in their eyes.

A weird thought about all the times I'd been unconscious lately popped into my head as I fell:

What a helluva way to go through life!

*

I came to with the sweet young thing just focusing in, and beyond her the black-and-white bespectacled kisser of Harrison.

"I made it," I said, duck-rasp.

"Yeah," he said. For the first time, the slob smiled. "There's money in this for you, Campus. Nice reward—totes up into four figures."

I grinned back at him, and my head started playing the *Anvil Chorus*. I could feel the adhesive pull of bandages on my arm and thigh. "Reward, huh?" I asked.

He nodded.

"Know what I'm going to do with it?" I asked.

He shook his head. "What?"

"I'm going to buy you a pair of roller skates, you creeping, crawling slob!"

He didn't smile—but what did I care?

From the Author the New York Times Calls
"THE SUPREME MASTER OF SUSPENSE"

FRIGHT

by CORNELL WOOLRICH
AUTHOR OF 'REAR WINDOW'

A man. A woman. A kiss in the dark. That is how it begins. But before his nightmare ends, Prescott Marshall will learn that kisses and darkness can both hide evil intent—and that the worst darkness of all may be lurking inside him.

Lost for more than half a century and never before published under Cornell Woolrich's real name, *Fright* is a breathtaking crime novel worthy of the writer who has been called "one of the giants of mystery fiction" and "the Hitchcock of the written word."

RAVES FOR CORNELL WOOLRICH:

*"You can palpably feel the agony
in Woolrich and his work."*
— James Ellroy

"One of the great masters."
— Ellery Queen

"The Poe of the twentieth century."
— Francis M. Nevins

*"One of the giants of mystery fiction…
one of my earliest writing heroes."*
— Harlan Ellison

"It is high time Woolrich was rediscovered."
— Los Angeles Times

**Available now at your favorite bookstore.
For more information, visit
www.HardCaseCrime.com**